Fogged In

Titles by Doreen Burliss

Fogged In
That Nantucket Summer
We'll Always Have Nantucket

Fogged In

Doreen Burliss

Copyright © 2024 Doreen Burliss

All rights reserved. No part of this book may be reproduced in any form or by any electronic or mechanical means, including information storage and retrieval systems, without permission in writing from the publisher, except by reviewers, who may quote brief passages in a review.

Paperback: 979-8-9861095-4-1
Ebook: 979-8-9861095-5-8

Library of Congress Control Number: 2024907970
Printed in Boston, MA

Fogged In is a work of fiction. The names, characters, businesses, places, events, locales, and incidents are either products of my imagination or used in a fictitious manner. Any resemblance to actual persons, living or dead, or actual events are coincidental.

I'd like to dedicate this book to you, dear reader, holding this novel and reading these words. YOU are who I write for, with the hope that my stories and characters will reach some place inside of you, make you laugh and maybe cry, and say YES, I totally get that.

Enjoy this little trip to Nantucket ~

"Years, lovers, and glasses of wine;
these are things that must not be counted."

—Anthony Capella

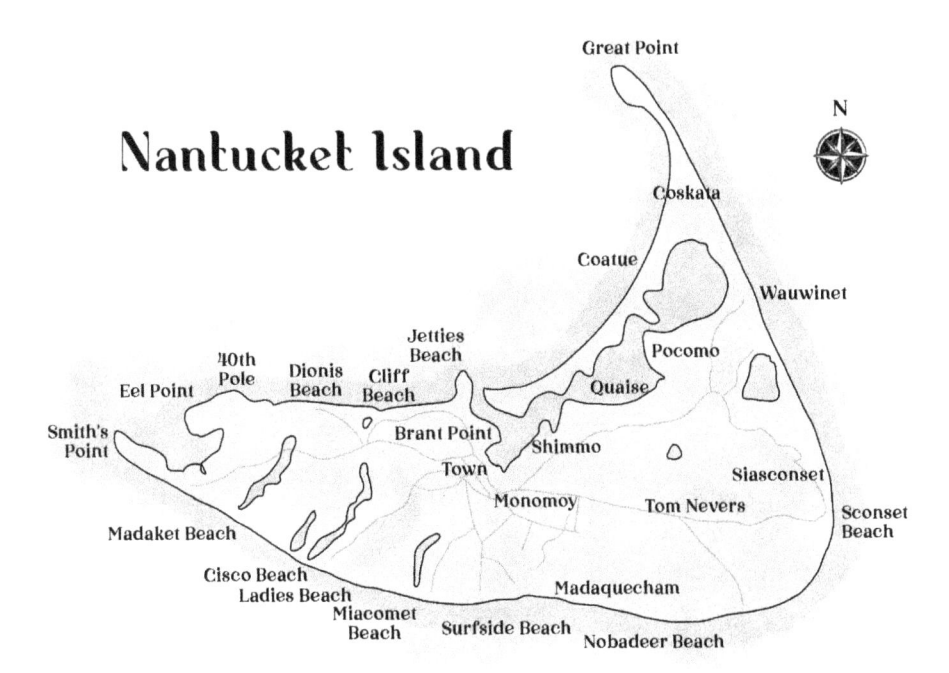

Nantucket Island

Chapter One

Sheri's heart tripped over its next beat as she sat alone in her truck at the mid-island grocery store. She'd come straight from her two-hour steamship journey and she noticed the sun was still high on the unspent day. She'd left her Vermont home at three o'clock that morning to make the nine-fifteen boat out of Hyannis and her hold on the moment was as insubstantial as the curled edge of a dream.

An abrupt rapping on her window pulled her to the surface and she jumped in her seat. Trudy. Her summer friend of twenty-five years. Sheri smiled and hurried to climb out of her Bronco and into Trudy's arms. Enfolded in her sinewy hug, Sheri breathed in the gulp of fresh air that was Trudy before stepping back to take in her five-foot, eleven-inch presence – a lemony beam of sunlight.

"*Girl*," Trudy said with a wide smile, "I can't believe you're finally here!" She stood back to look at her friend, giving Sheri's shoulders a light squeeze before releasing her. "Something's different," she said, with her golden retriever head-tilt and sky eyes, strawberry waves of hair falling over her sculpted shoulders.

"Well, yeah, I lost about one hundred eighty pounds since you last saw me."

It took Trudy a beat to realize Sheri was talking about her ex-husband. "That's right! With your mom's diagnosis and last summer being a bust, I haven't seen you since the divorce was final. Shit, come here, I need another hug."

Sheri's body went soft in her friend's arms, she hadn't realized how much she needed a hug that ran the length of her whole body. They rocked for a minute before letting go again. "I can't tell you how good it is to see your smiling face – how's Griffin, Ollie? Tell me everything."

"Tell you what," Trudy said, looking down at her watch," I have a Zoom call with my agent in, like, fifteen minutes. How about just you and me hang out tonight? We can make dinner or just have cheese and wine, whatever you want. As long as we do it at your place – I could use a new view, you know?"

Sheri loved Trudy for a lot of things, but especially for not being too shy to say, *pour some wine, I'm coming over.* "That sounds perfect, you know where to find me."

∞

Inside the grocery store Sheri's heart was doing that thing again, as she reached for the fruits her mom loved; deep red strawberries and sweet yellow peaches, then cherries and green grapes for her dad. She needed to stop. George and Rose would not be there waiting for her at the house. Nobody was. Unless you could count the cloying presence of *nostalgia* and its big, fat friend, *melancholy*. Enough, she told herself, as she pressed her shoulders back and grabbed a couple of Pink Lady apples and avocados for herself. Marching out of the produce section with renewed purpose, Sheri rolled her cart up and down the aisles with a mental menu for her evening with Trudy.

It took a minute to find her new Bronco in the parking lot, a belated post-divorce present to herself. Antimatter Blue – *reminiscent of the night sky – a refined blue with depth and intrigue,* it dazzled in the sun. It was perfect. The Bronco had definitely become the new it-vehicle on the island over the last few years and hers made her smile whenever she saw it. It was so cool. She was still waiting for the day when she felt as cool as that. The hardest part about getting rid of her old Honda Pilot was the loss of the rainbow of beach permit stickers on the bumpers. They'd represented so many shining summers rumbling over the sand. She was starting over now with only one sticker, hot pink.

∞

Crunching down her parents' shell driveway Sheri let joy roll in as she looked up at the house. How she loved the simple beauty of its faded cedar shingles and white trim that somehow caught the sun and kept it. It had a modest front porch with a bench swing and two sturdy white rockers, and the lush embrace of the ornamental grasses that surrounded the property. Her mom had been smart to replace the hydrangea bushes that the deer liked all too well. She loved how the fountain grass sprouted fluffy seed heads as pretty as any blossoms, and the ribbon grass for how it changed to beautiful purples and bronzes in late summer – they waved at her in the light wind. Looking up at her parents' beach house, *Moor to Sea,* sent a thrill straight through her every single time.

With groceries and her luggage, she had to make several trips up the porch steps into the house. She kept the swell of memories at bay until she was all the way in.

But then Sheri felt every past summer unspooling in her mind. Her heart was all over the place and felt as heavy as the bags she set down at her feet in the foyer. The air inside was old and hot, the windows stuck shut in its thickness. Sweat and angst rolled down her back as she moved from one window to the next, muscling them open to let the sea breathe life back in. It was impossible to reconcile stepping into this house alone – it had only ever known the fullness of family and the crackling energy of summer. Sheri heeled off one flip-flop after the other to feel the smooth maple floor underfoot before sliding open the wide glass door to the deck overlooking Dionis Beach and Nantucket Sound.

Oh, Sheri ... you'd be better off alone. She *was* better off alone, just like Steve Perry's song. Her divorce from Tommy was old news, two years old to be exact, though some days it still caught her by surprise.

Oh, I want to let go ...

A fog bank was gathering at the horizon mixing with the blue of the sky painting a lavender line. The obscured sun changed the sea from navy blue to steel, and the wind kicked up frothed whitecaps. The air was ambrosial and she filled her lungs with it, trying to let her heart and hopes rise with it. Her mother's Alzheimer's diagnosis was still fresh and the thought that her parents wouldn't be coming back to the summer house was irreconcilable.

We'd like to put your name on the deed, sweetheart, is that something you're comfortable with? Her dad had asked her. Sheri had barely taken ownership of her own life as a single mother – albeit of grown daughters – *was* she ready for this? But how in the world could she let it go?

Her sister, Mandy, wanted nothing to do with the place – not the house, not the island, not New England. She'd made northern California her home – she had wine country in her backyard and Ocean Beach and the Sierras. *What more could I possibly need?* Mandy had said often enough. Sheri couldn't argue, and wouldn't win if she tried. Mandy was an attorney specializing in environmental law, she literally got paid to argue. But still, Sheri couldn't help but feel deserted. They'd spent their childhood summers on Nantucket. Those days were solid gold and had meant everything in the world to Sheri. And to her sister too, or so she'd always thought. But Mandy was the more practical one, emotionally and in every other way. She'd defected to the West Coast after high school with her surfboard and her first big love, she never looked back.

Sheri's parents had children later in life and were older than most of her friends' parents, but they stayed young for a long time. Until last spring when they'd just gotten old. Eighty-three wasn't young by any standard, Sheri knew that, but she'd never pictured George and Rose not being around. She certainly knew plenty of people in their late eighties and even nineties still thriving.

But when her mom started putting her keys in the refrigerator, ice cream in the cabinet, and forgetting the ingredients for meals she'd been making for forty years, her dad couldn't brush it off any longer. And then everything changed; travel plans aborted, doctor appointments filling all the squares on the calendar, and the researching of quality assisted living facilities that included memory care. Life as they knew it had begun a slow but steady unraveling. George and Rose, eighty-four and eighty-three years old, had unknowingly spent their last summer on Nantucket.

The deck boards warped and splintered under her bare feet. Bowed and cupped. She knew the whole thing needed replacing, her dad had the project lined up. How could Sheri replace this thing that had held her parents in their chairs for so many sunrises and sunsets, then with her and Mandy in their laps, then Sheri's own daughters – the base, the support, the foundation of myriad schemes and reflections …

But salt air did a number on things and it was no longer safe. Like the railing up on the rooftop widow's walk and the fifty-seven steps down to the beach. All needed replacing. Why did everything ache so much? Why did so many things have to matter so damn much? It was just wood – a structure – a fixable physical thing. But to Sheri, it meant losing more of her parents than she already had.

She was being indulgent and maudlin when she just needed to take care of things. Her dad, a retired architect, had left meticulous notes at the end of last summer that he'd updated when they'd come for the Daffodil Festival just that spring. Right around the time of her mother's diagnosis. George had already hired a contractor for the job,

Folger & Worth. Sheri recognized the island-descendant surnames, letting a smile tug at her mouth picturing her dad wanting tried and true, antiquity over any young "upstarts." George had done all the legwork and Joe had already emailed Sheri that the job was scheduled to begin in two days, on Monday, July 8. *You got this*, Sheri coached herself.

The fog was lifting as Sheri stood there, vanishing as if she'd willed it, revealing a startlingly blue sky. The light was drinkable. Her phone buzzed in the back pocket of her shorts pulling her back to the present.

> Mrs. Steele – it's Joe from Folger & Worth. I hope you don't mind me texting, your father gave me this number. Are you on-island? We'd like to come out and take a look at the job again before Monday if that's alright. Please let me know – this number is the easiest way to reach me, thank you.

Sheri tore her eyes away from the horizon and all that it offered to go back inside. The air in the house was still musty but improving as the salty wind weaved its way in through the open windows. Her eyes darted around the familiar space, afraid to linger on any one spot lest the memories rise up and swallow her. The faded blue and white sofa that cradled all of them at one time or another in beach drunk naps and card games, the mantle over the fireplace where glass vases brimmed with scallop and jingle shells, and the big soap-dish sized clamshells holding stray hair ties and sea glass.

Countless days and years of beachcombing flitted in her mind. She could see her daughter's chubby hands, golden from days in the sun, offering up treasure, feel the salt drying on her skin, and hear her mother's laugh – like champagne bubbles popping in the air.

Sheri ran her hand along the backs of the kitchen barstools, where the biggest and smallest problems of the world were debated, and where heartaches were eased with Oreo ice-cream pie and milk. She felt her dad's strong warm hands rubbing her neck when she was sore from learning to surf, or stressed from planning her wedding in the backyard overlooking the ocean, and when her body was enormous and exhausted growing her first baby. And then when Tommy broke her heart.

Oh, Sheri, our love goes on.

Except that it didn't, Tommy.

She needed to unpack her things, return Joe's text, call her parents, and then her daughters. Thank God her girls would arrive the next weekend. The house needed laughter and spilled wine, and a fire in the fireplace on a cool damp night.

Chapter Two

"**Knock-Knock!**" **Trudy yelled** out, letting herself in the front door with a fistful of blooms from her garden in one hand and two bottles of Miraval Rosé in the other. It was France or nothing for that girl. With the evening sun pinkening the sky over the sea, Trudy stood there aglow in an oversize white linen shirt over vintage Levi cutoffs and strawberry-blond waves tumbling free. You almost didn't know what to stare at longer – her eyes that held every shade of turquoise or her Carly Simon smile that split her face. Trudy possessed the kind of unequivocal beauty that wasn't up for debate. It was a good thing she was such an excellent human or she would have been so easy to hate.

"Tru, did you *grow* these? They are amazing! Is there anything you're not good at," Sheri said, taking the flowers, knowing just the right vase of her mother's to hold the grand height of the deep blue delphinium stems and creamy yellow hollyhocks. "What would I do without you …"

"So, tell me something good, Sher, any new prospects in your life? In your pants specifically?" Trudy asked, pouring herself a generous glass of rosé and reaching in the fridge for some cheese and prosciutto like she lived there.

"Stop. And NO. I'm not even looking for that, Tru, not even on my radar. I mean, are you kidding me right now? I can hardly get out of my own way. I still feel like a dumpster fire – who'd want a piece of *that*?"

Trudy sipped her wine and let her friend talk. Historically, that made Sheri talk more, deny more, but Sheri didn't want to go down that road. She couldn't be more sick of herself, her problems, her poor-me crap. It was enough already.

"Enough about me. I'd rather hear about your new book and all the hot sex you and Griff are probably still having every single night after twenty-whatever years of marriage."

"Do you though? Really?" Trudy said, grinning over her glass.

"Shut UP, really? Still? I can't ... I mean, good for you, that's great, that's really, just, good for you." Sheri didn't have it in her to be jealous of her dearest, most selfless summer friend, but she sure wouldn't mind tearing a page out of her playbook.

Sheri and Trudy met on Nantucket in their twenties that singular enchanted summer between honeymoon bliss and having children when the cosmos seemed to offer itself at their feet. Griff, Trudy, Tommy, and Sheri were a gilded foursome; boating, beaching, surfing, and sunning. For two magical weeks they could see their entire futures in each other's eyes – the names of their unborn children, their dream jobs and rise to fame and fortune – and scheduling Nantucket summers around each other until the end of time. They got most of it right. But Trudy and Griff got more of it right – and were still impossibly in love and on the same page even after the shitstorms of life and loss, opportunity and defeat.

"Let's take this little soirée outside," Sheri said, "I think better with the ocean serenading me." She left the wide glass door open to let the island air in to snoop around the house, lifting curtains and bedspreads and having its way.

"George and Rose picked a winner with this place – rolling moors out front and the Atlantic as your backyard," Trudy said, setting the cheese board on the small teak table between them.

"*Moor to Sea*," Sheri said, "I've always loved its name." She lifted a conch from the railing beside her chair, wondering where it came from. To stare inside it was to see the whirl of a galaxy, the spiral of life itself, the wonder of what could be. Sheri's thoughts swam loose, buoyed by the wine. The shell blurred before her, glossy pink and peach swirling together. "I'm sorry."

"Say anything else you want, but do not apologize," Trudy said, "It's been a hell of a year for you, you're entitled to tears." Trudy drew her mile-long legs up under her chin and stared out at the ocean. "How's George – if it's okay to talk about this – I've been trying to imagine that man sitting still, and I can't, though I know he'd never be anywhere else than by Rose's side."

Sheri wiped her eyes on the hem of her Cisco T-shirt and reached for her glass before responding. "He's incredible. I mean, he's George! Right? My amazing dad – who'd never let on that he'd want to be anywhere other than where he needs to be right now. This is his journey too now, *their* journey. He and Mom go for drives, picnics, and he says it doesn't matter if they show up at a favorite restaurant and she smiles and says *oh, what a lovely new spot, dear.* It breaks my heart, but I don't think he lets it break his, Trudy, he just keeps putting one foot in front of the other. Every single day. With a smile and a kiss for his bride, telling her the story of their lives. It's like "The Notebook," I swear, my dad is too adorable, it's heartbreaking."

Trudy reached across the little table to give her friend's hand a squeeze. They'd lost Griff's uncle to Alzheimer's two years ago. "It's the cruelest thing, I know. I wish I could tell you it gets easier. I wish I could tell you it's worse for us instead of them. What I can say is that Rose and George are so lucky to have each other."

"A *freakin*men, sister. Cheers to you, Mom and Dad," Sheri said, raising her glass to the purpling horizon.

"Let's get some more liquid gold into that glass and change the subject. You know I am always here for you, but enough heavy stuff for now. Like do you at least have a hot contractor lined up for these projects? I wish George had asked for recommendations – Griff knows everyone."

Sheri let out a sloppy laugh, "yeah *right* – like this is some summer Hallmark movie where the sad divorcee hooks up with the hot fix-it guy in a tool belt, tan hardbody, shirtless and glistening."

"Not that you've given it any thought *at all* ... ha!" Trudy said, throwing her head back in a laugh, a golden waterfall of hair all around her.

"Please, Tru, you know me better. That's more Wyn's style anyway – hey, wait – Wyn's coming, maybe you're onto something! She's single and gorgeous ..."

"Well, you know my Oliver has always thought so – wouldn't it have been so perfect if that worked out?"

"They were so cute those few summers, weren't they? Jeez, we were practically planning the wedding," Sheri said, remembering their kids' crushes on each other, just never at the same time. She let out a sigh that could have luffed the neighbor's flag.

"Well *that* wasn't about Ollie and Wyn's ships passing in the night ... what gives?"

"I haven't told you everything. About Tommy, I mean," Sheri started. And when Trudy sat up to interrupt, Sheri held up her hand to stop her. "Let me get through this first, then you can respond. Tommy's *with* Stephanie. Still. I thought it was a phase, you know? That it wouldn't last. I get it – he was lonely, I worked all the time and what emotion and energy I didn't expend on social work clients was reserved for the girls. Fun Tommy needed fun Sheri ... I guess I let her get away from me, from us. I don't know, I don't know how or exactly when it happened. Anyway – Stephanie was supposed to be just some young rebound chick, you know? Just some hot career business owner that his company hired for their advertising ... except now they *live* together. With her six-year-old son, Aaro. That's *A-a-r-o*, but exactly like *a-r-r-o-w*, that thing that pierces your damn heart."

Trudy stood, pulling her friend to her feet and steered her into the kitchen. "I think we need more wine ..."

∞

A couple bottles deep, somehow the two women still managed to grill steak tips, asparagus, and portobellos to sublime perfection. They'd laughed the night and the anguish away – dissipating the hurt and anger, poking holes in the gathered energy of Sheri's private storm. They were drawn back outside for a last look at the ocean, in time to see that the moon had climbed out of the water, hanging cool and detached in the night sky, tipping the waves with silver.

Chapter Three

SHERI HADN'T BROUGHT HERSELF to fully move into the first-floor master yet but once Trudy had left, she sat at her dad's big desk in there to give his detailed note a closer look before heading upstairs to bed.

Deciphering her father's austere script was no easy task at her level of fatigue and intoxication and it occurred to her that she must have forgotten that the master bath needed a new toilet – she'd only been thinking of the outside work. This caused a new wave of dread to roll in her gut. *Dread* was probably too strong, but still, she wasn't in the mood for strangers in the house. And there were no plumbers on the list. Should she call her dad or just get a recommendation from the contractor coming on Monday? Which reminded her that she never returned Joe's text.

Sheri tried to feel happy that she *could* call her dad, that he was still in the world, even if he wasn't standing there in front of her with his wide, warm Geroge smile. Then she weighed her guilt at being at their beach house at all instead of in Vermont with them. Which was silly, of course, because her parents wanted her on Nantucket handling things, needed her to rise to the occasion. But still. It felt off. Everything akilter. And she missed her sister.

Oh, Mandy – I need you today.

Sheri wondered if anyone could hear her sister's name without hearing Barry Manilow's song. Their mother was the biggest Barry fan ever – would she remember him now, love him still? Sheri should play his records for Rose when she got back home. Mandy was named after that song but Sheri was not named after Steve Perry's song, "Oh, Sherrie" – which came out in the eighties after she was born, but it was becoming her anthem.

Oh, Sheri.

It still stung that her sister had waved it all away for the West Coast. Sheri hadn't gotten over missing her sister there by her side – in the summer bedroom they shared and combing the beach for treasure. But if she were being honest, Mandy never stayed there for long, was always rushing ahead – wanting to be the first to find the green sea glass, the unbroken conch shell, the first to catch a wave, a boyfriend, a life.

It had been Sheri's salvation when she met Tommy in college. Showing him her favorite place in the world that summer, getting to see Nantucket for the first time again through his eyes. He didn't run ahead, but instead, he'd folded her hand in his and matched her stride. Matched her joy, her curiosity, and her fear of sharks and the really big waves.

Teaching him to surf that first summer after junior year in college had empowered her like nothing had before. How incredibly cool she'd felt. Of course he'd picked it up fast – damn boys. She'd loved how open he was to trying anything and everything, ever-ready with an endearing smile, disarming anyone in his path, damn him. He couldn't help his laughing eyes, the impossible silver-blue of them. How her internal temperature would climb ten degrees when she was the focus of his gaze. How it still did. *Damn him!*

He wasn't the type of guy she normally went out with. He'd been so obvious in his confidence, so annoyingly extroverted. His energy demanded attention. But you couldn't always see your first red flag.

She wondered what Tommy was doing in that exact moment, if he ever thought of her. She still couldn't think of him without her heart folding. That even though he was the one who'd cheated, there was a part of her that shouldered some of the blame. It was never just one person's fault.

Her phone buzzed across the oak desk with an incoming text. It was late.

> Hi Mom, are you there yet? How weird is it without Nanna and Pops? Are you lonely? Have you seen Trudy yet? I'm still juggling my PTO – might have to change boat rezzy UGH will let you know! Love you

Her baby girl, twenty-three, adulting like nobody's business. Keeping up with all the acronyms of the day was a force, but even Sheri knew that PTO was *paid time off*. She was glad for the hybrid work model but liked it better when she had her girls all to herself all summer. Those days were gone, of course, her children were grown women now, having to actively schedule time to be with their mom. She worried sometimes that Wyn would take after Mandy, trade the East Coast for the West and never look back. They were alike in so many ways. But Wyn loved Nantucket more than Mandy did, and Sheri knew that no matter where in the world her work would take her, Wyn would always make it to the island and sink into it with her whole heart.

Tia too. Nantucket was gold to them both. But Tia was more practical emotionally, and in every other way, and wouldn't be one to let any place own her. She was like Mandy in that way. Good for Tia, Sheri thought, her financial wizard of a daughter, with her strict hair and nail appointments, barre and yoga classes three times a week, massages, and weekly facial masks. She was one put-together babe. Her boyfriend, Jackson, was basically the male version of that and Sheri worried if it might all be just a little too precise. She supposed time would tell. But then what the hell did time know?

Sheri needed sleep and the stillness it brought to her racing mind.

Chapter Four

DAWN PAINTED THE SEAFOAM walls of the room with peach. Sheri felt flannel-mouthed and dull. How had one glass of wine turned into ... well, too many. Drinking with Trudy was a slippery slope. She squinted at her phone that told her it was not yet five-thirty in the morning. She always forgot how early the sun rose on this island thirty miles off the east coast of Cape Cod.

Sheri had hauled herself up to her childhood bedroom. Even drunk she'd been unable to claim her parents' room as her own. If she agreed to have her name put on the deed, she'd have to grow up and get her shit together, and soon. Tia and Jackson would need the room she was in and Wyn would stay in the twin bedroom like always. Sheri understood what needed to be done but it was going to feel strange packing up her parents' personal things and the clothing that filled the closets and dressers. George and Rose were in every particle of air in that house. Sheri closed her eyes hoping for sleep to reclaim her.

Her head pounded in time with a distant knocking. And her phone was simultaneously buzzing. *What? Shit – was Joe at the front door?* Squinting through the texts on her phone she saw that she'd apparently told him that eight o'clock Sunday morning was good. *Good for what*, she tried to recall, reaching for her shorts and T-shirt on the floor by the bed. She gave herself a quick once-over in the mirror over the white dresser, leaning in to rub smudged mascara from under her eyes but nothing more. This was not a Hallmark movie, there would be no steamy affair with a hot contractor. Jesus, who even said he was hot – she needed to get it together.

She pulled the front door open and was met with a pair of sea-green eyes of indistinguishable expression and a smooth tanned face. Sheri knew she was staring and it took a beat too long to collect herself.

"Don't tell me," the bright white smile was saying, "you thought I'd be –"

"A dude, yes. Sorry, please come in. Hi, I'm Sheri."

"Josephine. But everyone around here calls me Joe," the adorable young woman said, "I apologize for any confusion, I …"

"You have nothing to apologize for if people jump to conclusions. My dad hired you so that means you're the best. Josephine was his mother's name, come to think of it, my grandmother who died before I was born. I actually love Joe for a nickname. I'm curious – did my father know your full name?"

"He did. Maybe that's why he hired me? Either way, I can promise you, Folger & Worth will not disappoint. Now, sorry to have to bother you on a Sunday, but I'd like a fresh look around, see if the winter laid any surprises on us as far as rot and that kind of thing. May I?"

Sheri invited Joe in and took in her compact form in her forest-green polo shirt and khakis as she followed her through the kitchen to the deck outside. Her arms were lean and tan. Hair the color of rich honey was stuffed under a baseball cap but there was no disguising its abundance in the low bun. Sheri tried to remain neutral about the work that needed to be done, tried to channel her dad as she stepped into this new role of being in charge.

"Looks pretty straightforward – complete deck, full stairs and railing rebuild here, and let's take a peek up at the widow's walk – I have here that we're just replacing a few banisters, is that right?" Joe asked after they'd ascended the vertical ladder-steps to the widow's walk. "I don't mind telling you that I don't feel comfortable with that," Joe said as she pulled a rotted post away from the railing with ease. "See this? There's no way the rest of these aren't splintering and compromised also. We'll need to replace the railing and posts all the way around."

"Absolutely. And sorry if this is a stupid question, but are we replacing all this with more wood that will eventually rot and need replacing again? Or are we considering newer, more weather- and moisture-resistant composite materials?"

"Excellent question," Joe said, "I think you'd want to maintain the traditional look of your home and stick with cedar. Pressure-treated wood is another option for decks and stairs but it's not as popular here on Nantucket, aesthetically speaking." As they went back down the ladder and closed the trap door to the widow's walk, Joe continued to fill Sheri in on the differences between cedar and the pressure treated.

The early sun was gathering its July strength as they stood on the back deck. Sheri loved how it lit the huge expanse of the ocean before her to a jewel-toned green-blue. Her headache was ramping up instead of dissipating but she knew she'd earned every bit of it. With a hand to her forehead as a visor, she could see the steamship in the distance coming in. The Eagle, filled with *summer people* and their Jeeps, Range Rovers, kids, dogs, surfboards, and giant joy. Summer was officially ramped up with the Fourth of July already in the rearview and the island population would continue to swell from about fourteen thousand people to over eighty thousand.

"As I was saying, pressure-treated wood is regular softwood lumber, such as southern yellow pine or Douglas fir, that has been placed in a pressurized chamber and infused with a mixture of insect- and water-resistant chemicals – it really shouldn't be used where there is direct human-to-surface contact. Another drawback to pressure-treated lumber is its appearance. Larger boards have thousands of tiny slits cut into the surface to allow the chemicals to penetrate deep into the wood. These slits are visible in the finished product, and the chemicals can give the wood a greenish tint."

"Can't have that," Sheri added, feeling like the least sharpest tool in the shed.

Joe tucked a stray curl behind her ear and continued. "Cedar is popular for outdoor furniture, decks, and fences because it is naturally resistant to rot and decay, and doesn't require chemicals or stain to stay protected. You'll notice if you take a look around at your neighbor's properties and all over the island, cedar shakes are also used for roofing or siding material."

Of course Sheri knew the siding of her parents' house was cedar, like almost every other home and non-brick building on the island, and that it started out almost pink but weathered to silvery gray inside of two years. Her father had undoubtedly already had cedar in mind to replace what needed replacing – Joe was good to humor her. A dude would have been sarcastic and made her feel dumb. Was she going to pass out? She really needed to get a grip and a tall glass of water. She headed back into the kitchen while Joe took a trip down the fifty-seven steps to the beach for a closer look at what needed to be done there.

Sheri filled a glass of water for Joe when she returned and they took seats at the island. "Wow, this is really beautiful, soapstone, right?" Joe said, running her hand across the smooth charcoal counter surface veined with white.

Sheri leaned back in the high stool remembering how happy her mom had been to finally redo the 1970s kitchen. "Yes, my mother had a vision – after living with the original Formica counters, linoleum flooring, and dark oak cabinets for too long, she finally got what she wanted."

"I can't imagine it any other way," Joe said, "and these gorgeous cabinets – don't tell me – Benjamin Moore Chantilly Lace."

"Oh, you're good," Sheri said, taking in the bright kitchen with fresh eyes, appreciating all her mother's artful touches.

"Beautiful contrast with this maple flooring, your mom had remarkable taste."

"*Has*. She's still with us ... she's just–"

"I'm so sorry, I didn't mean ... George told me, please forgive me, Mrs. Steele, I–"

"Oh my God, call me Sheri, please, and no worries, it's just hard for me, you know? It sneaks up on me. And talking about her in the past, it just comes out and it's so wrong. Even though she's not *here*, and will never actually be here again, *she's still here*. Ugh – it's just so weird."

"I can't imagine. I really cannot imagine being either the person who slowly slips away from herself and everything she knows *or* the person she's slipping away from, I am so sorry."

Sheri tried to stop her eyes from filling, staring up to reverse gravity, at the oversize glass waterdrop pendant lights over the island. "Light Pool is the official color," she said of their translucent beauty, "Mom's only concession to color in her new kitchen." A tear slid down anyway.

"Hey, Sheri, I can come back if –"

"No, I'm good, sorry. So – what was the verdict on the stairs and how long is all this going to take?"

"As I discussed with George, my best guess is that this job should take at least two weeks, give or take," Joe said, "but judging from the height of your eyebrows right now – really excellent eyebrows by the way – you were expecting the job to take ...?"

"*Whew*, yeah, I mean I'm only here on-island for a month and I was kind of hoping to enjoy the peace and quiet for as long of that as possible, you know? And with my daughters arriving in a week, I guess I was picturing this to be done." Sheri was scrambling, surprised by her own lack of realistic expectations and trying not to put that on Joe. "Nothing against you, of course, not sure what I was thinking – I have exactly zero idea of what this job will take in labor and time. Sorry, I'm rambling ..."

"No worries, tell you what, let me make some inquiries. Maybe I can get more guys on the job and hammer it out quicker. Pun intended, ha. We'll have to demo the deck to rebuild that but good news – the staircase to the beach is in better shape than expected with actually only some of the steps needing help," Joe said with confidence, tucking her pencil behind an ear and lowering the small notebook she held. Her self-assuredness put Sheri at ease. She was a reassuring combination of professionalism and kindness.

"Oh, I'm so glad to hear that. And the widow's walk?"

"Can be done in an afternoon."

"And you can start …?"

"Monday at seven thirty a.m. Your neighbors may not be too excited about the noise but I assure you it's code-appropriate. I'll let you know more definitively how long it'll all take as soon as I hear back from some of my crew – I know some of them were looking for extra hours – does that work for you?"

"It does, thank you so much, Joe. Oh – I almost forgot – the master toilet needs replacing, can you point me in the direction of a reputable plumber?"

"Stay away from The Clog-Father and Royal Flush – but you didn't hear that from me – you can't go wrong with Hussey Brothers Plumbing & Heating, Coffin Cousins, or Heritage Home Service. Feel free to use my name."

As Joe backed her pickup truck down the driveway, Sheri allowed herself a ripple of satisfaction at getting shit done. A small ripple, but still. She changed into running clothes and decided today was as good a day as any to break in her new Hokas. *More cushion, more running*, was the promise as well as *why run when you can fly?* Sheri had a feeling there'd be more walking than anything, but as long as it was forward movement, she was good.

Chapter Five

SHERI JOGGED OUT TO North Pond and Lavender Lane, stopping every now and then to catch her breath and to try and understand why some of the new homes being built were so damn big. She hated to see it – besides being outrageously unnecessary, it was beyond the farthest thing from Nantucket's simple Quaker roots. Sweat poured. She couldn't let these things bother her so much. Instead, she looked out at the moors, the swishing grasses, and breathed in the salty-sweet humid air that was so different from Vermont's crisp earthy mountain air back home.

The outdoor shower was the best part of every run. She took a minute to be grateful that it wasn't visible from the back deck which meant it would neither be disturbed during construction nor her privacy compromised. She wished the repairs could have been completed in the spring rather than interrupt her precious time now – but that wasn't how her father rolled. He wanted her present and available should questions or problems arise. It really was the least she could do.

The rest of the day belonged to her and she wasn't about to squander it. She would make a lunch, pack her beach bag, then pick Trudy up for their Nobadeer Beach day. It would be insane there on a Sunday but that was part of the fun.

∞

"Hey, beautiful, perfect timing," Trudy said, stuffing her bag and chair into the back of the Bronco. She let out a wolf-whistle appreciating Sheri's new wheels, "Dang, girl, this is one gorgeous whip – what did you say the name of this sweet color was?"

"*Antimatter Blue* – weird, right? Who thinks up these names? I'm just glad it came out of retirement, I mean why would they discontinue this amazing color, I freakin' love it so much."

"It suits you, Sheri, I'm so glad you treated yourself, you deserve it."

"Such a funny word, I mean who deserves anything, you know? Such a strange way to think of things – does my mom deserve to have Alzheimer's? *Does anyone deserve that?* Because I went through a shitty divorce, did that make me somehow *worthy* of a new car? When bad things happen, do we feel like we should have good stuff coming – like that's our right or something?"

"Well, for fuck's sake, lighten up," Trudy said, adjusting the ball cap she wore to tame her wayward mane. "I guess I just meant that it's good to do things that make you smile, we need more people smiling. Maybe we need to stop with all the weights and measures, you know? And just be happy."

"I hear ya. And you're right, Tru, keep keeping me in line," Sheri said, pulling at her swimsuit top as they bumped over the sandy road to the beach. "But speaking of weights and measures, damn this bikini top is working overtime already. Do you find yourself staring in the mirror saying *where the Christ did these jugs come from?*"

"Um, *no*, and let's not rub that in, okay? How are yours still getting bigger? I wish you could pour some into my cups!"

"No, I don't want these things – talk about side-boob and long-boob, no thanks, I'm all set!"

"They look pretty damn good to me."

They laughed, ponytails flying, eighties playlist cranked. Tires deflated down to fifteen, off they went rumbling over the dunes onto Nobadeer Beach in search of the perfect spot to back up to the sea for the day. It was almost noon and they were surprised to find plenty of real estate still left. You couldn't control who was going to squeeze in beside you as the beach filled up and you could hope for a quiet couple or a nice small family. But what you might get is two jacked-up pickup trucks full of teenagers cranking Morgan Wallen and Jelly Roll, setting up Kan Jam and Spikeball, Yeti coolers filled with enough beer and High Noons to float a village.

"I could not be more happy than I am in this moment," Sheri said, plunking herself down in her beach chair next to Trudy. The waves were lit up by the sun and firing with a perfect offshore wind. "Lunch and a show!" she said watching the lineup of surfers, "but it kind of sucks now to be of the age where we watch instead of getting out there."

"Hey, Sher, hate to say it but we haven't gotten out there in more than a few years."

"Shh, I can't stand it. Our parents are supposed to be fifty, not us! It's too crazy. I mean, we still got it, right?"

"Yes, we definitely still got it. Were our moms still wearing bikinis at our age? I think definitely *no*. And isn't fifty the new thirty?" Trudy said, pushing her Ray Bans up on her head and closing her eyes against the sun.

Sheri looked over at her beautiful friend, stretched out in her low beach chair, long and lean, rose-gold hair glinting in the sun, such a contrast to her own chocolate-brown tresses. Yes, she thought, they were way younger than their parents had been. She pushed her fake Ray Bans up onto her head to soak in the rays. Then laughed thinking about how her girls always made fun of her *Ray-Dans,* telling her she really needed to grow up already and spring for a real pair of sunglasses. Tommy always had the real thing. He spared no expense outfitting himself in the finest gear for whatever he had going on. She didn't really begrudge him that, he worked hard for his money, it just seemed so unnecessary. *God*, she was hung up on essential versus excessive. Maybe she needed more excess in her life. Getting to spend a month on Nantucket was a start.

Her parents were frugal, she'd had a conservative upbringing. Sure, they'd had nice things, what they needed, and a lot of what they wanted, but it was never showy. And despite the growing consensus of what owning a home on Nantucket stood for these days, her parents' place was different. George and Rose bought the Nantucket house in the seventies, it was *different*! She wasn't even remotely in the same league as people who bought now, or even Trudy and Griffin, who could afford to buy their Nantucket property in the early throes of the island real estate boom, which, it appeared, would continue ever after. It was never going back to simple and quaint, it just wasn't.

"Pretty quiet over there," Trudy said, eyes still closed against the sun, "solving all the problems of the world? Or coming up with new ones?"

"You know me well. I could probably argue with myself all day – debating the what-ifs, the why-nots, what used to be, and what will never be again."

"Sounds exhausting. It must be wine o'clock."

"And the season of day-drinking has begun," Sheri said smiling, reaching into her cooler.

"Umm, Sher? Don't look now, and by that I mean look NOW – isn't that *Tommy* down there by the water? And is that the hot mom he – "

There were so many things wrong with what Sheri just heard coming out of Trudy's mouth that she sat paralyzed in her chair letting her drink drop in the sand.

Chapter Six

TRUDY COULDN'T TEAR HER eyes away from the scene unfolding before them. Leaning forward in her seat for a closer look, she said, "Damn, he's looking fine – that *is* him, isn't it?"

Sheri's heart galloped in her chest and she was white-knuckling the arms of the highboy chair her mother had preferred. Suddenly it was an old-lady chair. And she hated it as much as she hated what the sight of her ex-husband still did to her. Her traitorous body turning gummy and boneless, her heart expectant and quaking. There he was, giving surf lessons to that yummy-mummy's little boy. In her black cheeky bikini with a long mahogany braid down her back. Right there in front of them, on Nantucket Island, thirty miles out to sea, and some three hundred miles from his Vermont home.

"Sheri? Say something, should I be worried about you? We can move, we can leave, we can call the ex-husband police, whatever you want to do ..."

"I taught him to surf." It came out as an exhale. Expressionless and dazed, she couldn't look away. "Twenty-seven years ago I taught that jackass how to paddle, how to stand up on a board, how to wait for the best set, the right wave. Who does he think he is right now, I cannot ..."

"Soo that must be Stephanie?" Trudy said watching Tommy give the board a small push in a low breaker so the boy could ride it in. Stephanie, jumping up and down, perky boobs and butt bouncing in time with the braid slapping her bronzed back.

Anger would have been so much better, Sheri thought, as a hot tear rolled down her face. *Easier.* Memories unraveled in her movie mind of Tommy and her when their girls were little. Tia had wanted nothing to do with surfing, but Wyn wanted up on that board as soon as was humanly possible. *How many times could a heart break,* she wondered, fumbling for her dropped cup that Trudy was already refilling. Rooted to the chair she couldn't tear her gaze from the happy threesome walking back down the beach out of view.

"Well. What. The. Hell." Trudy said.

Sheri turned to face Trudy. Some unnamed storm crackled in her veins making her hands shake. She and Tommy had been divorced for two years, there was no good reason why seeing him should cause her blood to congeal and clog in her ears like a bass drum. But it did. "Why would he do this to me? He had to know I'd be here. How, why?" Sheri tried to remember anything she knew about Stephanie, which was decidedly little. Did she have a place here? Was Tommy just trying to mess with her? No, that wasn't his style. But WHY then, why Nantucket?

"I don't have those answers for you, Sheri – could it be a coincidence? I mean he loves Nantucket too." Trudy put her hand up to stop her friend from jumping in, "I know that he was only ever here in the first place because of you, I get that, but what were you guys, twenty-one? That was like twenty-eight years ago – that's a lot of summers he's been part of this place because of you ..."

"Whose side are you on?" Sheri said, taking a healthy slug of her drink. "Don't answer that, I know it's a trick question. Do you and Griff still talk to him? That would be weird but I know you're his friends too. God, I hate this. Sure as hell didn't think I'd have to be thinking about

Tommy while I was here." As soon as the words had left her mouth she felt them crawling back down her throat. Who was she kidding? Summer memories here with her parents and sister were second only to the magical memories of falling in love with Tommy. And how lucky she'd felt every summer thereafter, building their little family, adding onto the precious Nantucket memories like a dribble castle.

You couldn't delete a person out of your heart the way you could from your Facebook page.

"You know what? I bet you anything he's just here for the weekend or maybe wrapping up a Fourth of July week – he knows that's not your usual time here, right? And what are the chances of running into him again?"

"Umm, on an island fourteen miles long by three and a half miles wide? I'd say pretty damn good. And by good, I mean bad. Did you *see* her body, Trudy? She looks like a twenty-year-old, Jesus. How can I compete with that?" Sheri looked down at the folds in her belly, bared to the world in a bikini, and felt ten kinds of foolish.

"You're *not* competing with that, Sheri. He's moved on and so have you," Trudy said, sitting up in her chair to face Sheri, her lithe body absolutely on a par with the yummy-mummy's. "Or, what I mean is, you will. You are beautiful and funny and smart and a total catch. So what do we know about this Stephanie anyway?"

"What, besides the fact that she's basically an infant and has a six-year-old son named Aaro with hair as long as hers? Well, I know that *she's* not worried about her tits and ass hitting the floor any time soon. And I know that if my daughters were to stand beside her there would be no telling the age difference. I know that she makes Tommy younger while the whole thing is making me older. And that while he's trotting full-speed ahead like a stallion, I'm treading water. Or going under – I can't tell anymore."

"Hey, let's get outta here, Sher, maybe move this party to Sandbar at Jetties for mudslides?"

"Sure," Sheri said, staring out, "in a minute, okay?" The wind had shifted to onshore and was trashing the waves. No more clean barrels, the breakers were spilling. The experienced surfers bowed out while newbies got tossed trying to catch waves that broke short. Things can change on a dime, Sheri knew that. She also knew about shoveling shit against the tide and how that ends up. Clouds scudded in over the sun mirroring the quick disenchantment and murk that coiled in her stomach.

Chapter Seven

WHILE THE BEACH DAY hadn't played out quite the way she'd imagined, Sheri was glad they'd gotten Nobadeer out of their system for the time being. A quieter day at Smith Point or Ladies Beach was in order for next time. The girls would definitely want to hit up *Nobes* when they arrived. Wait, would their father still be on-island? Did Tia and Wyn *know* he was there? She decided she wouldn't bring it up when she Face Timed the girls. Nantucket wasn't supposed to be so complicated. It was her place of peace, sacred, she had to let this go.

Oh, Sheri.

The first thing she needed to do was move herself fully into the master and out of her childhood bedroom. Maybe she'd splurge and hit up Nantucket Looms for some new fun pillows for the bed and a handwoven throw to make it her own, periwinkle or lavender. She'd put away her mother's faded mauve chintz bedspread and wouldn't give herself a chance to feel bad about it. She'd have plenty to feel bad about the day her mother no longer remembered who she was. *Stop it,* she scolded herself, chanting her mother's words: *don't borrow trouble from tomorrow.*

She needed to check in with her dad. But as she reached for her phone it was already summoning her – a FaceTime call coming in from

Tia in New York, and Wyn being added to the call from Santa Cruz. How she loved seeing her daughters in living color, even if it was only on a screen in her hand. Which still seemed like a miraculous thing to Sheri.

"Hi, Mom! I can't believe you're *there*," Tia said, "I can't wait to get out of the city!"

"I bet! But weren't you just in Montauk with Jackson's family over the Fourth? I mean how bad can I really feel for you?" Sheri said.

"Yeah, seriously dude – boohoo poor Tia," Wyn said.

"Shut up, Wyn, look who's talking," Tia said, the rivalry morphing her pretty features. "And very funny, Mom, I know, but it's not Nantucket – nothing is! So how is everything – how weird is it to be there alone – have you talked to Nanna and Pops since you arrived?"

"Slow down, kiddo. I was actually just about to call them when you rang, and yeah, it's very weird to be here alone – I'm not sure I ever have been. Not without at least one of you girls, and one parent or another …"

"And Daddy," Tia added.

"Right …" Sheri's heart rate tripped at the mention of Tommy, who she was trying to forget she'd just seen at their favorite beach, frolicking like he was in some MTV video, with his infant-girlfriend and her kid. Impossible to swallow– like the razor-sharp corner of a Triscuit – it poked and stabbed all the way down. Sheri wondered if Tia was hinting at knowing Tommy was on Nantucket, or if she'd just always see her parents as a unit, unable to think of one without the other. Sheri decided it was easier to just let Tia do the talking, she usually had a lot to say. Sheri would throw in a few appropriate questions and *mm-hmms* for good measure but for the most part, it would be the Tia show – just the way she liked it. It was too easy to say the wrong thing.

While she loved seeing her daughters' faces right there in front of her, she was less crazy about her own image in the corner. The way one pictured oneself was not always commensurate with reality. But this wasn't about her. Her daughters took turns interrupting each other while Sheri tried to keep up and respond in the right places. Easier said than done. She knew they'd mostly be sweet to her face but the injustices of being a parent, a mother specifically, knew no bounds. Children, especially ones of divorce, were time bombs. Even the happy and successful ones were walking around holding onto a lifetime of inequities waiting to detonate in the heat of a moment.

It was a hard thing to reconcile. One day you're Mom to these beautiful little darlings and you have all the power and star status. You decide what they're eating, wearing, and doing, and who with. Then suddenly the power is gone. Your advice incites anger, your opinions are dated, and everything is an unasked-for judgment. So you try to step back and hold your tongue. And then they tell you that you don't care. All you can do is tell yourself over and over that it's their life. Their decisions, their mistakes, *their life*.

Sheri tuned back in to hear Tia scolding her younger sister for poor planning, for turning *Planes, Trains, and Automobiles* into a series.

"WHY would you want to fly to Boston from San Francisco then have to get a bus to Hyannis *then* a boat to Nantucket?" Tia said to Wyn, "Because you kept putting it off like you always do and just couldn't book it when I told you to and that was all you could get, that's why."

"Looks like you don't even need me for this conversation," Wyn said to her sister, "and *yay* for you and your boyfriend flying straight to the island – you're my freakin' hero."

"Girls," Sheri cut in, "Enough. File it away as a lesson for next time, now give me your dates and times."

"Oh, that's just it, Mom, it's all happening on the same day. Except now you'll be going back and forth from airport to boat to pick us all up – how ludicrous is that?" Tia said.

"Okay, okay, take a breath – do you two do this for my benefit?" Sheri could see Wyn rolling her eyes as she folded her laundry. *If what she was doing to her clothes could even be counted as folding.* "And I can see that you do actually have fun together sometimes, you know, I see your Instagram stories and Snaps, so why—"

"Mom. How many times do I have to tell you that social media is *not* real life?!" Tia scolded. Again.

Sheri was definitely not asking the girls now if they knew that their father was currently on Nantucket. One shitshow at a time. They signed off on a high note with a suddenly smiling pair of sisters giddy about Nantucket being around the corner.

∞

After a quick shower to rinse away the sea and sunblock, Sheri found herself excited to get to Nantucket Looms before they closed, then maybe grab a drink and a bite somewhere in town all by herself. That was progress, wasn't it? Isn't that precisely what she'd been telling her younger colleagues at work – that they needed to be able to sit at a bar alone? It was time Sheri put her money where her mouth was. And it wasn't like she'd never done it before – it's just that Nantucket was her happy place, the place of so many love-drenched memories, and it just felt wrong not to be sharing that with someone.

Now, what do you wear for a date with yourself?

Chapter Eight

SHE FINALLY DECIDED ON her white jeans. They fit her like a glove and had a frayed hem at the ankle that suited her. She paired them first with a flowy boho top but landed instead on a navy linen halter-tyle top with tiny fabric buttons down the front. She wore her LOLA pendant, a gold compass rose, she loved how it looked embedded in the silver medallion on a chunky silver chain. It was a gift from Tommy and one of her favorite pieces of jewelry. She wouldn't let herself go down that candlelit road remembering the night he gave it to her.

She decided to make herself a gin and tonic, tall, lots of ice, and with two slices of lime. She brought it out to sit on the deck one last time before it was to be ripped out and replaced. The soft sun was low on the spent day, the light defied description. Nantucket Looms would have to wait another day - this was more than worth it to Sheri.

Rubbing the compass at her throat she could feel the memory cartwheeling in. It had been their fourteenth wedding anniversary but Tommy thought it was their fifteenth. He'd booked her favorite corner table at Galley Beach to celebrate their June anniversary. Sheri had felt like a movie star – the Galley always was and always would be the place to see and be seen. It smelled like garlic, warm bread, and expensive perfume and as they walked passed the zinc bar to their table, the piano man was playing Sinatra's "I've Got the World on a String." She remembered staring out with undisguised awe at the wide beach where people sat in divans and papasan chairs surrounded by tiki torches as the sun sank into the sea. Everyone was electric and beautiful.

After dinner, he'd presented her with a box wrapped in a Nantucket map. Inside the bigger box was a smaller one, LOLA's iconic ice-blue box with a white satin ribbon. Nestled inside the box was a note: *Under the stars, I'll always be where you are.*

Looking out now at the Atlantic rolling in and rushing out, Sheri remembered the next thing Tommy had said as he clasped the pendant around her neck. *And y'know, so you'll always be able to find your way back to me.* She pressed at the tear trying to escape from the corner of her eye and took a long sip of her drink.

She gathered up her handbag and keys before she lost her nerve. She wasn't wasting the outfit *or* the gorgeous island night.

∞

On her way into town, she thought about all the cool bars and restaurants with cutting-edge menus and the vibes to match and contemplated what atmosphere she was craving. Bouncing over the cobblestones of the narrow section of upper Main, past impressive homes built by whaling fortunes in the 1800's and around the Civil War monument centered there, Sheri was reminded of the island's storied history that began more than two-hundred years before that monument existed, and the contrast of yesterday's island against today's.

A *billionaire's playground* it was called now, home to famed artists and authors. It was hard to imagine its humble and fraught beginnings. That for the better part of a century, the little island of Nantucket was the whaling capital of the world. So while many people visited this small island thirty miles off the coast of Cape Cod for its charm, miles of unspoiled coastline, high-end boutiques, and five-star restaurants, hotels, and inns, Sheri often wished for a time machine to take her back, just for a day, to the simpler times, simpler dress – cottages instead of estates, horses instead of SUVs, farms, and family.

She couldn't resist the early love stories that brought the feuding founding families together, the audacious women who rose up to run things while all the men were at sea for years at a time, and all the people of color whose indomitable spirit changed the course of history. She wanted all of that to still matter. More than the rows of yachts lined up in the boat basin – each taller and longer than the summer before.

How had it become so elite, coveted? It was New England for god sake – not some tropical paradise – fogged-in half the time with no coming or going. She just didn't get it. But then she laughed at herself, sliding her shiny new Bronco into a prime spot and checking her hair and lip color in the mirror. Not exactly dismounting a horse covered in dust and dirt. The present day wasn't all bad, she conceded, having decided on the bar at Straight Wharf Restaurant for a Goombay Smash and their smoked bluefish pâté.

It was still early, the bar quiet, and awash in the peach glow of the setting sun. The light was honeyed and Sheri let her mood join the party, appreciating the space before it filled to overflowing with young beautiful people as the bartenders crafted one iconic rum punch after another. She let her mind wander like the people passing by outside either just arriving or hurrying to catch a boat. The scene was timeless; the happy new arrivals to the magic of Nantucket – smiles taking over their faces, hoisting bags, babies, and dogs, and then the departures – harried and hurrying, burdened under the weight of more bags than they came with, sun-crisp skin, and the gloom of having to leave such a spellbinding place.

She'd been both. Everyone had.

It never got old taking in the outfits parading by, the youth and beauty, and then those trying overly and obviously to preserve it. She let a sigh escape, dreading the inevitable *preservation* of things – her looks, her memory. The house! She would rise to the occasion, dammit, and do her parents proud by taking over its ownership and care. She needed to escape her undertow of self-pity and slogging around in the past for Chrissakes. She loved how easy and possible it all felt while her brain was dancing on a pillow of rum.

"Is this seat taken?" Sheri turned to the familiar voice and stared straight into the silver-blue eyes of her ex-husband. Nothing could have prepared her for that moment – or what it did to her – the jackhammering of her heart, the sweat that pricked at her armpits, and the blank her brain was drawing. The bluefish pâté hadn't come yet, her second drink was on its way – she couldn't, *wouldn't* leave now. She looked clumsily around for Stephanie, the infant-girlfriend, before being able to form her mouth around words. "Of all the gin joints in all the towns in all the world, you walk into mine …"

"*Casablanca*, very nice," Tommy said, looking better than a cheating ex-husband had a right to.

She tried not to notice how white his smile looked against his tan skin and tan hair and how in summer both took on a sheen of gold. Or the cream trousers that sat perfectly on his slim hips, or how the linen shirt of the palest blue was cuffed above his forearms of lean muscle – the muscle of someone who never stopped moving but who also never intentionally exercised. Her mind spun its feeble, rum-slick wheels trying to figure out what bothered her most about the moment.

"You look good, Sher," he said. Then she saw his eyes get all silky as he noticed the compass rose at her throat. "You're wearing the necklace," he said, with a shadow of something in his voice.

"Yeah, well, it sure as shit isn't because I'm lost without you or whatever scenario you're imagining. I'm fine, you know, just *fine*. What are you doing here, Tommy? I mean, really." Sheri was surprised at the strength of her voice when there were years of dominoes falling inside, collapsing on each other in slow motion. Her drink arrived just in time to give her mouth something to do. Over the thrumming in her ears, she heard him order his usual, a Miller High Life. The most boring drink on the planet. For a man, the only man, who'd ever made every soft place inside her feel like magma. Precarious and volatile.

He stood with his arms leaning on the bar while she sat. And while Tommy had never been the type to make her feel like the only person in the room – everyone in his radius was the beneficiary of at least a flicker of his silver-gazed regard. But when he did turn to her, fully, his attention was incandescent, it filled hollows she didn't know existed. Holding his gaze felt like a public indecency.

"The girls told me about your mother. I'm so sorry, Sheri, was it a sudden onset? Jeez, I just can't picture Rose as anything but razor-sharp, never missing a trick," Tommy said, angling his body closer. The bar was filling up, getting louder.

He smelled as she'd remembered – sunshine mixed with the leather and cinnamon tones of the Aramis cologne he still wore. At least Stephanie hadn't changed that. Fuck Stephanie. She didn't even want that name in her brain at the same time as her mother's.

"Which is why she was able to mask it for so long," Sheri said, temporarily relieved to have something else to talk about other than why the hell her ex-husband was standing close enough to breathe in his hoppy High Life breath in a bar on Nantucket. "That and she'd convinced herself that forgetting things was a normal part of getting older. She got really good at all the little tricks - writing detailed lists and keeping an exhaustive calendar of appointments, bills, and her medications."

"And your dad didn't think anything was out of the ordinary?" Tommy asked, then doubled back to rephrase. "Strike that. George is one of the brightest human beings I know, I didn't mean to imply –"

Sheri's rum-tickled brain allowed her to view her mother's dementia through a more detached lens. If not exactly detached, then distant and with oddly more clarity. "I'd asked myself that at first too –

looking for something, *someone* to blame. But it's not like anything could have prevented it or changed its ultimate course, you know? And, you're right about my dad, he really is the smartest guy, but don't we all have our blind spots? Especially about someone you know as well or better than you know yourself? He would have made the same excuses about her forgetfulness. Aging *sucks*. But when she got lost coming home from the supermarket she'd been going to for forty years, well, that was that."

Tommy let his arm lean against hers. The heat of his bare skin against her was too much. And not nearly enough. She felt drunker than she should only two drinks in. Well, three, if you counted her seaside gin and tonic back at the house. "I'm just so sorry, Sher, it isn't fair. I know that doesn't change anything, but—"

"Let's change the subject, Tommy, like *what are you doing here*? You didn't answer that question." Sheri spoke without getting caught in the storm of his silver stare. Tommy rubbed his clean-shaven jaw. Buying time? Thinking up a lie? Did it matter?

"Stephanie's father just bought a place here – stupid amount of money – I know, don't give me that look."

"What – because she apparently represents everything we always said we hated about people like that suddenly wanting a piece of Nantucket? Forget it, Tommy, I really don't care what you do or who you do it with. Do our daughters know you're here?" At that moment the bartender placed two drinks in front of them.

"From that enthusiastic group of ladies over there at the end of the bar," the bartender said nodding in their direction, where they stood sipping their own drinks, smiling and waving, "they think you two are, and I quote, *adorable* and *couple goals*."

"Oh brother," Sheri said, "let's not divest them of their wildly off-the-mark misconception. Bottoms up, cowboy."

"Should you really – never mind. Cheers. And no, our girls do not know I'm here. It was all pretty last minute, and to be honest, I didn't think you'd be on-island yet. Sheri, when will you believe that I'm not on this earth for the sole purpose of screwing with you?" His silver-blue eyes shone with that impossible mix of sincerity and seduction that Sheri had no defense against.

She looked him dead in the eye and let the question hang. He wasn't an evil person, she knew that. It always takes two. Not that anything excused cheating, but she'd let their relationship come in last – after the girls, after her job, her parents, and even, sometimes, her friends. And Tommy was not a man who could or should ever be put at the bottom of the pile. Hindsight was, well, a clearer view. Which was more than she could say about the view at the moment with her eyes threatening to fill. "We did have some good times, didn't we though?" she said, braving eye contact again.

Tommy let go of the breath he'd been holding, nudging Sheri's arm with his own and moving his body closer to hers, "Better than good, Sher, come on, please don't cry."

The memory of meeting Tommy edged in. It was her junior year at the University of Vermont and she'd slipped on the sidewalk one snowy January morning hurrying to class. She'd gone down hard, slick Bean boot soles no match for the layer of ice under fresh snow falling. Books and papers flew out of her tote fanning all around her, the icy wind knocked right out of her lungs. She remembered lying on her back, too stunned in the moment to do anything but watch the snowflakes drifting down on her when Tommy Steele leaned into her view asking if she needed help getting up. She did, and *yes, please*, she'd told him. Tommy had missed his class to help Sheri to the Student Health Center where it was determined that her ankle had suffered an avulsion fracture.

"We did," she said, "so many great times." They almost had to yell to hear each other now. The bar had filled, spilling over into a line outside of people waiting to get in. The bluefish pâté was long gone and they decided to give up their spot to make room for the younger crowd. "Tavern chicken wings! That's what we need right now," Sheri said, almost falling off her bar stool.

"It's the UVM late-night munchies all over again," Tommy said, steering Sheri out the door onto the uneven brick sidewalk, "except that it is not late-night by any standards!"

"Well, we're kind of old now. Hey, remember Howard Johnsons and potato skins? And, *ohmygod* – Nectar's fries and gravy!" Sheri said, almost sure she wasn't slurring her words.

"How could I forget *HoJo's*? And how did we not die driving there at two o'clock in the morning – after quarter drafts at Last Chance and pitcher after pitcher at What Ale's You?" Tommy said as they rounded the corner to the Tavern.

"And the Chicken Bone baby! And Jeannie drove, Jeannie always drove. She was fine, we were fine, it was *fine*!" Sheri said, catching a toe on a brick sticking up and grabbing Tommy to stay upright.

"Ah, how it all started," Tommy said, supporting her as she leaned on him the rest of the way to their patio table. "How about we slow down, start with some waters ..."

"No. Way. No way! What's happened to you, we gotta keep the party going!"

"Sheri, you are adorable right now, don't get me wrong, but memory lane is a dangerous place."

"Oh, please. Let's eat wings then you can go home to your precious Stephanie."

"Let's say we eat some wings then I drive you home – I'm assuming that new ride of yours is parked around here somewhere?"

"How gallant of you! But then how will you get back to wherever Daddy's mansion is? And why aren't you *there*? With *bow* and *arrow*? Ha! I crack myself up – see what I did there?" she said, watching as a drop of wing sauce landed in slow motion on her white jeans. "Dammit!"

"Not a mansion," Tommy said, handing her a napkin, "it's a lovely old home on Pleasant Street."

"Ha! And by lovely and old you mean an eighteenth-century whaling captain's home with like six bedrooms that's been completely renovated in shades of white, white, and oh yeah, more white. What did you say he does, in the music industry? Rap was it? Is he like Bad Bunny's manager or some shit?"

"I always loved it when you got all fired up," Tommy said, eyes dancing as he leaned in to wipe away a smudge of wing sauce from Sheri's cheek with his thumb.

Sheri could feel the heat of him, sneaking up on her like his incurable charm. She imagined they were still married, out on the town to celebrate another Nantucket summer. It was so easy. So natural to pretend they'd have this night out alone – while their girls and her parents did their own thing. It's what they'd waited for all those years, what they'd earned after all. His eyes stayed on her as he fumbled for a napkin. She missed his touch when he took his hand away.

"Remember Wyn's obsession with fried calamari that summer?" Tommy said, with a wide smile transforming his features, "Jeez, what was she, ten?"

"That's right!" Sheri said, her own laugh bubbling up, "and Tia saying how gross it was – that it looked like she was eating rubber bands – how could I forget? And I'm with Tia – *ew*!"

"And then the Shirley Temple phase that followed the chocolate milk phase..." Tommy said, resting his hand on Sheri's leg. "Will we ever get used to them ordering *cosmopolitans*? When did *that* happen?"

"It's crazy. Time's sleight of hand, I'll never get used to it ..." Sheri could feel her voice and her mind drifting off.

"Aw c'mon, Sher, don't do that, don't fall away. Kids grow up, they all do. It was great when they were little, watching them go from tutus to prom gowns, soccer cleats to stilettos, Razor scooters to cars ... Just think of all that's ahead. Can't live in the past, no matter how great it was, right? Can't let it make you sad." He'd inched his chair closer to hers and the past had all but slid into her lap. "And *we* were great, weren't we, Sher?"

She could crawl right into his lap and melt there. Just move forward from this moment, with him. Could she forgive him? The question dropped into her mind as if whispered in the air.

"Shots!" she said.

"I'm going to save you from yourself," Tommy said with a half-smile signaling to the waiter for the check, "and I'm driving you home." A familiar warmth flooded Sheri at being taken care of. She'd missed that. It felt so nice.

Chapter Nine

CRUISING OUT EEL POINT ROAD with the windows down had a sobering effect on Sheri, or maybe that came from the fact that her ex-husband was currently behind the wheel of her new divorce present to herself. It was pretty messed up from any angle. Which is what alcohol was for! "Gin and tonics! That's what we need," she declared as they crunched up the shell driveway. "How the hell are you getting home now anyway?"

"I'll get an Uber. Don't worry about me – it's you I'm worried about."

"Well, don't worry about me. I'm fine, it's fine, we're *fine*!" What was she saying? What was she *doing*? What she knew was that she didn't want her good buzz to disappear, she didn't want to consider that she wouldn't be in this position without it. Her body flooded with some base desire that she'd missed and she needed to keep her brain quiet. Choosing her cushy thoughts, her rose-colored view that she was frantic to hold on to, Sheri filled two glasses with ice then tonic with just a splash of gin on top. Then she carried them out to Tommy who had wandered onto the deck.

"Ah. This never stops taking your breath away, does it – the massive Atlantic as far as you can see, the roar and boom of the surf, then its hiss rolling back out over the stones ..."

All Sheri could focus on was the draw and spill of the tide inside her, its rush and rolling. Was he feeling that? Or was she just way too caught up in a moment that was so far off-limits?

"It always blows me away, how clear the night sky is here," he said, still staring out instead of at her, "every constellation visible – the light of stars long dead, diamond points on black velvet."

Sheri's heart skittered hearing Tommy's poetic mind, she'd repressed so many of his more earnest qualities. Their eyes snagged then and she felt a warmth gathering at her core. His smile unfurled from one corner of his mouth, not quite making it to the other side. Their drinks stood forgotten on the deck railing but she tasted the herbal edge of gin tangled on their tongues as their mouths met. Heat was pooling inside her and her pillowed thoughts slow-danced. She wanted only this perfect moment – nothing more or less.

A warmth gathered between her legs. Tommy always had that effect on her and she had no defenses against it. There was something about his silver gaze that pulled more from her than she meant to give, the feather feel of his hand behind her neck drawing her into him.

"This was always so good," he whispered, moving his hands down her body, his eyes cartwheeling with mischief. She craved more of it. She pushed against him lightly, then harder, feeling the rush, the swell, the want. Whether it was an old want or a new one, she didn't care. It wasn't the time for talk, she wouldn't fish for information that might break her heart.

She wouldn't remember how they got to her bed. But she'd remember that they couldn't stop kissing, their smiles colliding, and the searing places where their skin touched. She wouldn't remember getting out of their clothes but she would remember the feel of him stiffening beneath her, and how her body rose to meet him. She would remember need stretching out in every direction, waking up her nerves, her blood, as she clenched and pulsed around him. And she would smell the warm pocket their bodies made – his sweat and detergent and deodorant knitting together to wrap her in a quiet comfort.

She would remember the gasps of her heart and that she never could take him in small doses. One taste only ever made things worse. She wouldn't remember their bodies breaking apart or what time he left. But she would remember waking up alone.

∞

An anxious feeling curled in her stomach. What had they done, what had *she* done to the careful dignity she'd been rebuilding? She laid her head heavily back down on the pillow and stared at the ceiling. The room was too bright for her blooming headache which meant it was well past sunrise. She bolted upright – Joe and her crew were due at seven thirty which was in exactly twelve minutes. Sheri decided to get right into running clothes so she could neither blow off the run nor wait too long to get it done. It also occurred to her that while she couldn't run away from the staggering fact that she'd slept with her ex-husband, she could punish herself for it.

The doorbell was ringing as she raked a brush through her hair. And as she reached to open the door she wondered how many workers Joe had been able to pull together for the demolition part of the job. Sheri was more than a little surprised to see only Joe standing there. "Good morning," they said at the same time.

"Come in," Sheri said, "Where's the rest of –" Her question was no longer necessary when she heard the sounds of the deck being dismantled. "Ah, never mind. Coffee?" Sheri said, as the two women walked in the direction of the kitchen. "I don't know about you but I need some caffeine *stat*." Putting a Keurig pod in the machine, Sheri wished she were more of a grind-your-beans, culture-coffee drinker. Instead of the self-loathing that came with the overuse of environmentally unsound single-use plastic crap. Giant laundry detergent bottles were hideous enough – where was it all going? And how was there even room in her brain for more self-loathing after last night? She was piling on – that's what she did.

"Sorry," she said in Joe's direction, as if Joe had heard the diatribe in her head, "my brain isn't firing on all cylinders this morning."

"No worries. So, as you can see I was able to round up a couple extra guys for today so all the demo work will be completed, and maybe the framing will begin by the end of the work day."

Sheri followed Joe's gaze out back to what looked like four guys getting to it. A lot of rippling muscle under sunbaked skin out there – it was hard to look away. "I know, right?" Joe said, "It's not the worst view. And they're good guys. Now, I should have clarified with you the other day, but in the interest of cutting costs, your dad had originally provided for bathroom access in the house for the workers should the need arise – is that alright with you, Sheri? Because we can get a portable toilet out here on the property if you'd rather."

"What? No. I mean *yes*, it's fine for them to use the bathroom down here – no, you don't need to bring a Jiffy John – but thanks for asking." What was her freakin' problem – staring out at the workers, stammering like an awkward horny cougar. Who fucked her ex-husband the night before. "Is that all?" Sheri said to Joe, regretting the dismissive tone she heard in her own voice. She felt so messed up after last night and craved the perspective a hard run might provide. "Don't get me wrong – I just, I have to get out of here, you know? Get some miles under my feet." Sheri said, scraping her hair into a low ponytail, trying to smooth out her expression and tone down the crazy. From the look on Joe's face, Sheri was acting borderline bananas.

"Is everything okay, Sheri? I promise you, these guys won't be any trouble. And Rocco – the dark dude out there – he's in charge when I'm not here, any questions you have, he's your guy." Joe was unflappable and Sheri realized, again, that she was in capable and professional hands.

And as if Rocco had heard his name, he straightened, sable eyes seeming to hone right in on Sheri, gave her a two-fingered wave, and went back to work. "You're leaving?" Sheri said to Joe, noting the keys jingling in her hand, "That's fine, whatever, like you said, they know what they're doing. Okay, so I'll see you when I see you I guess?" Jesus, she sounded like a fifteen-year-old worried about being left alone with the varsity football team.

Chapter Ten

SHE RAN THE LONG loop, the one that's two and a half miles out then two and a half back, forcing the five miles. It struck her that her life was a loop, ending up every day right where she began. That felt mildly pathetic. But also somewhat of a comfort, if she were being honest. Was she having a midlife crisis? She'd read that women experienced those later than men. That was about as convenient as women peaking sexually ten or more years *after* men. What sense did any of it make? She needed to get her shit together – her daughters, *their* daughters – would arrive in less than a week. But with every footfall thoughts and images of Tommy pressed in. That was not the direction she should be going. That was the problem with loops.

∞

Being back from a run was the best part. And as long as she didn't stare out the wall of windows on the beach side of the house, she could think straight. What was a little banging, a pack of sweaty ripped men, she thought as she blended a smoothie. She was the ice queen after all. At least that's how Tommy had started to think of her twenty years into their marriage. *When exactly did things start to shift*, she asked herself for the thousandth time. Tommy always had been just this side of flirtatious, generous with his smile that rode all the way up into his eyes – he wanted people around him to be happy, feel seen. And he was good at it. When had she stopped being able to return the favor?

She'd told herself it was because of her job as a social worker – the consuming nature of it – and co-running a nonprofit parenting program for underserved communities, which was not for the emotionally fragile. Looking back, she could see that it took more space up in her heart than she had to spare. Or maybe it had been Sheri wanting more of a life for herself once the girls were grown and needing so much less of her – like nights out with girlfriends, thirsty Thursdays, Dukes & Boots at their favorite country bar – they were all finally a little freer. They'd earned it. Hadn't they?

Why had Tommy been a casualty in all that? Why hadn't they been able to adjust to the new terrain before the train went off the track?

Stephanie happened. Stephanie and her hip women-owned-and-operated ad agency. Of course, the greenest advertising agency in Vermont was an inevitable pairing with Tommy's work as an urban planner. It was just her luck that it was run by a pack of females. The long hours spent on research, business strategizing, design, and then the measurement of performance. Together with the white-hot passion of the sun, the planet crumbling around it, and then the eight million forms of life that exist on it, Sheri never stood a chance. Sheri, who was too blind to see her husband drawn toward all that power and light, like Newton's apple to the ground.

Speaking of power and light, heat was rolling through her again thinking about last night. She was torn between shutting it down and giving herself over to it. Where was Tommy right now? She never did find out how he ended up with a night to himself – were things on the rocks with Stephanie? Were they ending? She scolded the part of her brain that seemed to suddenly be rooting for that. No. Her run hadn't given her the perspective she craved at all.

As if she'd conjured him, a text from Tommy buzzed in. She didn't like this post-shower sweat gathering in all the inconvenient places.

Hi

Really? That was it? Not even any blinking bubbles? Had he really just lobbed the ball so insignificantly into her court? She was absolutely not responding to that.

Hey

God, she was an idiot.

What are you doing rn?

Really? He couldn't type out *right now*? He was not a teenager. And *she* was not a damn teenager texting her boyfriend who already had a girlfriend!

Nothing. Errands in town maybe

Had she lost control? What was she doing?

Meet me for lunch?

Had he lost his mind? Where were Stephanie and Aaro? What was going on?

What are you doing, Tommy?

1:00 Slip 14

As IF. She was definitely not doing that.

She changed out of her Levi's cutoffs and tank top. She wasn't about to look like a cheerleader at a carwash fundraiser when she sat across from her ex-husband at Slip 14 on timeless Old South Wharf.

∞

She avoided direct eye contact with herself in the mirror as she brushed her teeth and added a second coat of mascara. She told herself she was straightening her hair for herself, and that she chose the pale pink sundress not because Tommy loved that color on her but because it was the only one without wrinkles. She was a live wire on the inside, there was a thrum she wasn't used to. It felt fan*freakin*tastic and she wasn't shutting it down. It changed the way she moved. She was liquid, pouring herself into her Bronco before the real Sheri noticed.

Boston's "More Than a Feeling" was playing. It seemed everyone loved eighties tunes these days. So, she lost herself in a familiar song. And she overthought the lyrics – *faces fade as the years go by* – but not everyone's did. Tommy's never would – she saw it every time she looked into Tia's eyes. Silver-blue, at times glacial and then fathomless. *As clear as the sun in the summer sky.* She kept singing, hoping for maybe a Foreigner song next, or Journey. Anything but "Don't Look Back" – it really had been too long since she'd felt this way.

A parking spot opened up in the center of town, it was a sign. She was on the right path. It felt so much better than grief or regret. Why had she wasted so much time trying to do what was expected of her? *Dump the cheating ex and move on, you deserve better, get yourself online and shop for a new man,* they'd said. Her heart was mincemeat back then, she wasn't in her right mind, or any mind at all to be swiping right. Couples survived infidelity all the time, she'd told herself, she just couldn't convince anyone else.

Fun, fearless Sheri walked with purpose on the blinding white shells of Old South Wharf past Bar Yoshi, debating a pre-lunch drink. Then she laughed at herself for thinking she needed that, she was on top of the world. She almost got hung up on the jagged memory of having to picture Tommy fucking someone else – her alter ego tapping with force on her shoulder in case she'd forgotten. But she pushed that bitch right off her shoulder.

It was a little before one o'clock, she was early, she would choose their table – with views of both the tiny galleries and boutiques lining the shell lane as well as the yachts rocking in their slips. She ordered a glass of chardonnay and sat with her menu and lust disguised as freedom.

She'd promised herself no mindless scrolling or taking photos and exiled her phone to her purse. She decided to just be part of the beautiful scene instead of documenting it. Sadly, that required a conscious decision. The sky was a limitless blue and hydrangea blossoms as pink and as round as pompoms pushed through white railings. Everything was lush and abundant, matching her new joy perfectly.

"You beat me! That never used to happen," Tommy said, sitting at the square patio table across from Sheri. Her stomach curled a little but she met his eyes better than she'd been able to meet her own in the mirror. Which might have been a mistake, it struck her, since the look he wore only ever reflected hers. "I half-expected you to cancel," he said, "or not to show at all."

Sheri felt a wave of disappointment at his apparent lack of confidence. She craved his self-assuredness, his cockiness, though it had often been their tipping point. Sitting there with her handsome ex-husband, her instinct was to consider, maybe, possibly, starting over with him. To forget about the past. The ugly parts anyway. She was only mildly aware of how tightly braided those two things were and of how impossible it may be to embrace one without the other. They had daughters to consider. It didn't matter that they were grown, in fact, it probably made things weigh more. She took a long sip of wine to banish doubt for the time being.

"So, what's good here do you think ...?" Tommy said, looking down at his menu then back up at her, "I see they have a chardonnay you like? California, I'm assuming?"

"Yup, Hayes Ranch. Pretty low price point – not that you'd know from the cost of *this* glass but – and Mandy wouldn't touch it -- but it's okay. A little on the gold side, but smooth enough with vanilla, slight oak, and an apple-ish vibe."

"You always did know what you like." His bare knees pressed into hers and heat furled between her legs. She hadn't felt that in a while – the almost painful weight of wanting.

"Well, with wine it's easy. Sometimes it's not at all what I was expecting but really good in a different way. Or sometimes it's what I'm eating it with that makes it explode in my mouth and go straight to my head."

"Umm ..."

"Oh, no. No. Do not do that, Tommy, how can you make anything *filthy* – Jesus, it's like a gross superpower or something." But she couldn't keep a straight face. It *was* funny, her words barely needed twisting. And his eyes were doing that thing – she caught his vulnerable excitement before he could cover it up. It undid her careful composure.

"There's something different about you, Sher, I can't put my finger on it," Tommy said, taking a long pull of his Cisco draft beer and pushing his white linen shirt up past his elbows. "I assume you're still healing the world, one family at a time? I know there's nothing easy or sexy about homelessness and poverty but something agrees with you."

She was confused at first because optimism and hope were hard won in her line of work, weighing bureaucratic red tape slashes against tallies in the *win* column. But she knew every single step she took with young parents in need was one in the right direction. And while that fueled her most days, that wasn't the glow he was talking about. "You know what? Getting out of dodge has made me feel ten times lighter. I've taken a whole month off. Can you believe it? I can't remember the last time I took an actual chunk of time away from work like this for myself."

"No kidding. No judgment, Sher, but that was a big part of the problem for us."

Sheri put both hands up to stop the direction of the conversation, "Let's not go down that road again, Tommy, and ruin *this*." Whatever this was, she was resisting a definition of it. She wasn't weighing pros and cons or asking herself what the hell she was doing. She was sitting with the moment, in it, feeling the chair stick a little to her bare legs on the Nantucket summer day, swimming with her wine-softened mind, and the heat that grew where she let Tommy's legs stay leaning against hers. It was a date with a handsome, successful man whose attention was 100 percent on her. It was a deep pool of anticipation that she wanted to skinny-dip in.

"Well, you do look wonderful, you really do. Aging like fine –"

"Don't. Tommy Steele, don't you dare talk about my aging at *all*, or compare me to wine," Sheri said, hackles rising in the summer heat thinking about her ex-husband's young girlfriend, "I really do not want–"

"Stephanie wants to have another baby," Tommy blurted, eyebrows shooting up over rounded eyes, looking like a ten-year-old handing his father a bad report card. Stupidly, this pierced her.

Sheri raised the wineglass to her mouth for a gulp of wine, swallowing around the golf ball in her throat. Unsure what was expected of her just then, she sat and waited for more. For Tommy to say something, *anything* at all that would make what they were doing make sense. What. Were. They. Doing?

Running a hand through his short hair, Tommy continued. "I just ... I can't see it, Sher, I don't think it's what I want ..." He looked so contrite sitting there that Sheri didn't know who to feel worse for, Stephanie or Tommy. And it occurred to her that she should probably add her name to that list.

She reached across the table for his hand, his vulnerability striking some irrepressible empathetic instinct. "Does she know you feel this way?"

His silence was answer enough. Stephanie probably already had him depositing his sperm into sample jars at a fertility clinic for optimum fertilization. It wasn't information Sheri could digest at the moment, although it spoke to Tommy's current bachelor behavior.

"Listen," she said to him, "you have some stuff to figure out and it's not my place to help you do that." Sheri couldn't help the subtle lift in her heart at being chosen over Stephanie, at the thought of maybe getting to have him back. It wasn't something she could process – it was like her brain was shouting *access denied*. But there was something going on between them, a thing she felt powerless against.

Chapter Eleven

SHERI BARELY REGISTERED THE men loading up their trucks and leaving for the day or the dumpster of demolition debris. She didn't owe Rocco or anyone else an explanation as she marched up the porch steps into the front door with Tommy so close she couldn't separate his body heat from her own.

On the way back to the bedroom, she fended off the judgement pressing in and kicked off her sandals by the door. She was stumbly from the wine and conscious of her nerves revving without the veil of night. A sea breeze rode in through the open windows. She wanted to drag it in so deep it became part of her. The warm whip of the air dissolved any uncomfortable silence. And there was a pulsing bank of feeling so much that she was incapable of thinking anything.

"Is this okay?" he said softly into her ear, "Oh, Sheri, I want you so much ... I want this back." She jumped with both feet into that sentence as his hands on her hips burned through the thin cotton of her dress and his mouth dragged hot breath across her jaw and up to her lips. She could feel his teeth on her bottom lip when he smiled. Heat rushed into her mouth, into her, with the force and flood of a river. Want swelled in her, setting fire to all the spaces between their bodies.

Her pink dress pooled at her feet as she let him lay her back on the bed, divesting himself of shorts and shirt. Desire chased rational thought away as she arched under him. Her whole body was begging for more, lifting toward him like a magnet, locked into his silver gaze, like their first time on her mattress on the floor of her UVM apartment on Pearl Street.

It was wonderful and it was horrible.

She wanted to be that hopeful girl again, she wanted that future back.

The evening sun changed the sky and she watched the shadows move across the walls over Tommy's sleeping form beside her. Her heart ached, but with what, she couldn't name. Were they moving ahead to something great, something better? Or were they just taking a dangerous dip into the past ... What did any of it mean? What about Stephanie – could Sheri be the kind of person who did this to another woman? *How could she?* And she could barely consider what this said about Tommy.

But, above all, what would it do to their daughters? That was an ache twice as deep.

∞

After Tommy had gone and the spell broken, Sheri wanted nothing more than to be sitting out on the back deck keeping company with her wild ocean. But empty space yawned where the deck used to be. The rotted stairs down to the beach had been removed, preventing access, and her heart paced inside her, a lion behind the bars of a circus wagon. Even if she'd been able to get away from the house, she knew she couldn't escape herself.

Settling on the front porch, she let go of the breath she didn't know she was holding. She sat in one of the big white rockers, wishing her mom was in the one next to her. But cringed thinking of what Rose would have to say. *What have I done*, she asked of the purpling sky and the twilight hum of the crickets in the tall grasses, pulling her knees up under her like a child.

Trudy walked up the few steps and took a seat beside her – how had Sheri not heard her Jeep rumble up? "Okay, spill it, I thought you were dead. Way to respond to my texts and calls. Actually, hold that thought," Trudy said, taking a closer look into her friend's eyes, glassy and distant with unresolved emotion, " it looks like this conversation is gonna need alcohol, don't move." Trudy squeezed her friend's shoulder on her way into the house.

Sheri sent out a quick prayer of thanks for the intuition of good friends. She felt like a terrible one at the moment. And a terrible mother and daughter too for that matter.

"I don't know how you drink the buttery shit," Trudy said stepping back out onto the porch, handing her friend a glass of chardonnay, "thank God you still have some Miraval left." She tapped her glass to Sheri's and got comfortable in her chair. "Okay, shoot."

Sheri had no perspective or any idea where to start.

"You slept with Tommy, didn't you," Trudy said rather than asked.

"How do you do that? And yeah, *no*, it wasn't exactly sleeping," Sheri said, turning to her friend, feeling stripped of clothes and maybe even skin. She was torn between laughing and crying. And afraid of how much more she wanted.

"Holy hell. When? *How* … weren't you just wrecked the other day at the beach by his unexpected appearance on-island? I don't even know what to say …

"Then be my friend and don't say anything. Anything *mean*, that is – don't call me a slut, don't hate me!" Sheri studied her friend's face for what she might really be thinking and not saying. But her features were inscrutable.

"C'mon, Sheri – I would never do that. I mean, call you a slut or hate you. But screwing around with your ex? Shit – not judging – but talk to me!"

"You're yelling at me! And I *know*! Aw shit, Tru, now I'm the *other woman*!"

Trudy paused for a hot minute, her ambivalence matching Sheri's. "The other woman ... no, I don't think this counts. It's not like they're married ... or have kids together."

As grateful as Sheri was for the loophole Trudy was offering, it wasn't sticking. "But she wants that. Stephanie does. The marriage and a baby with him," Sheri said, plowing ahead despite the shock on Trudy's face, "I'm not even entirely sure how I know that! Or how it didn't take up as much space in the bed as we did."

"Lust does that," Trudy said, eyes pinning Sheri's to see how that word landed.

"Is that what you think it is? Is that what this is, Tru?" she said, touching her bare feet down and leaning forward in the deep rocker with her face in her hands. "Why am I so stupid? Why does it feel so much like when we were falling in love a million years ago? What if he's tired of running around trying to keep up with a child and her child, Tru, what if he's changed? What if I'd be *enough* this time?"

"Stop. You were always enough, Sheri. The fact that you were made to feel like you're not, says it all. You know I love Tommy, I loved you guys together – we had some great times, absolutely. But this – this doesn't feel right." Trudy set down her wine glass and massaged her temples, her long fingers moving in slow circles as she seemed to search for the right words. "I know you're feeling vulnerable right now. And you might just be in a place where you need comfort above anything else, someone to hold you and tell you it's all gonna be okay, something, *someone* familiar. I mean it's totally understandable that you'd be reaching back to grab something from the past to find that, where things felt easier, safer, happier. But what would the girls think, Sher? It killed them when he left, crushed everything they thought love was or could be. That's not a small thing."

Sheri ran her hands through her tangled hair and cast her gaze up to the sky as if answers were written there. "You're right, I know you're right. But then *why*, when we're together now, does it feel so damn good and so right."

"That's just sex."

That landed like a gut-punch. Sheri thought she was more intuitive than that. But was it? Just sex? Sheri wasn't sure if she wanted that answer to be yes or no. *Just sex* would be easier to let go of. Again. But being back in love with Tommy? And having it go south *again*? She wasn't up for that at all.

Night had fallen, the only light coming from the pinpricks of stars in the huge sky.

Chapter Twelve

SHERI AWOKE TO SAWING and hammering and it took her a minute to remember where she was. It was barely seven thirty in the morning. Staring up at the ceiling, her eyes searched for that spot where her grimy little-kid hands had left their mark so many years ago. She felt one corner of her mouth lift in a small smile remembering that summer night sitting atop her dad's shoulders.

She'd probably been five years old and had gotten into the dirt while her mother was replacing the hydrangea bushes destroyed by the deer with fountain grasses in front of the house. Her mother had begged her father to get her into the tub and he'd turned it into a game, a ride on an elephant. How silly and loved she'd felt, and tall, so tall she could touch the sky.

A single hot tear rolled into her ear lying there in her parents' bed. All she'd ever wanted was a love story like her parents had. It may have taken them a while to find each other but every single day they'd found ways to show each other it had been worth the wait. Sheri was certain they still did. But she wasn't ready to think about that – to picture her dad bustling about their new space in an assisted living facility, busying himself with her mom's comfort, her care, her joy. Even in a place as gorgeous and new as *Evergreen Estate*. Fending off her sadness and his own, George would lean into the good moments and memories and not dwell on what was getting left behind. Alzheimer's really was the devil's handshake.

She threw the covers off and got dressed. By some miracle, her hair was still straighter than not, though, from the looks of the fog pressing in through the screens, that wasn't going to last and it'd be in the next area code by lunch. Which, she told herself on the way to the kitchen, was the least of her problems.

Coffee, without a view, she sighed, the gunmetal Atlantic was barely visible beyond the gray curtain of fog. She laughed then thinking how her daughters would prefer the view of men at work to the ocean beyond. Should she introduce herself or stay out of their way, what was the call? They were making decent progress on the deck and she wondered about the status of the steps down to the beach. She could walk around from the front and see for herself, why was she hiding?

Because she felt like she may as well have been wearing a scarlet letter. Or maybe a sign that said; *I'm fucking my ex*. Shamelessly. Was she without shame? And did it matter? She was a grown-ass woman.

Making the mistakes of a much younger one.

Rocco was there with just one other dude, she looked up at them from the lawn below shading her eyes with her hand. Maybe the sun was trying after all. "Morning," she said. The hammering stopped as both men peered down at her. The blond one leaned his forearms on the newly framed railing and smiled while Rocco stood brushing sweat from his forehead waiting for her to say more, possibly not thrilled about the interruption. The last thing she wanted to say was *when will you be done*, but it was also the only thing she cared about.

"How's it going?" she landed on. Then added, "Looks good so far." She was overcompensating. For thinking they'd *see* her as some rich, bratty, entitled, impatient bitch slut who saw them as lower life forms. She wasn't any of those things. But maybe they could tell from the simple house, an *un*-McMansion, that had grown shabby around the edges, that she was in no way a card-carrying member of the one percent.

"It's goin'," blond guy said, "Nice spot you got here."

"Thanks. It's my parents'. They bought it in the seventies, back when things were a little more normal around here, not like some of these monsters being built now." Why was she compelled to downplay the Nantucket house, persist with her I'm-just-a-regular-gal schtick? She really needed to start owning shit. "You guys must see your share of crazy construction."

"You have no idea," Rocco said, "We should be out of your hair before the end of the week." Sheri felt pinned by his gaze. Everything about him was dark – his sable eyes, the ebony gloss of his hair and impressive thick mustache (apparently making a comeback from the seventies porn-star era), and the sheen of his brown skin – but not in any sinister way. Darkly curious maybe, possessing great depth possibly. Sheri liked to believe she could read people but she really was going too far – trying to work her way around the cliché sexy Italian staring down at her probably reading her like a book. Then she caught the flash of his gold wedding band as he picked up his hammer and went back to work.

Sheri wrapped her hands around her coffee mug and looked out at the ocean beyond the modest lawn, chastising herself for her preconceptions, wondering where making observations stopped and judging started. Human beings were a flawed species. Then she turned to head back into the house, feeling robbed of a cleansing beach walk, as the empty spaces in the wooden staircase grinned up at her like a jack-o'-lantern.

She'd exiled her phone to the mantle over the fireplace, punishing it for its silence. It punished her back by not ringing or pinging. What was she expecting exactly? *Something*. She felt singularly powerless having again put the bulk of her happiness in someone else's hands. She didn't know when she'd lost her power. What she did know was that she needed to get out of the house and do something that wouldn't remind her of anything or anyone.

∞

She found herself at the bottom of Broad Street shelling out twenty-five bucks for the Whaling Museum. Immersing herself in anyone else's history was better than grappling with her own, and this was the flagship site of the Nantucket Historical Association's fleet of properties. She hadn't been since the girls were little so she channeled their excitement and started a fresh journey into Nantucket's fabled four-centuries-old past.

The forty-six-foot-long sperm whale skeleton suspended from the ceiling was the first thing you noticed, that *ooh-aahh* moment, the jaw-dropper, and Sheri knew exactly how it came to be hanging there.

She remembered the news that New Year's Day in 1998 in Sconset when the young whale, after floundering for two days in the surf, finally died. She'd read how the heartbroken community had looked on as the leviathan beached itself for the last time on Low Beach, but how it would be preserved for all to take a closer look – a fitting acquisition for the museum.

The suspended whale skeleton was undeniably the star of the museum, but Sheri thought it was the scrimshaw collection that showed an even more personal link to the island's whaling past. Scrimshaw was the art of engraving images on bone or teeth and was a way for nineteenth-century sailors away at sea to pass the time between whale sightings. Sheri tried to picture the sailors sitting on their trunks in cramped quarters polishing the teeth then using their jackknives to create intricate images of whaling and portraits of their sweethearts. She considered the irony – that the discarded parts of the mighty mammal came to serve as the canvas upon which the most enduring artistic reminders of Nantucket's great whaling period were preserved – the hunt and the hunted.

She remembered the two-story lever press of the old candle factory from her very first visit, the only original whale oil lever press still in place in the world. She remembered being both grossed out as a kid and captivated learning that the spermaceti was taken from the giant heads of the whales – wanting to picture that process but also not! Her mother had let her buy two spermaceti candles – lumpy, yellowish, uneven things that Sheri treasured, wanting to save them for something special, imagining herself as a young Quaker girl. They were still wrapped in their tissue and in a box today back at *Moor to Sea,* too precious to burn.

Now, as then, she tried to imagine what Nantucket would have looked like, smelled like sounded like, with all of its industries revolving around whaling; barrel making, blacksmithing, ropemaking, and candle making.

Did anything in the current world measure up to whaling as a way of life? Fraught with danger and death a constant threat? Sheri was transported, rounding the corner of one exhibit after another, trying to put herself on Nantucket in the 1800s. She felt the dark sea, the tumultuous rise and fall of the ocean, of the island's ultimate economy. She looked at maps, timelines, and artifacts while she listened to the story of the tragedy of the Essex. The real Nantucket whaleship stove by an eighty-seven foot whale, Melville's inspiration for *Moby Dick.* Though he didn't visit the island until after the book's publication in 1852, it was said that Melville wrote his famous tome from the journal of First Mate, Owen Chase, whose house could be found at seventy-four Orange Street! The whole of Nantucket was a living museum.

Sheri was at once channeling the struggles of a whaling wife left behind, trying to put enough food on the table in between years-long whaling expeditions, taking over town and community positions left vacant by the men at sea, and finding a way to be both mother and father to her children. She was relieved to move on to a sunnier exhibit, *Summer on Nantucket: History of the Island Resort,* telling the story of Nantucket as a summer destination from the opening of the first tourist hotels in the 1840s to its current multi-billion-dollar real-estate economy. Nantucket's *high season* being defined in new ways across generations.

No museum visit was complete without a trip up the circular stairs to the roof walk. The panorama of the harbor tingled her spine. How that view had to have changed with the decades, weather, seasons, and all the layers of history that make Nantucket such a storied place.

She was startled by the buzzing in her bag against her hip. She hadn't thought about her phone all afternoon. Having been firmly planted in yesteryear, the interruption of technology was wildly unwelcome. But when you had kids, you were ever bound by it. She resisted reaching into her bag, unwilling to leave the past, its simplicity. And her heart had suddenly kicked her in the stomach remembering Tommy.

Sheri wound her way back down the circular stairs that had taken her to the roof of the whaling museum. It was time to exit the past and deal with her own present. Poured back out onto Broad Street, she took a seat on a sidewalk bench to look at her phone. There were two missed texts; one from Trudy and one from Tommy. She hated the gratification that speared her and the hot delight that tagged along. She opened Trudy's first, saving Tommy's as dessert. Then chided her infantile mindset.

> Hi! Griffin's coming in early from Boston for the weekend – how about a sunset sail on Wednesday? You don't have to do a thing – unless you want to bring along your famous lemon bars. Text me ☺

Sheri was 99 percent ecstatic about the invitation. Hating herself for the one percent of torment that lurked thinking about locking herself into anything that might lock her out of seeing Tommy again.

Then Tommy's text:

> Can't get you off my mind. Not that I'm trying. I need to see you

That flood of rapture again, a deep pool of it weighting her to the bench, lifting the corners of her mouth into a grin on a gray island day. She tuned in and out of the restless kids pulling on their mother's arms for ice cream, the line already forming for waffle cones at the Juice Bar. Couples using the overcast day to buy hoodies and tchotchke – anything with the word *Nantucket* or a whale on it – and to hit up Rose & Crown for lobster mac and cheese and day drinking.

She steered her mind in the opposite direction of self-loathing and leaned instead into happiness. Not overjoyed or giddy – but that low steady hum of better-than-fine that she'd let ride underneath everything else, a buffer between her and the world she walked over, that she knew had the power to open up and swallow her at any time.

She replied a simple *yes* to each text and then sat with her full heart, letting her joy mingle with all the happy tourists'.

She weighed going back home to Eel Point Road against doing a little shopping or day drinking herself. She decided that the weather practically begged her for chowder and a beer at the Brotherhood of Thieves, a quintessential mid-nineteenth-century whaling bar, before heading back home.

Chapter Thirteen

Sated with a healthy dose of Nantucket history, local fare, and still firmly wrapped in her bubble of *better-than-fine*, Sheri drove home. The workers were gone and it was quiet. Too quiet, but for the dull baseline beat of a familiar song. It was riding on the wind outside her house but there was an echo bouncing it around and she couldn't place it exactly. Until the wind shifted and brought the strains of "Pour Some Sugar on Me" right to her.

It was coming from next door where she could see people moving in and out of the house to the massive deck overlooking the ocean. It was a grander property than her parents' but not terribly so. She was surprised to hear Def Leppard cranking because the last owners she knew of were an older couple with one grown son. Stan and Ida, if she remembered correctly, with a son, Phillip, her own age.

Had it sold? Another question for her dad. Whom she needed to call! But that felt weird given the muddied waters of her life at the moment. She couldn't sully the sea of challenge her parents were riding. *Later*, she told herself, she'd call later. Peeking out at her new, albeit unfinished, deck, she wondered if it was okay to step out onto it. Oh, why not – she was feeling bulletproof.

She poured herself a glass of chardonnay and wondered if she might be able to lose herself in a good book. But her mind wasn't still enough for reading and she'd need to haul up a chair for that anyway. She stood looking out at the giant Atlantic heaving – tearing in, tumbling out. Her hair bending into crooked waves in the humid wind.

"Hey, neighbor!" she heard coming from the Def Leppard house to her left. "I'm Leo!" He was shouting over the wind and the song and Sheri was already laughing at her response before she spoke it.

"Need some sugar?" she yelled, cracking herself up ... But he either didn't hear her or didn't get the joke. He couldn't have been more than twenty-five but you never knew. A blush pricked at her face and she considered going back in the house. The music got quiet and another dude of indecipherable age stepped out onto the deck.

"Sorry! Kids these days ..."

"No worries," Sheri said. "So did Stan and Ida sell?" she tried to enunciate, their attempt at conversation hijacked by the wind.

"What?" both guys said. "Hey – you should come over!"

Oh, this was rich. But why the hell not? It was summer and it was Nantucket – *no rules*, as they'd always chant.

Sheri went back through the house, put her wineglass down on the counter, and headed out the front door over to the neighbor's. She'd gotten curiously skilled lately at stripping away the caution tape she'd hung inside herself – the stuff that would have stopped her from going out on the unfinished deck in the first place to see what all the fun was about next door.

Would she go back to old-Sheri once her daughters arrived? Was she feeling like a kid herself with no parents around and no kids to parent? She shut down the silent interrogation she'd started when she got to the neighbor's front door.

∞

Should she ring the bell? Would anyone hear it over the music that had been cranked – should she just walk right in? The door opened before she'd decided, "Moving in Stereo" met the open air with a blast, flooding the evening like a concert.

"Hey, come on in! You like the Cars, right? What can I get you to drink?" Second guy's age was more decipherable up close – late forties at least – but what was he doing partying in Stan and Ida's house with a pack of Gen Zers?

"Let the good times roll," Sheri said, oh, she was on.

"I see what you did there, excellent. Welcome, I'm Cooper Madden," he said extending his right hand.

"Sheri Steele," she said, giving his hand an almost too-firm shake. Why did she always do that? It only seemed to make a man want to hold it a beat longer. She followed him into the grand home beyond the curved staircase into the big open kitchen. Music embraced her with some kind of cinematic surround sound.

There weren't as many people there as she'd thought but everyone looked happy. "What's the occasion?" Sheri asked loudly over the music as she followed Cooper over to an actual bar in between the kitchen and living room, complete with high-top seating, cozy pendant lighting, and a jade-green stone counter. He stood behind it like a boss, pointing like Vanna White to the many pretty bottles of booze. Was this guy for real?

"No special occasion. My son has a few friends over and we're just happy to be here. Gorgeous part of the island out here away from the fray, isn't it? What can I make you?"

Stunned for a half-second, expecting solo cups of ambiguously fruity punch to match the music, she blurted, "Gin and tonic?"

"Beefeater's or Broker's?" Cooper said, with a smile in his eyes.

"I've never heard of Broker's ..."

"Broker's it is," Cooper said, with an endearing grin that rode a little higher on his left cheek. "Trust me. Beefeater's disappears into the tonic, you're gonna love this one, it's serious stuff." Sheri watched as he filled two highball glasses with designer ice. His hair was the color of wave-kissed sand, bending a bit at his collar and his eyes put equal time on her and the drinks he was making. "It hits you with a blast of juniper upfront, chased by crisp citrus and spice, with root flavors at the base – I hope you're not afraid of flavor." What sorcery was this, Sheri wondered, getting caught up in his full gaze, eyes some nameless color between amber and gold. "This London Dry Gin commands a full sensory experience, you'll find it assertive yet smooth, punchy yet balanced."

"If you had to guess?" was all she could come up with. "Gin snob," she said, laughing, trying to read this beguiling man who was so at home in her neighbor's house.

"Ha! I like nice things. I appreciate quality," he said, tapping his glass to hers, "Salud."

"Salud. Italian, right? I mean I know it means *cheers* but—"

"It's Spanish and if we're being literal, it means *health*."

"There you are, Dad, isn't it enough with the 80s rock already?" First guy from deck said.

"Sheri, meet my son, Leo."

Leo stood at least an inch taller than his father, putting him at about six feet, two inches, and had the leanness of youth. And while his hair was longer and lightened by the sun and his eyes a darker hazel than his father's, he exuded the same quiet self-confidence and grace.

"Oh, hey, you're the lady from next door, right? Good to meet you," Leo said, turning back to his father for an answer to his playlist question, "C'mon, you like Greta Van Fleet, maybe some Soundgarden – trust me, alright?" Leo said. Cooper could have spit him out, they looked so much alike, but there was more ownership in Cooper's countenance, the way he held himself compared to the restlessness of his son's youthful energy. But of course, that was one of the gifts of age, she thought. And then a shadow of joy surprised her at the thought of there being actual gifts to aging.

"Not too loud. Can't have it bouncing off the water breaking the sound barrier. Having the cops show up at our door is not the first impression I, *we*, want to make – got it?"

Thanking his dad, Leo practically bounced out of the room. Was he on something? Sheri wondered, then shut the thought out. Where was Leo's mother, she wondered, Cooper's wife – was there a wife? "Ah, so you are new, Stan and Ida *did* sell?" He wasn't answering right away, Sheri was being too nosey, she shouldn't stay too long. The air felt thick, or maybe that was just the gin-slicked wheels of her brain making things up – the drink had punch for sure.

Cooper came around from behind the bar to stand next to where Sheri sat. He had a gentle way about him, Sheri thought, but he was just a little too good-looking for her to take it at face value. They took their time with their drinks and skimmed on the surface of small talk: was the sun always so fickle there, could you get a dinner reservation *anywhere* without a month's notice, was the ice cream at the Juice Bar really worth the forty-five--minute wait in line?

"First-timer, huh?" Sheri said, looking into his eyes over the rim of her glass as she sipped.

"That obvious?" he said, swirling the ice in his glass, the corners of his eyes crinkling as he smiled. "I wanted to spend some quality time with my son, we've had a rough go of it in the last year. And since he's a surfer I wanted to see what all the fuss was about with this island of Nantucket. This place became available and we jumped on it. Leo is an environmental scientist and can do a good percentage of his work remotely – but so far he's not disappointed that he also had to use a chunk of his personal days."

"The surfing's been good, there are some decent breaks here for sure – I bet he's loving it," Sheri said, setting her glass down and tucking a strand of hair behind her ear. She liked how easy he was to talk to. He had a quiet charm and he reminded her a little of Gerard Butler.

"A surfer yourself, then?" he said, surprise rounding his eyes.

"Former, anyway," she chuckled, "I grew up surfing summers here. My youngest daughter is the surfer in the family these days. She—"

A loud crash coming from the kitchen had them both hurrying out to see what was going on. Two boys were going at it, one of them was Leo. They'd plowed into the kitchen table knocking over a chair and the other kid was on the floor. Maybe they were younger than Sheri thought.

"That's ENOUGH!" Cooper shouted, coming between them, "Shane, get up and look at me. Are you hurt?" Sheri watched as Cooper checked out Leo and Shane for injuries and how neither wanted to be treated like a child, shoving away Cooper's careful inspection. She was getting doctor vibes. He was calm and thorough deciphering the source of what little blood had been spilled.

Sheri suddenly felt like an intruder. The carefree mood vaporized. She'd see them again, she figured, but for now, she was craving the familiar comfort of her own space. She thanked Cooper for the drink and he walked her to the front door apologizing for the commotion, assuring her she didn't have to leave. Part of her could see them hanging out and talking easily for hours, but another part was saying *what are you doing – isn't there enough going on in your life right now?*

∞

She headed back to her house. Her house ... was it really going to be *her house*? The mist had thickened and the sky was leaden and very low. From the edges of her vision she could see her hair springing into waves, and everything she wore felt damp. *The gray lady* was out in full force, the diabolical Hyde to Nantucket's blue-sky Jekyll. Sheri didn't mind it every now and then, it made the sun so much brighter in comparison.

Still stuffed from her late lunch at the Brotherhood and her *punchy* gin and tonic next door, Sheri decided to stay away from the kitchen and catch up on correspondences. She couldn't worry whether or not it was a good time to call her father – couldn't talk herself out of it again assuming he was busy tending to her mother. She was painfully aware of the cop-out and hated that she had to gear herself up just to talk to her parents. Did growing pains ever end?

She tucked her legs under her and got settled inside on the couch overlooking the ocean. It was fading to black by the hour. She took a deep breath to steady the throbbing of her heart, exhaled, and tapped her dad's name in "favorites" on her phone. While she waited for him to pick up, she acknowledged that part of her wanted him to answer, with his booming reassuring voice that hugged her across the miles, while the other part half-hoped the call would go to voicemail. It was weak and awful of her to even think, but she wanted only happy news, for things to be as they'd always been, which she knew was unlikely and childish.

It went to voicemail. But not immediately, so at least he had his phone on. That was frustratingly not always a given. Her dad tended to view his cell phone, and technology in general, as available for *his* convenience, not anyone else's. Secondly, she was able to leave a message, which was another plus because it meant his mailbox hadn't filled to capacity. And lastly, she was off the hook, for now.

Hugging her knees, she stared out at the monochromatic night, forcing herself to think about her parents and what she currently knew about what her mother was experiencing. Her father too, for that matter. Denial had been her go-to when it came to her parents' aging. Which didn't fit at all for a social worker who'd made it her life's work to help struggling young families and underserved communities of parents to get the support and services they needed. Her skin had had to thicken across her career, but the things she told herself about not getting attached to clients wouldn't work now.

She let go of her knees and sat up like a grownup and tried to eliminate the soupy layer of emotion and think about the science and how they'd all made excuses for Rose's symptoms, not seeing them as symptoms as much as the normal forgetfulness that accompanied aging, like misplacing car keys, forgetting recent events, having trouble finding a word but then remembering it later, or forgetting the name of an acquaintance. But there came a day when they had to admit it was more. And that they were seeing Rose having trouble paying attention, saw the disconnects with judgment and problem-solving, and her reasoning compromised. And probably hardest of all were the changes in her personality. Her sudden anger and lashing out that was so unlike her dear mom.

Her dad was leaving no stone unturned, she knew that, being certain every cognitive and neurological test was being done and brain scans to identify changes in the brain's structure and function. He wasn't a man who took no for an answer and wouldn't allow those in his orbit to either. It was her turn to step up and see what she was made of.

Sheri knew there were no known cures for Alzheimer's disease and they knew it could progress quickly or last many years. Her heart sat like a cannonball in the dust.

Her phone rang in her hands, shrill and dissonant set against the soothing cadence of the steady surf beyond the open door. Her father's voice in her ear from so far away in place and time. She pushed an unbidden tear away with her free hand, trying to dislodge the stone in her throat. Her dad had a tired smile in his voice as he handed his phone to Rose who he said was anxious about her New Dawn roses.

"Hi, Petal, how's my darling girl? Tell me about my roses on the east side of the house, dear, they should be bursting about now." Rose's voice was coming through loud and clear – with only a little wobble. Sheri swallowed and swallowed again to get rid of the cry in her throat. She missed her mom so much.

"Mom, your roses are beautiful, that sweet blush pink and to the top of your trellis. I'll text a photo in the morning – it's a bit gray and dark here now. And I don't want you to worry for one second about the contractors damaging them, there's no reason they need to be anywhere near them. Now, how are you? Do you have a small garden there?" Sheri was conscious of trying too hard to fill the space and forced herself to slow down and just listen as her mom described their new place.

The moments of lucidity were gold. Sheri memorized each one, wanting them to go on forever but also to cut them short, on a good note, before they disassembled and broke away. Before her mother vanished before her eyes like mist or memory.

She pictured her father sitting beside her mother, holding her free hand, his thumb making smooth circles on her satiny skin, weary hope swimming in his eyes pleading with the universe for Rose to follow the thread, stay on track, and not say *who are you again?* Sheri prayed for the same thing every time they spoke. But she knew, they all knew, that the day would come when Rose would no longer know them. Sheri knew she wasn't supposed to skip ahead like that, but it was so hard. And all the denial and attempts at self-preservation in the world wouldn't protect her from the end. Or for however long the middle lasted. It choked her.

She had to stay in the present, had to stay strong for her dad, forcing a smile into her voice when he came back on the phone after the conversation with her mom. She could hear in his tone a mix of relief and renewed luster. "Let's talk toilets, have you found a plumber yet, honey?"

Sheri burst out laughing, good old George, master of the non sequitur. "Dad, I've got everything under control," she said, not terribly certain she did but not wanting to add one single thing to his plate, "don't give it another thought. Oh, by the way, why didn't you mention that Stan and Ida sold their place? Talk about the end of an era, huh?" Or had Cooper Madden said they were renting? Had she only half-heard him? Or had he only half-told her?

"What was that now, honey? I think you may have some misinformation. I would certainly have known about it if that were the case," George said before turning away from the phone to cough. The meatiness of the coughing worried Sheri. Of course, he was probably running himself ragged.

"Are you alright, Dad? That cough does not sound insubstantial. Or new. How long have you been coughing like that, and have you seen your doctor?"

"I'm fine, honey, don't you worry about me, and I've been surrounded by enough doctors to last two lifetimes. Listen, I need to ring off, your mother is trying to tell me something and I can't quite make it out. Now, you let me know when you've got that master bathroom toilet squared away, won't you?"

Sheri assured her dad she would and was smack in the middle of telling him she loved him when she realized he'd already hung up.. She wondered again about his hearing – so often it seemed he'd speak his piece, whether it was an accurate response to the conversation or not, and then be finished listening.

Leaving her phone on the coffee table, she sighed and stood to stretch. Wondering about her neighbors, and if maybe the Maddens were some extended family or something? Who knows what kind of health issues Stan and Ida may or may not be going through. Her brain was stuffed but it was too soon for bed. Reaching to the top shelf of the built-in bookcase beside the fireplace she found dad's copy of Nathaniel Philbrick's *In the Heart of the Sea: The Tragedy of The Whaleship Essex*. That probably wasn't the most uplifting choice.

Chapter Fourteen

COFFIN COUSINS PLUMBING WAS due in an hour. Sheri made the bed, straightened the bathroom, and stowed her personal things, trying to see it through a stranger's eyes. She wasn't entirely comfortable with the thought of a strange dude amongst her private stuff but the sooner he was in he'd be out. She hoped the toilet would be a quick swap out and that the tiles around the base would be undisturbed – for all she knew, they'd have to be completely replaced – and they were ancient, where would she find replacements? The doorbell yanked her from her ruminations.

"Good morning, I'm Wes, you must be Mrs. Steele?"

Jesus Christmas, was every single person on Nantucket a beautiful human specimen? Had she brushed her hair or checked her reflection for smudged makeup? "That's me, come on in. I'm glad you could fit me in – it was nuts getting anyone to even return my calls."

"You got lucky, what can I say? My guys are crazy-busy this summer, crazier every year. Now why don't you show me what's going on with your toilet."

Sexy opener, Sheri thought, then wondered why the hell that stuff popped into her head. Being with Tommy had lit her up and she couldn't help it and now she noticed every man in her path. What she did know was that she'd better get it together before her daughters arrived Friday night. And that she hoped her ass looked good in the shorts she threw on as Wes followed her into her bedroom. *What was wrong with her?* She combed her memory for why exactly George wanted a new toilet – besides the fact that it hadn't been replaced since the Carter Administration. Or possibly Reagan? A long time ago anyway.

"Here she is," Sheri said standing before the basic-looking bone-colored toilet. "I'm pretty sure it's original to the house. It doesn't leak as far as I know, it has a running issue sometimes, and *oh*, now I remember my dad mentioning that it was clogging more than usual last summer, that was the problem."

"Ah," Wes said looking down at the porcelain throne, "an American Standard from about 1977. The first water-saving toilet, believe it or not, which flushed at 3.5 gallons."

"Compared to ... ?" Sheri had no idea why she was asking except that it did occur to her that newer low-flow toilets would be more environmentally sound.

"Five to seven gallons per flush, if you can believe."

"Should I be embarrassed to say I've never given it much thought? I suppose you're going to tell me that new toilets use ... ?" She couldn't believe she was in her bathroom with a handsome stranger talking toilets. And that her body was defaulting to flirt mode.

"Standard is about 1.6 gallons per flush but there are toilets on the market now that use 1.28 gallons per flush. If you can believe *that*." Sheri couldn't tell if his navy-blue eyes were laughing a little. Or if he was the kind of guy whose second language was seducing his lady customers. She could totally picture it.

"How in the world can a toilet flush, well, *anything*, with so little water? I mean, my dad was a double-flush guy on a good day, I mean *is*, he's still with us, just not *here*." She was rambling and talking about her dad's toilet routine, could things get any weirder?

Wes took a beat before responding, "There are higher performance flushing technologies these days – some higher-end toilets even include features like UV lights for sanitizing and paperless cleaning – if you're into that sort of thing. Let's just replace this dinosaur. What did you have in mind?" Oh, this was just too much having to picture paperless cleaning.

Letting out a sigh, she backed out of the tight space wanting to finish the discussion anywhere else. He followed her back out into the kitchen where she asked him what he usually used for replacement toilets.

"Plumbers have their preferences and recommendations, of course, but ultimately it's up to the homeowner – style, what you want to spend – that kind of thing."

"Style? Hm. I have never, not once, ever considered *style* and *toilet* in the same sentence. Please – just tell me what you'd recommend without breaking the bank."

"I like the American Standard Cadet 3 for its efficient flushing and straightforward design that will run you in the neighborhood of three hundred dollars depending on if you want a round or elongated bowl –"

"Seriously? Three hundred dollars for a toilet? And they have *bowl shape* choices?"

"Oh, you have no idea, Mrs. Steele. Last month I put in a TOTO Neorest 750H Dual Flush Toilet for fourteen K. Forget gold. True luxury to the brand comes with a remote control, warmers, and multiple butt-cleaning functions."

"I can't ... And, please, call me Sheri. And seriously, just get me a normal toilet without all the bells and whistles, okay? And how soon can we get this done? Not to sound demanding or anything but –"

"I got you. I'll order your toilet and we'll settle on an installation day and time." Wes took in the expanse of the Atlantic beyond the living room. "Beautiful place you have here – I bet that view never gets old."

"Thanks. You must see your share of beautiful places here." Sheri wondered if he was a Coffin cousin, possibly a direct descendant of the original Coffin family who settled Nantucket in 1649?

"Oh, sure, sure, but this is stunning in its simplicity, luxurious without ostentation, cozy, perfect. Nothing like your neighbor's place," he nodded to the left, where the Maddens were staying, now that was a story she'd like more of. But she was also curious about Wes – his story – married, a dad? He gave away nothing. No wedding ring but he probably wouldn't wear it to work as a plumber anyway. And why did she care? *Jesus*. Her hormones were on overdrive.

"Have you been in that house? Do you know Stan and Ida?" Sheri asked.

"Sure, sure. They still own the property. Stan had a hard winter from what I gather, took a bad fall then had to have another stent put in, and their son convinced them to rent the place out for the summer."

"That would be Philip, right? Yeah, he would be all about the revenue stream, and with his own place in Amagansett have zero interest in Nantucket. Which blows my mind, but I've never been to the Hamptons, so what do I know? What do you know about the renters?" The second the question was out of her mouth, Sheri regretted asking. It was none of her business and she was putting Wes on the spot. "Sorry – you don't have to answer that, I'm just being nosey."

"No worries – I don't really know much. Got a call from Doctor Madden about the washing machine not spinning properly or draining – you know it's not uncommon for a sock to get into the drain system and clog the hose or pump– "

Sheri stopped listening to the details as her mind raced trying to put the few pieces she had together. Doctor – that sounded about right, the way he was so thorough when that kid went down. Can't mess with concussions, or lawsuits for that matter. But still no mention of a Mrs. Madden. "I actually met him last night, and his son Leo. I was out on my deck and I think they felt bad about the loud music and invited me over. They were having a little party, a few kids, friends of the son's. But there was some fight which kinda killed the mood and I left. Is there a wife?" Boom, no filter.

"I actually don't know the answer to that. If you'll excuse me …" Wes's phone started to jingle in his pocket, and when he checked the number, told Sheri he had to take the call, heading to the door, saying he'd be in touch. It was too quiet when he left which made her think of two things: one, how lonely she felt these days in her favorite place without her daughters and parents around, and, two, where the heck was the crew to finish up her deck and stairs?

Whatever. She didn't feel like wasting any more of the day thinking about contractors or the too-empty house. Or Tommy for that matter, and what world she may or may not be getting herself into with him. She picked her way carefully down the staircase with its missing teeth to the beach for a long walk.

∞

It never failed to fill her all the way up. The perspective of the Atlantic ocean there at her feet hugging the whole island was humbling. She wondered if she could actually walk the entire eighty-two perimeter miles of Nantucket, was it possible? Was any of it impassable on foot? Maybe she could kayak it … she felt a quick thrill pondering it.

The sand was confectioner's sugar under her bare feet and the sun was making its steady climb. It was still early enough for an abundance of shells and treasures before it had been combed of lucky stones and sea glass. It was all she could do to tear her eyes away from the ground to watch where she was going.

She recognized some of the usual suspects who tended to walk at the same time each morning. The tall, tan, white-haired man, all business with his sinewy stride and quick nod hello, the hat ladies with their navy tank suits, white coverups, and wide-brimmed straw hats – hands gesturing wildly in conversation. And the woman with the cornsilk hair flying and her two Golden Retrievers who so resembled her that they seemed to have stepped from the pages of a children's book by Jan Brett.

Sheri walked on, smiling into the wind, watching how it scalloped the water. Her heart was full at getting to be a part of it, while her mind ticked off the list of things she'd need to buy to make her lemon bars for the sunset cruise on Wednesday and all the other things she had to do before her girls arrived.

Her legs burned with the excursion of walking in the soft sand and she thought that no matter how fit she was, this was always so. But she felt strong nonetheless and good about her body. Oh, you could tell yourself a lot of things about the back end of your forties, and fall for all the excuses about how a woman's body changes, but she'd be damned if she was going to accept any of it. At the edges of her mind, she knew she was allowing herself a moment of vanity. After all, Tommy couldn't keep his hands off of her.

But she couldn't just pretend that he didn't have a girlfriend closer to their daughters' ages than hers – so there was *that*.

She stopped in her tracks and faced the sea. Let the waves suck at her feet in the sand leaving them teetering on small bars. *Girlfriend*. Her ex-husband's girlfriend. With her tight young body, flat stomach, and perky boobs. There were too many things wrong with the picture. And the Aaro stuck through it.

It was as if Sheri couldn't allow herself to just go with feeling happy. And desirable. And she had felt so desired by Tommy – wanted, sexy. But she couldn't let herself have it. Because where was it all going? Her thoughts ping-ponged. Maybe they'd changed, grown. Maybe they were ready to be together, and have the life they deserved. They'd raised great kids, now they could devote themselves to each other. Right? She picked her pace back up. And found a perfect heart-shaped rock at the water's edge. It was a sign.

Like the text that came in from Tommy, later, while she was at the store picking up fresh lemons, powdered sugar, and some Kerrygold Pure Irish Butter to make her lemon bars. He wanted to see her Thursday! But thought it was risky to keep showing up together in town. Sheri had just the solution – she'd make him all his favorites and they'd sit out on her new deck, which she was certain would be finished by then. It was perfect.

∞

She stood taller and had a zing in her step as a giddy anticipation propelled her around Bartlett's Farm. She would make her garlic-herb-butter roast chicken, Tommy loved that. She'd pick up some fresh potted herbs: rosemary, thyme, dill, and basil – she didn't care that she wouldn't be there for the whole summer, she could give them to Trudy or bring them home to Vermont.

She didn't even want to think about Vermont yet! She never wanted Nantucket to end ... not as a kid, not now.

She'd do the grilled Brussels sprouts from that old Met on Main recipe they'd all loved, and her garlic mashed potatoes. Oh! And for dessert, a salted caramel mud cake! And then her girls, *their girls*, would arrive Friday – what a week this was turning out to be after all.

Chapter Fifteen

SHERI HAD WORRIED THAT Griffin would call off the sunset sail with the lingering fog but, true to form, the island weather had shifted in their favor. Threatening storm clouds had been whisked away offshore leaving behind soft blue skies that promised a beautiful evening out on the water. After Sheri wrapped the lemon bars in parchment and stowed them in her mother's vintage woven pie basket, she had only to decide what to wear.

Layers were always the answer, even in summer, and though Sheri wasn't much of a boater she knew it would be cooler on the water. Her white jeans would be the perfect look but she didn't trust herself not to spill *something*. She landed on white linen shorts and a sleeveless top of the same fabric with a light cashmere pullover in a pale creamy caramel. That sweater remained one of her favorite go-to pieces – even though it didn't come with a romantic story. In fact, it came with the opposite.

It had been the only thing Sheri had asked Tommy for on her birthday one year – she hardly ever asked for anything. It felt wrong to ask for a single thing when she had it all; a husband she was madly in love with and their two healthy, happy daughters. But he'd asked, he wanted to get her what she really wanted – to make a birthday wish come true for someone who always used her wishes up on everyone else. Which was the sweetest thing.

Until her birthday came and he'd either totally forgotten asking her or he'd gotten stuck somewhere along the way with the follow-through. He meant well, he always meant well. But she ended up buying the sweater for herself. And while she loved it and the way it caressed her figure, it was a reminder of Tommy's priorities – and where she sometimes fell among them.

Interesting how, caught in the affair, he'd been able to list the ways Sheri no longer seemed available to him. Had he forgotten his own lapses? He'd been so busy polishing his halo that he didn't notice the horns poking through. She wasn't going there now. She wasn't the same person anymore and maybe Tommy wasn't either. She was too excited about getting to watch the sun set over the water on a sailboat. She decided to keep her dinner date the next night like a secret gold doubloon in her pocket.

Walking to Straight Wharf after parking, Sheri tried to remember the last time she saw Griffin and the names of the other two friends Trudy and Griff had invited. Her brain had been scattered at best getting Trudy's text that day on the other side of Tommy's. She hadn't been in her right mind. Wasn't still.

"Yay, you're here!" Trudy said, hugging Sheri as she approached the launch, "and looking fabulous I must say. Hand me your pie basket while you get in, everyone else is here."

Griffin offered her his hand from in the launch and Sheri almost fell into it stepping off the dock when her eyes caught Cooper's, already in the small vessel that would motor them out to the mooring. Her brain was a gameshow wheel, spinning so fast it blurred the possibilities. "Cooper? This is so weird, how do you know Trudy and Griffin?" Sheri said, as they maneuvered around the mooring field to the sailboat.

"Wait," Trudy shouted over the low wind, "you two know each other?"

How had Sheri forgotten to tell Trudy about her handsome new neighbor? She had summer-brain, where every thought was a pretty colored ball in a slow-motion bouncy house. "Um, we're neighbors?" Sheri said, questioning the sentence herself, and noticing another man in the launch. *Cooper's friend? Boyfriend, possibly?* She had to concentrate not to fall into the sailboat. It was gorgeous with a navy-blue hull and teak toe rail. Her senses were in overdrive.

Once the last of the provisions were loaded into the boat, Trudy made the introductions. "Well, I guess you've already met Cooper Madden, you must've forgotten to tell me *that* story," she said with a wink in Sheri's direction, "and this is Noah, Griffin's new partner who's known Cooper apparently since undergrad at Brown – small world, right?"

"You have no idea," Sheri said, avoiding looking straight into Cooper's eyes, more gold than amber in the evening sun. And while that night had been filed away under the heading of Def Leppard in a fog of Broker's, there was something about Cooper Madden that stirred her up inside.

"Now it's my turn to be curious," Cooper said with a disarming smile, looking from Sheri to Trudy and back again, "How do you two know each other? I must have won the lottery to be included in this lovely adventure."

"Smooth, Coop," Noah said, then turning to Sheri, "you'll have to excuse Doctor Madden – he has much more finesse in the operating room."

Sheri was anxious to get out of the harbor and into the summer wind that might blow away her tangled thought parade. She'd let them race through one last time: *Was Trudy trying to set her up with Cooper? Or Noah? How to tell her she was not* at all *in that headspace! Trudy would kill her if she knew everything about Tommy, would lock her up if she knew about the Met on Main Brussels she'd planned, and throw away the key with the salted caramel mud cake. Her girls! Was she setting them all up for another disastrous fall?* Breathe ...

Once out of the fray of moored vessels, Griffin cut the motor and steered the bow across the wind. Sheri could tell by looking at him that this was the moment for him when the world fell away. She watched the pattern on the water, dark specks rippling across the surface toward them. Wind. Then – *woosh!* – the sails filled and they were off. The magical force she felt carrying them along was not unlike the power she remembered of a wave under her surfboard, that feeling of an invisible force.

As well as Sheri knew Nantucket, she was a nautical newbie, having clocked more hours on the steamship in her lifetime than sailboats. She wasn't even sure she'd be able to ask an intelligent question. "So, where does one sail for a sunset supper?" she asked anyway.

In his element at the wheel of *Fantasea,* Griffin's face was a timeless painting, a captain at the helm of his pride and joy. Tall and self-possessed with golden streaked hair blowing back from a tanned face, gently creased from seasons in the sun, Griffin had sapphire eyes that took in the light and shone it back. Rather than making her feel silly for her question, he directed his ocean eyes her way and said, "Well, the simple answer is – wherever the wind takes us! The prevailing wind is southwest which will take us past Brant Point lighthouse, through the jetties, and into Nantucket Sound then we'll pick a spot to drop sail and enjoy our lobster rolls. We can play the light by ear then get a closer look at the boats in the boat basin and mooring field and be able to check out the homes and beaches along the waterfront. How does that sound, Sheri baby?"

"Don't start with your Frankie Vallie, I swear. Anyway, Griff, this is amazing, thank you so much, and Trudy for organizing! Being out on the water is a whole different feeling."

"I'm thinking," Griffin said, "if the winds allow, we can sail up the head of the harbor along the Coatue Wildlife Refuge and anchor there for supper."

"Oh, it's going to be so, so beautiful, I can already tell," Trudy said, pouring Sheri a glass of her favorite chardonnay into the most glass-like plastic wine tumbler she'd ever seen, delightfully heavy in her hand. The lapping of the water against the hull soothed her and the soft warm breeze streamed through her hair. Ahead, Sheri watched a gust dance and twirl across the water's surface as the boat glided steadily forward. The color of the sun was ripening with the lateness of the day and it gilded everything it touched.

"Just look at him," Trudy said dreamily of her husband as she looked over at Griff, "you can just see him listening to the water moving beneath the boat, feeling the hull cut through the ocean, the tension in the sheets ... It's one of the only times I can see him connecting with something larger than himself."

Sheri envied her friend's relationship with her husband of so many years, wondering about the magic sauce that kept a marriage glued together for twenty-five years when so many others fell apart. And she was curious about how much of her own marital status Trudy had shared with Cooper and Noah – if any at all. She was still unsure of Trudy's intentions and her own place there on their little adventure. She felt suddenly careful of how she presented herself, protective of the things she hadn't even shared with Trudy. And as if her thoughts were bobbing overhead in a bubble, Cooper said over the wind, "So Trudy tells me you're divorced ..."

And there it was. Thoughts ricocheted while Sheri shot her friend a look that said, *so, you're pimping me out now?*

"Forgive me," Cooper started to say, "I don't mean to pry, it's clearly none of my business and –"

Sheri put her free hand up in the universal symbol of *don't worry about it*, took a gulp of her wine, and said, "It's fine, really. I am divorced." Those words didn't feel right in her mouth. Which was stupid. She was stupid. It was easier *not* to think logically about her situation, this thing she was doing with Tommy, her *ex*-husband. She just wanted to get back that sexy feeling, the new connection she and Tommy were feeling their way around. One that was neither ready to be scrutinized nor validated.

"And what exactly is your story, where is Leo's mother in all this" Sheri said. Whoa. What was she doing? That sounded so personal and pointed. And why was it suddenly just her and Cooper having this conversation? Maybe the wind had whisked away her question – had Cooper even heard her? Griffin unwittingly changed the direction of things.

"When I was a kid sailing with my dad," Griffin began, "I remember him steering the boat into the wind giving my brother and I commands: *Free the ties! Loosen the sheets!* And how we'd snapped to attention, aye-aye captaining him at every command. He'd tell us when to winch up the sails and we obeyed. Everyone understood that out on the water, he was king. My brother and I would lay on our stomachs and just stare over the side into the depths, at the rising and falling of the green below. Do you know how ecologically rich the Nantucket Sound is? A shallow basin of shifting sand and shoals – which also happens to be home to dozens of shipwrecks – pretty cool, eh?"

"Very," Sheri said, leaning forward, not wanting to miss a word, "so tell me about this boat, Griff, I know it's new to you and Trudy but it must have a story." Sheri thought how everything about Griff and Trudy had a story.

As they glided over the deep blue water out to Coatue, Griffin and Trudy reminisced about how the thirty-seven-foot Tartan came to be theirs.

"It must have been kismet," Griff said, "that Trudy and my dad both came across this beauty on YachtWorld. Trudy and I decided a while ago not to do big gifts for each other on our looming fiftieth birthdays and big anniversary - no wasted money on big parties either."

"Bro – so this doesn't count as a *big gift*?" Noah said, with a quick laugh that everyone joined him in.

"Okay, wise guy, I had a feeling that was coming, let me finish. This we consider to be more under the heading of *life experiences* than *material things*. Now, as I was saying ... Dad and Trudy sent the listing to our family text thread. We knew right away that this was our boat, that she was everything we wanted. *Wayfarer,* as she was called, was in Maryland and when I called the broker just before Christmas to see if we could take a look, he said that she was already under contract. Several weeks later my dad saw that the listing was still up, so I gave the broker another call. The other buyer had backed out! Talk about a sign, right? Turns out that the dude had gone through the whole sea trial and inspections but forgot one small detail – like not telling his girlfriend that they would be moving onto the boat!"

"Meant to be," Sheri said, getting swept up in the romance of the story and the beautiful summer evening, practically drooling in anticipation of the lobster rolls. "You've sailed practically your whole life, right, Griff?" Was that it? Trudy's and Griff's shared passion for sailing? Big love for something other than just each other? Sheri thought of a quote that stuck with her: *Love does not consist of gazing at each other, but in looking outward in the same direction.* When had Tommy's horizon become a different one than hers?

"Pretty much," Griff said, "I was fortunate to have grown up with two sets of parents - my actual parents and my godparents. My godfather Jack and my father have known each other since they were nine years old. Jack and his wife Laura hooked me on the sport of sailing when I was eleven with sails on their boat, *Contessa*. Then they gave me my first boat, *Sales Up* when I graduated from high school – my passion for sailing exploded from there."

"You're a lucky guy," Cooper said as Griffin tacked *Fantasea* around Coatue. "You both are, to have a thing you love together. Are you here for Race Week in August? That looks like quite an event."

"Wouldn't miss it. I'd like to catch the kiteboard regatta this year, right, Tru?"

"Yes! And the kids' races – they're incredible and they're not even sixteen years old! And the celebrity invitational is fun too," Trudy said, refilling drinks and setting up the lobster rolls as Griffin anchored and dropped the sail

∞

The setting couldn't have been more quintessential Nantucket summer but Sheri felt like she was never 100 percent relaxed out on the water. On one hand, she loved the fast feeling of skimming the surface of the ocean under the power of the wind filling her up, and bobbing on the inky depths while they ate with the setting sun in her eyes. But on the other, there was a restless unknown and powerful depth to the experience that frightened her. She couldn't imagine ever sailing across the Atlantic to the other side, but people did it. "How long would it take to sail to, oh, say, Italy? And could you do it in this size boat?" she asked.

That got Griffin's attention. "Absolutely! It would take three to four weeks. Entirely doable."

"Over my dead body," Trudy said, her hair a golden halo as the sun sunk lower to the horizon.

"I'm with you," Cooper said, wiping a buttery bit of lobster from the corner of his mouth, "too many things could go wrong on a trans-Atlantic voyage like that, no thanks."

"No sense of adventure in this group – you'd be with me, right, Noah?" Anyone could see Griffin was at one with the sea, alive with its heaving energy, the thin seam of horizon his true north.

For Sheri's part, the wine softened the edges of the unrest that rose and fell beneath the surface while the sea spray and succulent lobster answered the call of her senses. She felt respected and interesting in Cooper's company and a strange tingle when their eyes met. Competing desires rolled through her as they often did when meeting someone new – to know everything at once about them or to save it all for later. In some quiet corner of her mind, she knew there'd be a *later*.

Their conversation rode the low swells that rocked the anchored boat and time was suspended like the crimson orb in the deep pink sky. She learned finally that Cooper was a cardiothoracic surgeon on the other side of an ugly divorce trying to keep his twenty-four-year-old son on the straight and narrow. He'd rented Stan and Ida's place for the month with the hope that someplace new with no memories attached to it and killer surf would lighten Leo's load. Things had apparently been grisly at home for a while before the finality of divorce.

"Not that you needed my life story," Cooper said, apologizing for how much he'd laid out, "and why is the rum always gone?" He rattled the cubes in his empty glass with a smile unfurling on his face. His tiger eyes were glowing full force with the sky working its final magic. Sheri had so many more questions.

"So why this boat?" Cooper asked Griffin as he hoisted the sail to head back, "what were the standouts?" Sheri was surprised to feel a prick of disappointment at Cooper turning his attention to Griffin and a conversation that wouldn't include her.

Sheri could tell Griffin was sad to see their evening on the water winding down and that he would make it last as long as possible. He looked glad for Cooper's question and his face brightened, turning thoughtful as he answered. "The biggest selling point for me – other than the fact that a Tartan 37 is a superior vessel – was that she'd been repowered several years ago with a brand new YANMAR – really the best diesel engine out there. We love the teak interior and the two spacious double cabins make us feel right at home. I especially like the Navy cushions with red piping – it reminds me of the University of Pennsylvania's colors, my alma mater."

"I love the comfy sleeping quarters too," Trudy added, "and the gourmet galley with a big sink and good counter space – what's not to love? Sheri, let's go down so you can see what I mean. You boys help yourselves to drinks – we'll do dessert in a minute, Sheri's lemon bars are not to be missed."

Sheri couldn't believe the luxury below deck, she'd never been on a craft like it. It was beautifully appointed but she didn't know how she'd feel about spending any prolonged time living on a boat, any boat. "Wow, just wow, Tru, you guys went all out this time, good for you. Do you have any Caribbean trips planned?"

"We do – we're so excited. We're working around my rewrite schedule which I'll be wrapping up this month – let me tell you, the Caribbean in February is spectacular. Griffin has been busy planning our route – so many choices – constant wind, endless beaches, did you know there are over seven hundred islands in the Caribbean?" Trudy said, tidying every surface as she spoke, "Of course you know the more famous spots like the British Virgin Islands, Saint Martin, Saint Lucia, Turks and Caicos – they're all gorgeous."

"I think you should write your next novel about it. Don't look at me like that – I know you don't do romances but it could be dark ... rogue hurricane swoops in, or some scuba diving mishap? Or maybe a couple ending up at each other's throats being out in the middle of the ocean alone together for so long – endless possibilities!"

"That's not a bad idea actually. Hey, let's head back up, we've given the guys enough time to talk about you."

"*What?* Trudy? Look at me – what are you –" But Sheri was already looking at the backside of her friend as she went up the steep ladder steps to the deck.

∞

Griff had pulled the anchor and anyone could see he was happiest under sail. The sky was a deep red with streaks of violet. Sheri loved when the sky lit up like that after the sun had sunk into the sea. It wasn't a sure thing. So often a cloud bank would steal in and swallow it or the orange ball would drop unceremoniously into the water without a single splash of color left behind. This was her favorite kind of sunset.

"You almost missed the best part," Cooper said.

"It keeps getting better, look at those colors," Sheri said, kneeling on the cushion beside Cooper staring out beyond their little group at the way the water became the flaming sky. She hated herself for caving and taking her phone out for a photo. She knew that palette could not be captured.

"Never quite does it justice, does it?" Cooper said.

"I was thinking the same thing," Sheri said, "but I still can never stop myself from trying." She dropped her phone back in her bag, noticing, not for the first time, Cooper's thoughts echoing her own. She sat back and tried to just be in the moment. To feel the smooth glide of the vessel, the summer wind raking her hair back, and taste the salty strands that blew across her lips. Trudy passed the basket of sweet treats to Sheri so she could do the honors.

"Look at these perfect triangles," Cooper said, before lifting his off the napkin it rested on and taking a bite. "Ooh and a shortbread crust, my favorite. My Scottish Grannie made the best."

Sheri didn't know if she should tell him he had powdered sugar on the corner of his mouth. She had to repress the urge to brush it off with her thumb. *What was wrong with her?*

"Did your Grannie grow up in Scotland?" Sheri asked, eager to flip the script in her brain.

"She lived her whole life there, in the village of Braemar, in the Highlands west of Aberdeen."

Was she picking up a sudden brogue, Gerard Butler-style? "You spent time over there with her then?" She could see it. Great, and now scenes from *Outlander* were playing in her head.

"I did. Every summer growing up. My mother brought my brother and me with her to visit for two weeks every July. She was very close to her Mam – and never did quite forgive herself for leaving Scotland to attend university in America. And once she met my father, there was no going back. They visited a few times together but my father had little use for the Highlands of Scotland – he was Wall Street and Madison Avenue to his core. But those were the best two weeks of my summer, every year. Mmm, and this shortbread takes me right back. Well done, Sheri."

"Sounds wonderful. I've never been to the UK at all." Sheri said, pleasantly adrift in the scenes and memories Cooper painted. Before they knew it, Griffin and Noah were easing *Fantasea* into a slip at the Town Pier. She'd forgotten Trudy saying that their slip reservation had opened up a day earlier than expected and that they didn't need to return to the mooring field. She felt like some kind of VIP as they tied up to the dock under the magical sky in a row of majestic yachts.

Cooper also seemed to suddenly realize that they'd docked. The wistful look he wore matched Sheri's – hoping the night wasn't ending already. Griffin announced that he was ready for a beverage and that he hoped the party didn't need to stop.

"This is incredible, Griff," Sheri said, relaxing deeper into her seat, "now you can finally join us in a drink or two – thank you so much for this." Stars were beginning to splash across the indigo sky and the glow of boat lights mingled with the low murmur of gatherings around them. "Cooper was telling us about Scotland, where his mother is from." It was as though she wanted to keep listening to the sound of his voice. And she was buzzed enough not to question it.

"*Was*, I should say," Cooper added, "My mother passed away almost thirteen years ago, cancer. My Gran outlived her own daughter by almost two years, never letting go of the belief that had she made Scotland her home she'd never have gotten sick."

"I could never live in a different country than my daughters," Sheri said, "that must have been so hard."

"I imagine it was. But I can understand why Grannie had no interest in leaving, Scotland being the most ruggedly beautiful of all four United Kingdom nations, with its deep history, striking mountains, castles, and misty lochs. And of course, its mythological monsters."

"The Loch Ness Monster!" Sheri said.

"Yes, Nessie is probably the most famous. The Scottish Highlands are a special place," Cooper said with a faraway look in his eyes. Sheri could tell he was right back there in the Highlands playing hide and seek with his brother in the clover and tall grass after a snack of milk and his Gran's shortbread cookies.

"Sounds dreamy. Do you think your mom ever had regrets leaving?" Trudy said.

"Not that she'd admit – I think she wanted more of a metropolis, you know? Braemar is a pretty little village with strong royal connections –"

"Wait, that's where Queen Elizabeth's Balmoral Castle is, right?" Trudy said.

"Exactly. But my mom had no use for the Royals and their behavior."

"A soap opera even then?" Sheri asked, laughing.

"Always," Cooper said, "though, to be honest, I do remember my mother telling us about being quite enamored with the story of the brand new Queen Elizabeth II, taking over the throne at just twenty-five years old. Mom was just a child at the time, and the current King Charles was just four years old."

"Royalty, a *monarchy*, seems like such an antiquated idea to me," Trudy said.

"Isn't it tradition more than anything else now?" Noah asked, "I've spent some time in London and what seems clear is that in this era of reality-TV obsessed people, the House of Windsor never disappoints – supplying tabloid readers with a steady thrill of glamour, wealth, and blinding fame. But actual British public support for the monarchy is historically low."

Sheri thought how well-spoken Cooper was and that she liked listening to him as he expertly steered away from a political discussion. She wondered about his wife, was she beautiful, brilliant? Why did they split? She also wondered whether or not they ever got back together – for sex or a second chance. Questions she wouldn't have thought to think before.

She was finally settling into vacation mode. She felt transported – like being in a good book, or the perfect outfit – she felt elevated into another version of herself. It was like when the salty ocean air curled her hair up in a way she loved and she'd think – maybe I could be this way at home too.

The water slapped lazily against the hull and the boat rocked against its ties. Trudy tried to hide a yawn and Sheri realized it might be just this side of overstaying their welcome. How was it almost ten o'clock already? "Well, we should leave you two to your sleepover," she said, winking as she collected her pie basket, leaning in to hug her friend.

"This was so much fun – I'm glad Griff got out here early. This was the best sunset of the summer so far," Trudy said.

"With many more to come for you, I hope," Cooper said shaking Griffin's hand, "can't thank you enough, Captain. Congratulations on your new boat, well done. May your anchor be tight, your cork be loose, your rum be spiced, and your compass be true."

"Classic Coop," Noah said, clapping his friend on the back, "always knows the perfect thing to say. Now let's heave-ho and leave these kids to it, shall we?"

Stepping onto the dock was like having to get her sea legs in reverse, it took a minute to get used to solid ground. Flanked by Cooper on one side and Noah on the left, off they headed into town. "Not sure if I look more like Mary Poppins or Little Red Riding Hood," she said, with the pie basket swinging in her hand, "Either way I need to lose the basket, my car is right around the corner." she said, feeling not awkward, but cute and fun instead. In keeping with her vacation vibe she thought how free she felt walking down the street to a bar with a couple of handsome men she barely knew – she could do whatever she wanted to do, be whoever she wanted to be. There were no stakes!

"Well then you'd better watch out for this big bad wolf," Noah said with a wink, "I hope you don't mind my bowing out – meeting a friend at Cru."

At the same time Sheri was thinking how oddly convenient that was, Cooper said, "you have another friend on-island? Isn't that a coincidence ..."

"Serendipity my friend" Noah said, with a mischievous head tilt in his friend's direction and an endearing side smile. "don't do anything I wouldn't do."

"*Is* there anything he wouldn't do?" Sheri asked Cooper playfully as Noah took his leave.

"Excellent question. He was a wild child, and while I think he's a tamer man, he's as unmarried as ever," Cooper said, with his hands in his pockets and a side glance at Sheri as if to say *you know the type*.

"Should I use my imagination or ... ?"

"Let's change the subject. What do you know about Gaslight – Leo says it's a happening spot?"

"It is. But do you think he wants to run into Dad there? I mean they have live music and I'm game if you are," Sheri said, a bubble of excitement rising up. Just look at her – out on the town – not crying over being in her parents' house alone. And if she were being completely honest with herself, totally enjoying Cooper's company. It was easy and new and it came without baggage.

"Yes, then, let's," Cooper said. Letting Sheri's body bump ever so slightly into his as they navigated the cobblestones in the dark on their way to Gaslight on Union Street. More tingles. Who even was she anymore?

∞

They could hear the music before they got to the door and feel the night buzzing. Inside she felt a pull of energy, that happy chaos that seemed to live behind the doors of a crowded bar when the music is good. She slipped her cashmere sweater off over her hair, barely giving a thought to wrecking her 'do. She tied it around her waist and almost missed the look on Cooper's face as he forgot to camouflage his delight at her generous décolletage in the deep white V-neck of her top. Averting her own gaze she stared up at the board of fun drinks and a ping of excited thirst hit the back of her throat anticipating the cu-cumba margarita.

The band was Easy Honey and Sheri loved their indie surf-rock sound. She couldn't stop staring, they were so cool, like the guys you wanted to party with in college. It was like folk music meets fun rock and they were kind of reminding her of the Kinks and Raconteurs. Wyn would absolutely love them and Tia too – maybe the band would be playing again during her daughters' visit. Maybe they'd all come back together. Maybe fifty *was* the new thirty.

A sideways glance at Cooper told her he was enjoying himself too. Men were so cute the way they could make standing and swaying look like dancing. Cooper looked particularly adorable with one hand in his khaki shorts pocket and the other wrapped around his beer bottle, alternately watching the band and watching Sheri. She felt his eyes on her and let herself feel sexy without censoring or analyzing it. It felt good to let go of some things and just be.

Sheri made her margarita last because she knew she'd have to drive home. It was getting close to midnight, which was well past her usual bedtime, but she wasn't worried about losing a glass slipper or her Bronco turning into a pumpkin. Things were good, she felt good.

Main Street was quiet and Nantucket town twinkled like a child's toy village. Cooper walked Sheri to her car before getting into his Range Rover and heading home. Weird that "home" was next door to each other on Eel Point Road. The ride back was quiet in comparison to the night she'd had, but she wouldn't allow herself to start feeling lonely. She shoved the memories away of her little girls asleep in their beds and her dad in the bedroom waiting up for her with the television on low while her mom read in the bed beside him.

That was a punch to the solar plexus. All the rooms were empty. Before changing into her nightie she took one last look at herself in the mirror. She was still rocking the outfit. Mascara still where it belonged, and her hair – she had to admit – looked freakin' great. Would this be the summer of new Sheri? Fantasizing about the *ex* probably wasn't the best start. Damn, being alone invited way too much self-examination.

Climbing into cool sheets with the lights out Sheri could still feel her body buzzing. It was electric and while it beat the flatline her love life had become the last couple of years – it was a little overwhelming. She'd been funneling all her excitement into her dinner plan with Tommy but spending time with Cooper had her confused. Not knowing where these thoughts of Cooper belonged, she decided to put them away up on a shelf for now.

Burying herself deeper under the covers as the cool night air swirled in through the windows, she laid back wondering if Tommy was thinking about her. If he was wishing he was with her instead of Stephanie. She did her best to tamp down the memory of the things she'd ignored the way you do when you're trying to stay married. He was different now, she was different – they would be different. Wouldn't they?

She almost felt sorry for Stephanie. And Aaro. And the baby Stephanie thought they'd have together. Of course Tommy wouldn't want that – his girls were everything to him and he wouldn't let anything, *anyone*, take away from that. That's what you get for falling for an older man, Sheri thought, *someone else's* man.

It was a dangerous thought path she was on, all of it, she was aware, and she wasn't psyched to be *the other woman*. BUT – what comes around goes around, right? She had him first, and she'd have him last.

Chapter Sixteen

SHERI WAS HAPPY TO be awakened by the sounds of construction – finally her deck would be completed, and not a minute too soon. *Her* deck, that had a nice ring to it, she decided. She was anxious to set out the new teak furniture that her parents had bought just two summers ago. She had the energy of five people anticipating her daughters' arrival tomorrow night. Tommy coming over for dinner was the icing on the cake. Or was it the whole cake? She wasn't going to analyze it to death. She also wasn't going down the road of her parents never getting to enjoy their teak loungers on their new deck that they'd most likely never see again. No, no, she was definitely not going there.

Instead, she would photograph everything when it was completed and send photos of Tia and Wyn waving from the new deck and raising a glass from the chairs with their regatta-blue cushions, bright beach towels draped over the railing the way her mom liked it, showing that life and love lived there. It was all she could do.

Maybe she could get Rocco to help her get the furniture out of the shed and up the deck stairs – she'd want it to be all set up for twilight drinks with Tommy. Would she have time to string some bistro lights along the railing? The girls would love that. Speaking of the girls, she needed to text them for a grocery list of all the things they hoped to find when they opened the cabinets and the fridge.

That was one small benefit of the empty nest – how her daughters were now guests who she wanted to shower with every good thing, fulfill every wish. The culinary ones anyway, and all the little creature comforts that they couldn't always afford for themselves. So much else was beyond her reach! She couldn't buy their happiness, put a down payment on the perfect job or boyfriend, but dammit she could have sweet fat strawberries in the fridge, chunks of aged cheddar, bresaola instead of salami, Sicilian green olives, and Reposado Tequila. Cinnamon frosted Pop-Tarts and Captain Crunch in the pantry just in case. Spoiling her girls was a fun side-effect of losing them to their own lives. A pleasure instead of the chore it once seemed – their happiness so fleeting and tenuous then.

And the bonus surprise of their dad being on Nantucket - did they know? Surely they'd have mentioned it if they did. *Sheri was clearly avoiding yet another road – the very ragged one with the giant pothole named Tommy.* Happiness bloomed in her chest and she decided to go for a run on the beach to make the most of her revving engine and the perfect summer day.

She went out the front and around back to the beach steps not wanting to encourage conversation with Rocco and the blond guy. She felt weird about that but whatever, let them work and get it done. She took the fifty-seven steps down to the sand. The tideline was an unforgiving slope regardless of the tide and she hoped her knees wouldn't complain. Days like this, with her mood carrying her along, she felt no pain. Which isn't to say she wouldn't feel it later, but for now she was good.

Passing through the drive-on section of the beach called 40th Pole, she expected more vehicles to be backed up to the water, but it was still early in July and not as crazy as it would be in August. She dodged kids as she jogged along the waterline and their castles, rafts, and a few dogs – the reward just beyond, where the empty beach stretched, no longer open to vehicles.

Memories of her own childhood and of those as a young mother rushed in like the clear shallow water delivering glinting treasures. Striped scallop shells, peach and yellow jingle shells, coveted green bits of sea glass, and the small eager hands that reached for them, filling pails too heavy to carry. Her heart was a full bucket swinging in her chest. She stopped, leaning her hands down on her knees to catch her breath. Sweat poured and mingled with tears stinging her eyes. Happy tears, she told herself, she'd had it all. It had just gone by too fast.

Had she loved it enough when they were little? Had she appreciated their complete devotion, their distinct and singular trust? The love and adoration that poured from their whole faces, filling her up with importance, self-worth. Where does it go? When your whole identity is wrapped up in those sweet babies that grew not only under your heart but in it - into people with their own ideas, their own opinions, and an address that no longer matched yours.

Sheri had friends who were glad when the kids flew the coop – finally time for themselves, an orderly house, crap-free surfaces, date nights again with their husbands. What had she ended up with? It had been the loneliest she'd ever been when the girls moved away for college and Tommy was moving away from her in his heart. On some level she knew none of them were ever coming back. It didn't seem real. It had been impossible to reconcile. She'd buried herself in her work, in the lives of her clients with so much less who needed her more – a roof over their head, food, healthcare. Love was a luxury.

Had she squandered hers? If she and Tommy had stayed married, had found a way back to each other, would the girls have lived at home longer after graduation? Or were they already gone? Of course she blamed herself – if only she'd done things differently, better. God, why was she such a mess half the time? How did she ruin the simplest best things like a beach run on a quintessential summer day? Why did the past, the really great past with her happy little family, make her cry?

Because it was g-o-n-e. Because it was exactly that, the *past*. She had to find new ways to grow and feel meaningful and productive in this second half of her life. Yes, some things were over and not coming back. Her children wouldn't be climbing into her bed on rainy summer mornings to watch *Beauty and the Beast* again, or beg her to get out the watercolor paints and Shrinky Dinks.

Everything ends, her insightful youngest daughter once told her. Indeed.

She straightened herself out to see a fellow jogger headed in her direction. Something about him was familiar but he was still too far in the distance to tell. He slowed to a walk, putting his hands on his hips. She dried her eyes and stretched her hamstrings before getting going again.

"Sheri?" It was Cooper coming toward her. How did he know it was her, with her hair tied back in a ponytail under a ball cap – she felt generic, anonymous. "Gorgeous morning," he said, shielding his eyes from the sun, "and I see you're no worse for the wear?" His smile was bright as he posed his observation as a question. He'd pretty much matched her drink for drink between the boat ride and the bar – so she could say the same of him.

"One of the lucky ones, I guess, I don't usually have to pay too much of a price for over-imbibing."

"Lucky? Well, I guess that depends how you look at it," Cooper said, using the shoulder of his T-shirt to wipe away the sweat that started to run down his face.

"Ah, Doctor Madden is in the house. Yeah, I know, I know, drinking is bad for me, we can skip the lecture," Sheri said good-naturedly but a little defensive too. She turned her body to catch the breeze off the water. "How lucky are we with this for a backyard to run ..." She kept her focus on the lazy sea, ripples pleating the surface, the horizon an unreachable lavender line.

"I couldn't agree more," Cooper said, standing beside her facing the water. "How long have your parents owned the property, did you get to spend all your summers here growing up?"

"A lot of them. Let's see, my parents have had this place for over forty years now – could that be right?" Sheri said, turning to face Cooper as if he'd have the answer. "Yes, they must have bought in 1979 because I was four years old that first summer here."

"So that would make you –"

"On the wrong side of 40 ..." Sheri laughed, reaching up to tighten her ponytail.

"And how old did you say your kids were?"

"I don't believe I did," Sheri said with her hands on her hips, "but twenty-five and twenty-three. I wanted to be a young mom, what can I say?"

"Good for you. Leo falls right in the middle of that – and you said they're coming to the island?"

"Are you taking notes?" Sheri said, chuckling but starting to feel exposed with all the questions. Probably a consequence of sneaking around with her ex-husband while also flirting easily with her handsome neighbor. "They'll be here this weekend actually," she said, anxious to continue her run before her muscles cooled completely and started to stiffen, "Lots to do! Have a nice run, Cooper, I'm sure we'll see you around." With that she continued on her way in the direction of Smith's Point while Cooper headed back home.

∞

The steaming outside shower after her run felt especially good knowing no contractors were around and the deck was done. She did a mental checklist of things she still needed to buy before her girls arrived: their favorite bodywash, shampoo, conditioner, body lotion, and Coppertone.

Or did they want Beach Bum? Was that the one that was PABA-free? And reef-safe? Were they the same thing? Could you protect your skin *and* the coral reefs? Life was getting more complicated.

Trudy was blowing up her phone asking her about her night with Cooper, if there would be a second date. A *second date?* Had there really been a first? Sheri still hadn't taken those feelings down from the shelf for closer examination, but she'd be lying if she said she didn't sense the background flare of something hovering quietly. Sheri was trying to focus on Tommy, which already came with a bag of rocks, and sensing Trudy doing everything in her power to get her off Tommy only served to make it heavier. But she was a grown-ass woman, dammit, taking care of herself.

Then why was she hiding stuff from Trudy?

Because. Because Trudy knew better than most the pain and heartache that Tommy's cheating and ultimate defection from the marriage unleashed upon Sheri's heart, her well-being, her sense of self. But what she didn't understand, or wouldn't if Sheri confided in her, was that people can change. That it was not only possible for Tommy to change but he was doing it! He was choosing her over the *bow and arrow* that took them down. He'd had an epiphany, Sheri was sure of it, that Stephanie and Aaro didn't belong to him the way Sheri, Tia, and Wyn did. And from where Sheri stood, she had every right to take back what was hers.

She wanted to get back to her good mood, her bubble of excitement about the evening ahead and her daughters arriving. A text from Tommy boosted her to the next level.

> Seven hours ... but who's counting?

She was whirling inside. Not even tempted to ask him what he'd planned to tell Stephanie, or how was he getting out of the father's house. To do so would be to acknowledge that Stephanie meant anything at all.

When all she really was, was the catalyst for the reunion of Sheri's family. The sunny wind blew through the open windows of her Bronco on the way to do errands and Journey came on her 80s playlist, "Separate Ways."

That song used to kill her. *True love won't desert you ... you know I still love you ...* Her blood slowed, felt thick in her veins. Maybe she wasn't really ready to hear that one. She switched to Bob Marley. Reggae was what she needed.

Her heart picked up its regular pace and she went back to looking forward to dinner with Tommy, and their daughters' arrival. She floated from shop to shop fulfilling her lists and her heart.

Chapter Seventeen

Tommy was due at seven o'clock and Sheri walked back the meal prep in her mind so she'd know just when to begin roasting the chicken and then the Brussels sprouts and garlic mashed potatoes. The first thing she had to do was make the lemon herb butter to put under the skin of the chicken.

Reaching for the glass measuring cup to melt the butter, she suddenly felt like her mother. How many times had her mom put that to use measuring, melting, and measuring some more? Sheri would never be the natural cook Rose was, but she did okay. She tried not to hold the glass handle so tenderly or attach more nostalgia to it than necessary. But every little thing weighed too much.

She had to coach herself to be in the present moment, to not let it drag her to some melancholy place. Things change, nothing stays the same. It's not supposed to. It was as simple and as impossible as that. And even though her parents were still living she had a right to her feelings of loss. Because enough was certainly lost, knowing that her mother, at least, and very possibly her father, would never be standing there in the Nantucket house with her again. Rose would never again ask Sheri to peel the garlic cloves to stuff in the chicken or to help her lift the heavy roasting pan out of the oven. All Sheri could think of were the things she hadn't asked her mother and might never have the answers to now. Recipes Rose had never written down because she either knew them by heart or they were just a part of her.

But Sheri could be the kind of mother to her daughters that Rose was to her.

She peeled and minced the garlic then combined the rosemary, thyme, lemon zest, Kosher salt, and ground black pepper, adding it to the melted butter. She separated the skin with her fingers first and then with a spoon to create deeper pockets for the herbed butter. She could hear her mother's voice telling her how rubbing the herb butter under the skin kept the chicken juicy and tender as it roasted.

She got out the large roasting pan and arranged a vegetable bed for the chicken so the skin wouldn't burn, then she placed the chicken on top. Looking down at hands so like her mother's, she rubbed the remaining herb butter all over the outside of the skin, seasoning it with salt and generous grinds of pepper. It felt like so long since she'd gone through these motions, making this beautiful dinner for someone who'd enjoy it so thoroughly.

Seduced by the perfect summer evening and the illusion of her single life and loneliness coming to an end, Sheri set the big farm table for an intimate two. She arranged her newly collected scallop shells around the fat pillar candles of varying heights that she'd nestled in powdery Nantucket sand inside hurricane vases. It was picture-perfect. If only there were someone she could share a photo of it with, trust with her unbound hope and fevered heart. But she kept it for herself right now, away from her protective friend who might tell her things she didn't want to hear and didn't believe anymore.

A one-time fling Trudy could get behind, but not this. And Sheri told herself all the things she needed to hear to justify not confiding in her. Trudy wouldn't understand that Tommy had changed, that he regretted ever leaving his family, that he'd come to his senses. That Sheri had changed too. But what about the girls? There was no way Sheri was ready to see them in the equation yet.

Your journey is unfolding exactly as it should, her mom always said.

The chicken had begun roasting and everything else was prepped and ready. Sheri wanted nothing more than to pour a glass of wine to enjoy out on the new deck and to light a couple candles out there to enjoy the sight, sound, and smell of the sea. She would leave her phone inside – endless, mindless scrolling had no place in this night she'd created with painstaking, deliberate detail. She was aware that Tommy would be dipping out on Stephanie for the evening, that he hadn't explained everything to her yet, that it wasn't the right time or place. And while something about that scraped at something somewhere in Sheri, she understood the position he was in.

A memory drifted in of Rose and George sipping gin and tonics on the deck while the sun made its descent ... her mom in a blue paisley patio dress, "At Last" by Etta James playing loud on the radio, her dad sweeping her mom into a waltz.

At last, my love has come along ... my lonely days are over ... and life is like a song ...

∞

Sheri found herself going back and forth from inside to make sure everything was timed just right. Certain everything was cooked to perfection, she placed the chicken on a platter and each side dish in one of her mother's elegant China-lidded bowls and set them all on the table. Tommy would pull into the driveway any moment. She lit a match to the fire she'd built in the fireplace and turned only a couple of the lamps on to their dimmest setting.

The old photo albums lined up on the shelves flanking the fireplace caught her eye. She grabbed one and lowered herself to the couch to flip through a few pages. The nostalgia of her younger parents, her younger self, and her baby girls with Tommy made the pages swim before her. Grabbing a box of tissues, she headed outside with the oversized album and a bottle of wine to refill her glass and to slow the march of her thoughts.

Sheri could feel herself coming undone seeing the way Tommy looked at his little girls, how he adored them – and how he adored being adored by them. And then her young and hearty parents! Their vigor so distinct, enduring. Until it wasn't. When had the decline even begun? She'd barely noticed. Until seeing them in the photos, how she pictured them still.

But they weren't those people anymore, none of them were.

Her head was swimmy with wine. How long had she been sitting there lost in the years? The candlelight blurred before her and the huge sky showed off its crimson magic. She hadn't even realized the sun had already sunk into the sea. How had she missed it, what time was it? After nine? She set the album on the small teak table and went inside, tamping down whatever it was that rose up, jagged and familiar inside her.

It was late. Well past what she and Tommy had agreed upon. She looked around for her phone – surely she'd missed a text from him explaining. Where the hell was it? Why was she such an idiot that she could never remember where she put her damn phone? *Why was she so stupid?*

She reached up to the mantle and there it was, its blank screen staring back at her, mocking her foolish anticipation. There and then it dropped out of her, the hope she didn't know she was holding onto – that he'd changed.

She wanted to scream away the ugliness that was building inside her, the hatred she felt for herself looking upon the extravagant meal that sat waiting by candlelight for *nothing*, for *no one*! How could she have been so stupid? The ringing doorbell tore into her frenzy of self-loathing. Tommy after all? Would she have to walk back all the things she'd just ripped herself apart about and move forward? Again?

Everything after that happened so fast.

She tried to arrange her features into something good on her way to the door, pulling it open too abruptly. "Cooper?" she said as he pushed past her outside to the deck engulfed in flames.

"Where's your hose? Didn't you hear me screaming your name?" he said running down her new deck steps to the spigot with Sheri on his heels. "I called 911 but I think we can get this out – here, *pull!*" Sheri ran up the steps pulling the hose as it filled with the gushing force of the water. Cooper came up behind her to help aim it at the blaze as it consumed the candles, tissues, photo album, and the small teak table with flames licking out at the loungers. "It looked a lot bigger from my house, you're lucky," Cooper said, as they heard sirens peel in the distance coming closer.

"*Lucky* ..." Sheri said, considering the word, tears rolling down her face. Emotions collided and she had a hard time parceling out which weighed more: shame, shock, fear, or embarrassment. She could have burned her parents' house down, or reduced the new deck to a pile of rubble. And for what? How had she not noticed the tissues blowing into lit candles in the wind – how could she have left it all unattended? What had she been thinking?

She hadn't been thinking at all. She was such a fool she could barely stand herself. And now she had to face the firefighters – people who risked their lives every day for the foolishness of distracted people doing dumb things. The pendulum from high to low was too much.

Chapter Eighteen

ONCE THE NFD TOOK every measure to be certain the fire was extinguished and lectured Sheri on preventative measures for the future safety of her home and the homes around her, she was properly admonished and took note of the disturbing fact that she'd had no idea where the fire extinguisher was in her parents' home. Things could have been exponentially worse. She was spent.

She put the uneaten meal in the fridge and dismantled her tablescape so it could no longer taunt her and she went to her room and closed the door. Against what? She was alone in the house. Felt alone in her life and like she deserved to be there. What must Cooper think of her? Once the firefighters had gone, he'd asked if she was okay, noticing the table set for a romantic dinner for two. He'd been too polite to ask.

What would have happened if he hadn't raced over from next door with his quick thinking and action? She was practically paralyzed with shock and disbelief at the pyre she'd built. The photo album was torched, as was her parents' little teak table. Ash. Her heart was sick about it.

It was an accident. It could have happened to anyone. They're just objects, no one was hurt. She could recite these things over and over but it wasn't easing her heart or her mind. How would she sleep? How would she meet the next day? Had she literally set fire to the past? Her phone jangled on the nightstand.

She hated what that did to her insides, the thoughts that rushed in unwanted. Of Tommy. The hope that still betrayed her. But of course the text wasn't from him. She wanted to throw her phone against the wall. Or smash it with a cast iron pot against the stone counter. She quaked with nerves and hurt and shame, and most of all, anger with herself.

The text was from Wyn. Her dear youngest daughter. Who was so full of life and had the energy of six people. But who, like Sheri, was forever either on the ceiling or in the cellar. Sheri didn't have the bandwidth to deal with whatever was most likely on the other side of that name lighting up her screen. But ignoring it and waiting until morning to open it would only add heat to the lava already roiling.

She swiped before she could overthink it. Really, what was more shitty news?

> Can't stand my job. Hate that I'll be pulled into at least one meeting while I'm there – I put in for my time off but the stupid project takes precedence – UGH. And I swear to God if my flight's delayed. Adulting sucks I want to spend the whole summer on Nantucket.

Sheri sighed and slapped the phone down on the bed. Staring up at the ceiling in the dark she tried to think of what to say, any response at all that wouldn't incite further frustration. There were, of course, no answers. Adulting *did* suck. And especially now for twenty-somethings. She hated that they all seemed so collectively hopeless – she hated that no matter how hard they worked or for how long, affording a home seemed hopelessly beyond reach. It *was* depressing. *And that is why no one our age wants kids, Mom, because we can't even afford ourselves,* Wyn had said often enough.

Where was it all going?

And what about Tia and Jackson, with all their analytical discussions – they both made decent money working in finance, but money wasn't everything. They talked things to death, Sheri thought. *Way* too much sharing in her opinion. Yes, there was such a thing as overcommunicating! Damn kids today had to dissect every little thing and how it was *making them feel*. Where was the tolerance? Where was accepting a certain percentage of crap in a relationship? But that definitely sounded like bad advice.

Wish you were here already. It'll all work out. I love you.

It was the best she could do.

Sheri pleaded for sleep to come, for the perspective and light of a new day. She felt like she was grappling for purchase when everything under her was made of sand.

∞

The dawn of a new day helped. Her mind was marginally clearer and she came to accept the futility of beating herself up. People screw up, that's what it was to be human. And she didn't exactly write the book on the foolishness of second chances. She was almost used to the numbness that replaced the anger, grateful for it. She had the day to get her shit together for her daughters who would be arriving at six-forty and seven o'clock respectively. One by boat the other by plane, God forbid they would get *their* shit together. She wanted to vacuum, dust, put sheets on their beds, and make sure the towels smelled fresh. Seaside living could be a force, the damp salty air was an uninvited guest.

She couldn't wait for company – to *not* be alone in the house another day, she was way inside her head. And she was nowhere near ready to think about what her heart was up to. She did need to thank

Cooper – maybe get him to help her dispose of the scorched table, damn, she was angry with herself. Maybe Marine Home Center would have a suitable replacement. She deserved whatever it would cost.

A tentative rapping on the screen door frame startled her and she tried not to allow herself time to guess who it was. She saw that it was Cooper, but her gut had hoped it was Tommy. Her own body's betrayal! She hated herself.

"Hey, good morning, Coop – how do I thank you for last night?" Sheri felt awkward and embarrassed without the veil of alcohol, what must he think of her?

"Thank *you* for the fireworks," he said with half a smile. "Too soon?"

Sheri just stared. Her face was starting to flame and her stomach twisted. She suddenly felt inept at conversation, a buffoon in the presence of his composure. As if she didn't deserve the affection and kindness of this decent man.

"No, you're good. I'm an idiot. I can't believe I let that happen, I mean an open flame and tissues hanging out together on a breezy night. Duh! I'm embarrassed. So, what did you say – you were on your deck and saw the flames? I think I blocked everything out. Again, I'm so sorry for putting you through it." Sheri dared a look up at him and his warm hazel eyes set her at ease. There was nothing accusatory or impatient in them. He was probably one of those doctors who also had a great bedside manner. But maybe he was also a cheater – who knew? She wanted to ask him to carry off the table wreckage down the steps for her but she also didn't want to invite conversation – like who she'd been expecting last night.

"I was sitting out on my deck watching the moon on the water when I saw the quick flame in my peripheral view. I called out to you but the wind must have swallowed my voice and you didn't hear me."

"I just feel so stupid. Anyway, I'd really appreciate it if you could help me get rid of the evidence. My daughters are both coming tonight and, well, we can't have them thinking I'm losing my shit, you know?"

Cooper nodded, with a small smile that said he did know. He really was a kind man, Sheri thought, and in possession of excellent neighborly qualities. She felt like a disaster in comparison – she hadn't asked him anything about his son or the kid from the fight in his kitchen the other night. It felt like ages ago, but had it been only a couple of days?

"How's Leo by the way? You said he was needing kind of a reboot or something? Maybe it was just a change of scenery, is he finding it?"

"It's been a slow start. Taking a swing at that kid in our kitchen wasn't part of the prescription, you know? But he'll come around. He's been frustrated with the surf, or lack thereof I should say, but big swell coming in tomorrow I heard him say," Sheri giggled at Cooper's air quotes around *big swell*, it felt so good to laugh.

"Oh, I feel your pain. My Wyn is the exact same way about the surf. It's extreme – definitely falls under the heading of addiction. I mean, safer than some other options but still ..."

"Because they need their fix. And too long without it makes them ..."

"Crazy. Not fun to be around. So how's that gonna work? You know, long-term, in real life?" Sheri said.

"I ask myself the same question all the time. Live at the beach? Or maybe finding some career that inspires them, or spilling some of that passion into a relationship ultimately? Making the surfing less of a do-or-die mentality?"

"I'd like to believe that, but I'm not so sure redirecting her passion for surfing would work for Wyn. Why is it such a challenge for kids to be happy these days? I mean just the fact that we're calling twenty-somethings *kids* is probably part of the problem. There's just this alarming degree of hopelessness about the future that we did not feel, do you agree?"

"I do. If it's not the decimation of the planet, ever being able to afford a house, the untenable political climate, or trying to date in an AI world, it's ten other things that spell anxiety." Cooper was shaking his head and the light went out of his eyes. Sheri could relate so hard to what he was saying, it was the exact conversation she'd been having with her own kids lately.

"All so true, I hate to say. I don't remember feeling that way at all at that age, do you?"

"Who had time for that?" Cooper said, sounding exactly like what he'd probably always been, a man on a mission, med school and all that came with it, with a plan and laid out path to get there. "I'll admit to getting frustrated with the whole woe-is-me bit, but I do have some respect for the challenges they face. I'd just hate to see it weaken their resolve, you know?"

"That's a good way to put it. I mean it's not like they can just throw in the towel because things are harder, right? But I hate to see them praying for a meteor to strike earth and end it all. It gets tough knowing what to say to them in response to all these issues though, how to encourage them, right? Sheri felt a sense of validation talking with Cooper and it was nice to not be alone with things in her head. Tommy was so infrequently there for the day-to-day.

"We need to toughen them up instead of sympathizing," Cooper said, "If they see us getting soft, feeling bad for them, they'll take that and run with it – can't have that!"

"Ha! Right, okay, enough of that," Sheri said, feeling lighter than she had been, despite the heaviness of the subject. Maybe it was having another adult to commiserate with, feeling seen and heard. She'd been feeling like a single parent for a while with good-time Tommy mostly only there for the good times. This felt like something different, an unexpected sense of comradery.

"Let me get out of your hair, Sheri, I hope you have a wonderful visit with your girls. And don't worry, my lips are sealed about your little accidental campfire."

Sheri smiled and clapped him on the shoulder as she opened the slider to the deck for him. He was muscled and warm beneath her

Fogged In

hand and it surprised her to notice that. It pleased her too. She felt a space open up in her chest where anxiety about Tommy had taken up residence.

Chapter Nineteen

Of course Tia's flight had been delayed, why would anything be easy? Sheri knew her daughter wasn't really trying to show off her bank account by flying instead of the traditional ferry from Hyannis, and that it was more about saving time and getting to Nantucket sooner, but it had backfired. Tia's island connection in Boston had been delayed causing precious hours to be wasted in a chair at Logan Airport while her fly-by-the-seat-of-her-pants sister managed to barely make it on the five o'clock boat, surfboard under her arm wheeling a bag behind her.

Sheri's heart took flight at the sight of Wyn deboarding the Hy-Line fast ferry. Her sandy hair looked adorable in a hastily chopped cut to just above her shoulders, Noah Kahan concert T-shirt, cut-offs, and beat-up Reefs on her tan feet. And while she looked exactly as Sheri had envisioned, lean and muscled from climbing mountains and surfing, shading her pale-blue eyes from the strong sun, Sheri was never quite ready for the sublime fullness that flooded her at the sight of her beautiful, strong daughter.

Sheri took too many photos with her phone of her daughter coming toward her. Why did she do that? Trying to capture every beat – though it wasn't even a thing that could be preserved, it wasn't a thing that *should* be. Emotions were fluid, rising and falling and as changeable as the sea and sky and Sheri needed to quit trying to freeze them for all of time because that did not make them *stay*. She'd stowed her phone in her back pocket by the time Wyn had zig-zagged down the gangway with the rest of the passengers – all gorgeous in their happiness.

She made space to hug around Wyn's surfboard and backpack. Sheri was the taller of the two and so she always got to feel like the mother – the one who held, while Wyn, though an adult, was still the child, the one being held. It would be ever thus.

"My beautiful girl, how was your trip? I can't believe you beat your sister after all."

"Right? Ugh, flying is such a joke. She should have just booked to Hyannis then we could have taken the boat here together. Whatever – you can't tell Tia what to do."

"Oh, don't I know it." Making their way to the luggage cart, Sheri looked around at Straight Wharf through Wyn's eyes, it was showing off in all the best ways. Hydrangeas nodding their fat heads in full bloom, a powder-blue sky showing no signs of night, and rows of yachts with their gleaming hulls of white and navy bobbing in their slips.

The cobblestoned streets and uneven brick sidewalks heaving with the roots of the ancient elm trees reminded them where they were, thirty miles out to sea on a historically preserved little island. The federal and Greek revival style buildings lining Main street took them back in time. Their preservation was striking, their survival and lasting charm long after the demise of the whaling days.

"It gets me every time, Mom, this place, its history …"

Sheri draped an arm across Wyn's shoulders as they walked, "me too, kid, me too. So, I think I've stocked up on all your faves but is there anything you can think of that you want to pick up while we're here in town?"

"Did you get ginger beer? Limes? I've been making these awesome mules lately … And Portuguese bread?"

"Bread and limes, yes, no ginger beer. Let's load your stuff into the Bronco and run into Murray's. Then we should head to the airport – I don't want to *not* be there when your sister lands."

"God forbid," Wyn said as they pulled up to Sheri's new Bronco parked in the grocery store lot, "*Whoa*, Mom, the photos you sent did not do this thing justice! This rig is beautiful, good for you, Mom. Gotta say, I'm a little jelly, this things is sick. And this blue is so pretty! Has Dad seen it yet?"

Sheri tried to head off the twisting of her gut at the mention of Tommy. But it couldn't be avoided – not any of it – not talking about him, thinking about him, or probably seeing him. She pressed some cash into her daughter's hand telling her to get what she needed at Murray's, that she'd wait there with the truck. How in touch with their father had the girls been? Was there going to be some plan that would knock her off her feet? *Deep breaths*. She was so angry with Tommy for not showing up last night! For. Not. Showing. Up. *Dammit!* She hated herself for believing he would! Thinking he could change, that he was ever going to be any different.

She would not, *could not* allow any of it to ruin her time with her girls. Nantucket was everything to them, more precious now than ever with them living on their own. Time together now seemed to take on such huge importance, and she could never quite figure out the right proportions of her full heart versus one that weighed her down. She understood it logically – that time spent together now was finite and would always come to an end. And Sheri could never quite handle the end.

"Sorry it took so long! I forgot Cisco's craft cocktails – of course I had to grab some Nantucket Cran and Blue for the beach. I'm so over the High Noons. Anyway – did you get Tia's text? They're back on schedule, let's head to the airport – it shouldn't take long. I can tie the board on top once we get there while we're waiting for them to deplane.

∞

It should only have taken about ten minutes to drive the three miles to the little airport, but it was a summer Saturday evening on Nantucket – all bets were off. Sheri wasn't shy about her lead foot and even though it took twice that time, they pulled into the airport lot just as Tia and Jackson were landing.

"I'll run in," Wyn offered, "see if you can just live-park here – we probably don't want to know how much luggage those two have."

Sheri's phone pinged form the cupholder, eliciting a trickle of anxiety and she felt like one of Pavlov's dogs salivating at the sound signaling a treat – except anxiety was no treat. Given her parents' current situation, her children out on their own in the world, and the constant weights and measures of the affections and intentions of he who shall not be named, the news being shot her way could be not only good, bad, or ugly, but the mutant collaboration of all three.

Got the toilet, is tomorrow ok for installation?

Jesus. Wes. She let out the breath she was holding and laughed at herself then typed:

No sorry - my girls just arrived - I'll text to schedule

Without waiting for a response, Sheri tucked the phone out of sight into her bag. She kept looking toward the doors from which Tia, Jackson, and Wyn would emerge, impatient to witness their unrestrained glee, the unquantifiable magic that was Nantucket shining in their faces. It was taking longer than she thought it should – she sent a prayer out into the universe that their luggage made the right trip. No one wanted to be around Tia if any of her precious things got left behind and she had to somehow make do, or, Sheri bit her tongue at the thought, borrow anything of her sister's.

Finally, the three of them pushed through the white-trimmed *arrivals* door of the quaint cedar-shingled airport that, like nearly every building on the island, resembled a large cottage. They were wheeling enough luggage behind them to cover a month's stay, was Jackson as bad as Tia about packing light? Tia was radiant in a sleeveless Lily Pulitzer sundress in bright-pinks and greens with her expertly highlighted, sunny, pin-straight hair. Jackson complimented her perfectly in shorts the same shade of pistachio and a white linen shirt rolled to the middle of his forearms, tanned and taut from sailing. Her daughters couldn't be more different, Sheri thought, watching Wyn hoist her sister's pastel Lily duffel to her shoulder, in vintage Levi's cutoffs with frayed white strings hanging.

She was glad they hadn't thought to put on sunglasses – the joy sparking their eyes was a sight to behold. Sheri wondered what they were saying to each other before they caught sight of her and waved. She already had FOMO and couldn't stand to miss out on a single thing. The closer they got to the Bronco, the faster Sheri's heart beat. It would be tight with everyone's things, the four of them, and Wyn's board, but Sheri really only wanted the two-door. She fully expected admonishment from her oldest regarding her impractical vehicle purchase. But she hoped she was wrong, after all it was her gift to herself and no one else. Having driven a mom-monster truck for years, it was her turn to have whatever she wanted.

"Sweet ride, Mom, *woohoo*!" Tia sang out, surprising Sheri in the best way. Wyn was already tying her surfboard to the roof and Jackson was fitting the bags like a puzzle. Sheri held her daughter tight, feeling her familiar form, strength, and length of the hug. The hair that hung to the middle of Tia's back was a shining curtain, feeling and smelling expensive – there was no way Sheri had bought the right products for that.

"It's nice to see you again, Mrs. Steele, thank you so much for having me," Jackson said.

"Please call me Sheri, I'm not your fifth-grade social studies teacher – get in here for a hug."

"Of course you already have all your crap piled into the front seat," Tia said to her sister.

"Of course I do – was I supposed to leave it available for you and sit in the back with your boyfriend like an Uber customer, you weirdo?"

"And so it begins," Tia said.

"And ends! Here and now you two, come on." Sheri said, shaking her head and grinning at Jackson as if to say, *kids these days* ... Sheri knew her girls couldn't help themselves when they were around their mother – it was the fresh audience thing – they didn't behave like that otherwise. She hoped they could control themselves and act like the twenty-somethings they were. Or was this par for the course with kids in their twenties these days? She wasn't having it.

Old South Road to Madaket Road was their best bet even though it would still take them about twenty-five minutes – it always felt like forever for an island so small. "So how does everything look, Mom, is anything different?" Tia asked leaning forward into the front seat, "I can't believe last year was the summer that wasn't and we missed a whole year. Everything looks the same, right?"

And that was the unexpected thing about her sophisticated, progressive daughter who liked nice things – you'd expect her to want the latest thing, the updated appliance or furniture. But she and her sister both wanted everything in the Nantucket house to be the same, to remain unchanged forever.

Sheri looked up in the rearview mirror into Tia's sea-blue eyes, expectant and childlike. "It is just as you remember, my darling girl, with the exception of the new deck, which as I told you, was a necessary replacement, and as luck would have it, construction was just finished."

"Aw, so no hot contractors on the property?" Wyn asked, "Damn, that would actually have been kinda fun." Sheri noticed Tia roll her eyes but restrain herself from commenting.

"Well, I am having the toilet in Nanna and Pops' room replaced, which as you know is where I'm staying, and while Wes the plumber is kinda cute, he's too old for you, Wyn."

"Are we really talking about this?" Tia said, "do you always have to have a boyfriend, Wyn?"

Wyn turned in her seat to face her sister in the back, sitting next to her boyfriend, "Really, Dude? When was the last time you were single?" Then to Jackson, who looked unphased by their bickering, "sorry, Jackson, this really isn't about you, but since she brought up ..."

"Okay!" Sheri interrupted, "who's hungry?" She said as they got closer to the house. "I'll heat up some things while you guys settle in, how does that sound? And who wants to be bartender, Wyn?"

But her girls were too busy looking out the window once they hit Eel Point Road, scanning the rolling moors, almost afraid of what new monstrous construction had popped up since their last time there.

"Like *who* in the world needs a summer house the size of a country club?" Wyn said, disgusted at one new place going up that looked like it would contain three separate dwellings, "I mean are sculpture gardens really necessary? Infinity pools? And eight-thousand-dollar shower curtains? Ugh! I hate people!"

Sheri hated that part too – the unwelcome juxtaposition of pristine nature with suddenly a giant house being carved into it. She heard Tia explaining to Jackson about the billionaire problem on Nantucket – so much had changed in just her kids' lifetimes. Sheri had forgotten it was Jackson's first visit to the island and started to feel the pressure to make sure he saw it through the right lens. With a heaping dose of history.

"It's just little old New England," Tia was saying, "with crappy weather half the time, even in summer. I just don't get it – it's not some tropical island with turquoise water and smooth sailing every day – why do these people come here and build these literal estates?"

"Because they can?" Jackson offered, "Nantucket gets press, it has this reputation – good or bad – and people with money want to do what the people with money are doing."

"Sucks," Wyn said, sweeping away sunny wisps of hair that had blown across her face and tangled in her eyelashes, "get off my island. And I still don't get why the super-wealthy want to be here."

"Hate to break it to you," Sheri said, "but as you know, Nantucket was once the whaling center of the world and it produced a lot of wealth because of it. Whale oil, and everything associated with it, was king. So if you think about it – maybe Nantucket has always been for the rich?"

"Have you been hanging out at the whaling museum again, Mom?" Tia asked, squeezing Sheri's shoulder lovingly.

"How'd you guess? It's fascinating though, isn't it, Jackson? From truly humble beginnings after farming didn't really work out, this little island struck gold with whale oil, and the ships' owners were the merchant princes of the era. You know Orange Street, all those mansions from the 1700s and 1800s? Those belonged to whaling captains and ship owners. And they built their homes on the finest streets, close to the water to be able to walk to the docks and with roof-walks to watch their ships come in. Shipping fortunes were real, Nantucket was on the map."

"Wow, I guess I never walked the wealth part back to that," Wyn said, "but still ..."

They wound the rest of the way along the sand road with only the sound of the breeze rushing in through the windows and the salty summer smells it carried.

"We're *here*! Oh Mom, Nanna would die to see how beautiful her grasses look."

"Great word choice, loser," Tia said.

"Nanna's not dead, *loser*," Wyn said, but her face was agreeing with her sister.

"Girls. I know this isn't easy, being here without Nanna and Pops. And we can talk about it. We can talk *to* them, FaceTime them too, okay? They wouldn't want us to be sad, I promise you. Come on, let's get all your stuff in and get some food on the table."

"And drinks!" Wyn said, a little too excitedly, "I'll be bartender." Sheri couldn't help but think *like mother, like daughter.*

Chapter Twenty

"It smells exactly the same," Wyn said with a smile, dropping her bags and wrapping her arms around her middle. Sheri, not wanting her daughter to have to hug herself, folded her up in her arms.

"Good," Sheri said to Wyn, "and now since I'm sleeping down here, I put Tia and Jackson in my old room. So you'll have the blue room all to yourself, Wyn." Sheri couldn't tell if Wyn would love that or miss being with her sister in the room they'd always shared. With the twin beds, it wouldn't have made much sense for Tia and Jackson.

"Awesome," Wyn said, gathering her things to head upstairs, "now I won't have to listen to your snoring. Works for me!" she said to her sister, "Good luck with that, Jackson." It was hard for Sheri to tell how much was bravado, knowing Wyn held an expectation for tradition and the comfort of the way things had always been.

"So what does everybody want to drink?" Wyn asked, "Mom has stocked up. I'm making a Moscow Mule for myself, anyone else?" Wyn's eyes were alight with joy and mischief. When in the wild world did her little girl go from SunnyD to vodka?

The kids took their beverages out on the deck while Sheri heated up her beautiful herb-roasted chicken and other painstakingly prepared delectables from the previous night. She kept her eye on them, hoping only for signs of relaxed comradery, no disappointment with change or sadness, and definitely no discovery of tell-tale ash or scarring. They were a rainbow set against the new cedar, radiant in their collective joy.

She loved setting the table for four. As it turned out, two was the loneliest number. She scattered her best scallop and jingle shells down the length of the table, inverting a few of the biggest ones to hold small votives and lit the thick stout pillars in their hurricane lanterns.

"Mom, this looks amazing," Wyn was the first to say as they came in from outside, "you always make everything so special. You know if Nanna were here she'd say, *it's like you waved a magic wand, so lovely, dear.*"

"Aw, honey, thanks for saying that. I really miss her, and you're probably right – that does sound like something she would say. She was always just a little more conventional than me, wasn't she?" Seeing the sudden sorrow wash over Wyn's expression, Sheri realized immediately that she'd referred to her mother in the past tense. "Of course, I mean, she *is* more conventional, not was! I'm sorry, I –"

"It's okay, Mom, I mean, I guess I understand – she's not really who she was anymore, is she? And she won't ever be again ..." Wyn's round blue eyes glistened with the weight of tears that refused to spill. Sheri needed to take her girls to see their grandmother sooner than later.

As if Wyn had read her mother's mind, she told her as they set the dishes on the table that she really wanted to go see her Nanna and Pops after Nantucket. "I was thinking the same thing," Tia said, "you know, before she doesn't know who we are anymore."

"Jesus, Tia, way to sugarcoat. But then you never were exactly Miss Sensitivity," Wyn said.

"*Girls*. And Jackson. Let's eat."

As Sheri began the task of slicing the chicken at the head of the table, Tia said, "Hey – isn't this Dad's favorite meal? The herb-lemon chicken? The roasted Brussels *and* garlic mashed potatoes? And do not tell me you made salted caramel mud cake too ... What's this all about, Mom?" Tia turned to her mother, smiling expectantly.

They were interrupted by the doorbell. Dammit, Sheri hoped Wes had gotten her message about *not* installing the toilet. It was too late for that anyway. Wyn rushed to answer the door while everyone else started the rotation of dishes. Sheri just about dropped her carving knife when she heard Wyn's voice yell, "Dad!"

Before Sheri could order her thoughts or arrange the expression on her face, Tommy was standing before them with a fistful of pale-blue hydrangeas and a smile. Of course he was.

"Daddy!" Tia sang as she came running to hug him, Jackson standing also to greet the father of his girlfriend. "What are you doing here?" Tia asked, smiling, then turning to Sheri, "Mom? Did you know Dad was *here*, on Nantucket? Wait – of course you did, *that's* why you made all his favorites, you knew he was coming to dinner! Oh, Mom, this is the best surprise!"

Tommy and Sheri exchanged looks over their daughter's head. Oh, this was rich, Sheri thought, Mr. Grand Gesture himself standing there with her favorite flowers after ghosting her last night as she served up his day-old favorite dinner.

Who could possibly get the wrong idea? What the hell was Tommy up to? *And why the hell didn't he show up last night?* Without a single phone call or text? While she almost burned down the neighborhood waiting for him!

"Let me set your place, Daddy," Tia said, heading into the kitchen while Wyn told him she'd make him one of her Mules.

"Quickly, girls, I don't want everything getting cold," Sheri said, with her best version of a fake smile, "*again!*" she whisper-scolded for Tommy's ears only. "What are you *doing* here – what is *wrong* with you?"

"Aaro got sick, I couldn't just leave!" Tommy whisper-shouted back, "and Stephanie had my phone. I think she suspects something's going on ..."

"Well you can tell her nothing is!"

"Nothing is what, Mom?" Tia said, toting silverware, a plate, and napkin, "Oh, we should light a fire! Wouldn't that be so cozy?"

"I can do –" Tommy started before Sheri cut him off.

"Sit, " Sheri ordered, "we're eating."

"To Daddy," Tia said raising her glass in a toast, "and you too, Mom, of course, for making this all possible! It's so good to be back and to be all together."

Glasses clinked and after everyone had taken the first sip, Wyn added, "and to Nanna and Pops, for really making amazing summers here possible for our whole lives."

"And welcome to Jackson," Tia added, tilting her glass to her boyfriend who looked only mildly nonplussed by the whole crazy thing.

"Let's dig in, kids, your mother obviously pulled out all the stops for this meal," Tommy said, with his irresistible smile – the one that started in one corner of his mouth then rode straight up into his silver-blue eyes – the one Sheri lost her virginity to, and her heart, her mind, and her happy life.

While Tommy asked Jackson about Wall Street, pretending he knew anything at all about high finance and investment – and succeeding with his charm – Sheri ate without tasting the food she'd so lovingly and expectantly prepared, trying to parse out if the girls had any idea that their father was on Nantucket with Stephanie. And *what*, if anything, they thought was going on now.

∞

"This is all *so good*," Wyn said with a mouth full of the garlic mashed potatoes, "you forget how amazing it is to have a home-cooked meal just waiting for you, *mmm* ... so, did you guys plan this or what, this is so weird you're both here, what'd I miss?"

"Yeah, what's up, parents, under the same roof – this is unexpected," Tia said.

The glare Sheri shot Tommy over the rim of her wine glass let him know it was all him.

He cleared his throat and took a gulp of his Moscow Mule before answering. "Well, it was the strangest thing – I ran into your mother at Straight Wharf Bar one night and we actually had a pretty good time." Did he think his daughters were going to let it go at that?

"Go on, that can't be it, and where's Stephanie?" Tia said, while Wyn looked wary of too much information. Wyn had taken the divorce the hardest of the two, was probably still not totally recovered, if a child of divorce ever was, but at the same time she wouldn't be the sister to participate in the *parent trap*. That would be all Tia. Expertly pulling the strings of some fortuitous and wildly unexpected tryst.

Sheri was curious how her ex-husband would handle the inquisition.

Without missing a beat Tommy continued, "Stephanie's with her father at his place in town. And Aaro, of course, the place is huge."

"Duh, isn't he some music mogul or something?" Wyn said, her voice thick with no small amount of disgust. "Why are they even here – like go back to LA, get off our island."

"Dad, you really haven't answered the question," Tia said, then turning to Sheri, "Mom? Is there something you're not telling us? Or something you want to say?"

Sheri said *no* at the same time Tommy said *yes*.

Sheri knew she'd better disavow her children of any fantasy their father might be about to spin. And maybe she hadn't realized it until that very moment but she could not do this anymore, the battering rollercoaster ride that was any kind of relationship with Tommy Steele. It was like her heart had crusted over for the last time – once again he'd chosen Stephanie and her son over her.

She was definitely not cut out to be the other woman. No matter what Tommy said, now or ever, she'd been a fool. Even though he looked so contrite sitting there at the head of her parents' table, adorable in a pale-pink linen shirt tucked into faded khaki shorts, completing the family they'd made and then broken. It gnawed a fresh wound in her.

Sheri couldn't let her eyes meet his, those silvery pools of humility and some reborn desire to be woven back into the tapestry of his family. Isn't that all Sheri had thought about the last few days too? Wasn't that what she wanted beyond all else? Had she been under some spell? Because *look at him*, she told herself, look closely. Can't you see his leg wiggling a mile a minute under the table? His furtive glances down at his phone like some duplicitous teenager? Saying all the right words but with body language giving him away? Like he might sprint from the table and their lives, again, on a whim?

It was a trap – all love was – a seductive, precarious, cruel trap. And she just couldn't be sucked in again – especially if one or both of their daughters thought they actually wanted some big reconciliation. What would it do to their sense of love and marriage if failure struck even harder a second time?

Wyn, with her sixth sense, forced the train to switch tracks before derailment. "You two obviously have some shit to work out but it's not going to ruin my first night back on Nantucket, if you don't mind. Now please pass the Brussels sprouts, Dad, and you better save room for the dessert Mom made – even though I'm starting to wonder if she made it for me or for you."

"What about me?" Tia said.

"What *about* you? Get over yourself. You know the salted caramel mud cake is Dad's and my favorite dessert."

Conversation went around the table while Sheri helped herself to more wine. As if there were a big enough, soft enough landing for the hurricane in her head. She sat back and listened – it always fascinated her to learn more about her kids when they spoke with anyone else. When did her daughters become these knowledgeable women? With their own resolute ideas about the way things could be, *should* be, about people, about leadership, life? When did they become so philosophical – but with an uncomfortable and alarming amount of angst about their futures, about the planet's future, the world's? How could she protect them anymore, from all of it, from any of it?

She really couldn't.

"I know," Tommy said, as the last plate was cleared, "I'll make some popcorn and you guys cue up *Jaws*, like old times!"

Tia and Wyn squealed with delight, turning off the lights, claiming their spots on the big *L* the couches made, making room for Jackson and spreading blankets across everyone's laps.

Chapter Twenty-One

EVEN BY JUST THE light of Amityville and Chief Brody arguing with the mayor, Sheri could sense Tommy stealing glances at her with each of his arms slung over a daughter as if to say, *see how great this is? This is where I belong.* She wasn't having it. Sheri was not having any of it. Something in her had shifted irrevocably as she'd sat waiting for him the night before, candlewicks drowning in their own pools of spent wax. How she'd been forced to picture him with Stephanie instead, choosing *her*. Again. And she knew, beyond question or doubt, that she would never put herself in the position again, *ever*.

She'd been swept away by the magic that was summer and Nantucket and certainly nostalgia. She'd been lonely and vulnerable with the echo of an empty nest and having to face her parents' inevitable mortality. But she had to face some things. Truths that would make her stronger instead of her own worst enemy.

Why couldn't she have a midlife enlightenment instead of a boring crisis?

Anyway, she'd foolishly allowed herself to want a different ending – one where her family was whole again. But she could see now how wanting that with her ex-husband was a backwards step. She loved feeling sexy again and desired – did she have to let that go? That was depressing to consider.

Sheri wondered what Jackson was thinking, sitting there beside Tia and her father, if he was thinking anything beyond Quint and Hooper getting drunk and comparing scars on the *Orca* waiting for the *big fish*. Her girls were rapt, Wyn especially. Tradition was tradition. What were *they* thinking? Sitting there with their father like nothing, like everything. Or were they just waiting for the bottom of the boat to be ripped out from under them...

The End would eventually scroll across the screen, the movie always ended. Everything did – the song, the dance, the story.

Once her own childhood ended, starting a new life with Tommy had been everything. And then their babies came and filled them to overflowing. It had seemed like they'd be hauling a diaper bag around forever and scheduling their lives around naps and then potty training. And then one day their daughters were charging down the soccer field, then asking for the car keys. Then the prom dresses and college letters – it was staggering what time did. When was the last bath? The last bedtime story? She was glad she hadn't known when so many lasts were happening.

And now, their museum bedrooms in the house they'd all shared in Vermont. *Past tense*. A monument to all that had been, to everything that was over. She needed to sell it. *She couldn't let it go*. Who was she anymore? From being a mom to little girls to a daughter caring for her aging parents. Where was she in all of it? The loss was profound. No wonder it had been so tempting to think she could have some of it back.

∞

The credits were scrolling, lights being turned on. "Aw ... that was so awesome," Wyn said, "as always. Why am I so tired?"

"Same," Tia said, "I could go to bed, how about you, Jax?"

"I'm totally beat, bed sounds good," Jackson said with a grin and a proprietary arm around Tia's shoulders. "This was amazing – I haven't seen Jaws in forever." Sheri gave him points for his diplomacy and good nature. But at the same time, felt bad about his being dragged into the dysfunction unfolding all around them.

"Do we have a breakfast plan?" Tia said, looking from her father then to her mother.

"OH! Let's get breakfast sandwiches from Bartlett," Wyn said.

"What? No. Downyflake!" Tia said, "Right, Dad? You love Downy." Sheri was glad at least that Jackson took the girls' merciless inability to agree on anything in stride. He must have sisters, she thought, she was probably supposed to know that.

Sheri was losing control of the situation Tommy had seamlessly inserted himself into. She'd bought food – even that Kodiak protein pancake mix they liked now instead of Bisquik – she wanted to make breakfast for her daughters, not her ex-husband! What was happening? She'd created this mess – they didn't know the half of what Sheri had set in motion.

"I do love Downyflake," Tommy said, but with the decency to shoot a questioning glance at Sheri over their heads, "Is it still there? But maybe your mom has something else planned ..."

Oh, like that was going to work – this was their father, their *daddy* who all but oozed charm and magnetism. She could see it in Tommy's liquid gaze, that he thought he could change Sheri's mind, bend her, break down this abrupt resolve of hers he didn't seem to understand. She suddenly pitied the hope in his voice.

"Aw, Mom, come on! We can do pancakes Sunday, like always," Tia said, with Wyn uncharacteristically agreeing. "I want Jackson to see the island!"

Was this happening? Was Sheri going to agree to breakfast out like one big happy family? Did she have a choice? No, of course not, she wasn't about to be the bad guy here. She wasn't about to wreck everyone's good time on the first damn day. How was this happening?

She needed air. So while the girls settled into their rooms with their father moving around the house with them as if he'd never left, Sheri stepped out onto the deck. The abiding draw and spill of the sea steadied her. That, at least, was everlasting, could be counted on to endure for all of time. She stood at the far edge of the deck, leaning with her elbows on the railing, breathing in the new cedar, appreciating the certainty of its refurbished strength to hold her up.

"Are there always this many stars?" Cooper's voice rode over to her from his deck next door on air as clear as the sky. It was dark and Sheri almost cried out, straightening as she gripped the railing. "Sorry – didn't mean to scare you. Did your daughters arrive uneventfully?"

"No worries. And yes to the magnificent spray of stars *and* to my girls arriving safe and sound." She was not about to get into how her ex-husband had shown up unannounced and unwelcome by her, or that her children were under some impression that she'd planned it all along, and how they may be under some deluded assumption of good old-fashioned happy family time on the horizon. What had she done?

"Glad to hear," Cooper said, reminding Sheri that she wasn't just talking to herself. They stood on their respective decks staring up at the diamond night. It occurred to her that Cooper was not uncomfortable with silence, that he wasn't the type of person who had to fill every silence with words, conversation, observations. That he could just sit with a moment and appreciate its beauty, its grandeur without narrating it, cataloging it. Whereas Tommy seemed to need to quantify things, say a thing was beautiful or terrible, as if he needed the clarity, the label, the definitiveness. There was always a pressure in that – to agree or disagree with him – Sheri realized suddenly, that it was so much more rewarding, comfortable to just be in a moment, sit with it, stand in it, let it in.

She didn't hear the slider open or Tommy walk up behind her putting one hand on her low back as he came to stand beside her. She sucked in her breath, spooked for the second time in ten minutes.

"Jesus, Tommy, *what* are you doing?" She was whisper-shouting again and hyper-conscious of Cooper overhearing them.

"Come on, babe, it's just us now," he said moving her hair off her neck and kissing her there. "I'd almost forgotten how beautiful it is out here, your folks sure bought at the right time."

Sheri stepped away from him craving distance from his heat and his intentions. And Jesus, did he have his eye on her parent's property now too? She was losing her mind. "I mean it, Tommy, what do you think you're doing? You can't just come here—"

"Sshh. I know you're still upset about last night, I'm sorry, Sher, but it was unavoidable – there was nothing I could do about it. Now, let's start over –"

"NO. How many do-overs do you think you're gonna get? I'm done, I cannot put myself in that position again, Tommy, I won't. Now, I'm sorry but we're not doing this – I just don't have it in me anymore, this goddamn roller coaster that is *you*. And just what does Stephanie and family think you're up to now? When does it end, Tommy? The lies, the sneaking around? God, I'm such an idiot."

∞

"There you guys are," Wyn said, stepping out onto the deck – Sheri putting another arm's length between her and Tommy. "What a gorgeous night, God, I love it here." Wyn looked up at the stars reigning over them like some spectacular dome then stood between her parents with an arm around each of them. "It's good to see you two getting along," she said, "I mean this is so much better than fighting, right?"

Sheri could hear it in her daughter's voice, the doubt over whatever was going on but the need to spin it in a way she could handle. It had taken her youngest daughter a while to even begin to heal after the divorce, and she'd finally come to terms with the fracture of her family and her father's defection. She'd taken it personally and she'd punished her father for a long time. Sheri knew Wyn would not abide further disappointment – another blow of that magnitude. And Sheri's heart folded at the thought of it, at what she'd almost done again.

Sheri rested her cheek on Wyn's head and gave her a warm squeeze around her waist, avoiding touching Tommy in their three-way embrace, before stepping away. "We're good, Pumpkin, you don't have to worry about a thing."

"Pumpkin? You haven't called me that in a while, Mom, jeez, what am I, twelve?" Wyn said with dramatic yet unconvincing exasperation.

"To me, you'll always be twelve," Sheri said, resisting patting Wyn on the head like she really was twelve.

"Interesting – not exactly my finest moments if I recall," Wyn said, laughing and giving her mother a hug with both arms and her whole self. Tommy seemed to fade to black beside them as they turned to head back inside.

Chapter Twenty-Two

SHERI WOKE UP with the sun the next morning. Something about the pearly pink light always pulled her from dreams before she was ready to wake up. Sometimes she'd be able to fall back to sleep until a more decent hour, but not this day, not when her daughters were under the same roof.

Every part of her churned with the magnitude of it, the preciousness of having them both there, a rare enough gift that she couldn't sleep through a moment of it. Intellectually she knew the pressure she put on herself for everything to be perfect was ridiculous, but it didn't stop the churn. Yes, they were adults and in charge of their own happiness and expectations, but wanting the fulfillment of her daughters' every need and wish wasn't a thing Sheri could turn off.

When did they go from being sullen demanding teenagers, for whom nothing was ever quite right, to these young women making their own way? They'd achieved guest-princess status. Sheri dusted and set out her best towels *for them* instead of begging them to scrub their toilet and the mildew farm in the shower. The role-reversal made her head spin, the speed with which time marched on.

It was still barely six o'clock in the morning, but Sheri's body was a live wire and her brain a mess of rubber thoughts. She could slip out of the house and go for a run on the beach before the kids were awake – but what if they woke up early and she wasn't there? She couldn't bear to miss a minute, not a single thing.

So she lay there, watching the room grow lighter and the shadows shift, thinking about everything they wanted to do while they were there. Ten days seemed so abundant on one hand, but at the same time altogether too short to get it all in. Why couldn't she just relax and let things unfold? Why couldn't she be more chill? Like Trudy, who was somehow able to hold on loosely, like her favorite 38 Special song …

She couldn't even lie still until seven. She decided to start with coffee on the deck in the pink morning, feeling unendingly lucky for it all – the warm mug in her hands, the softness of the air, and the girls asleep in their beds in their favorite place with the hourglass still filled with sand.

"We have to stop meeting like this!" Cooper said with a smile in his voice, loud enough to reach Sheri's ears but not loud enough to wake everyone up. It startled her nonetheless – Stan and Ida almost never enjoyed their outside space and Sheri was unused to the intrusion. *But it wasn't an intrusion*, she scolded herself, Cooper was a good person and a good neighbor – she just wasn't used to the company, or sharing the view and her thoughts about it.

"Right?" she said back, not exactly inviting conversation but not shutting him down either. "I physically can't sleep in through all this," she said, extending her arm across the 180-degree view of the rosy morning sky and the sea that went on forever.

"Agreed," he said, raising his mug like a toast then taking a sip from it, holding it by its handle instead of cupping it in both hands like Sheri, "So what are you all up to this fine summer Saturday?" Cooper had an endearing way about him and Sheri changed her mind about having company and a conversation.

"You know what? Why don't you come over here – it feels a little like we're shouting. Unless you have somewhere you need to be?"

"On my way over," he said, "I just made a pot of Italian roast, I'll bring it over."

There was an ease to Cooper that appealed to Sheri and settled her. He was thoughtful and uncomplicated at the same time, the opposite of fraught. It was a relief from how charged everything felt to her lately. His subtle strength and self-possession were a welcome diversion from Tommy's main-character energy. And he seemed to get better looking every time she saw him.

"Here we are, Mademoiselle," Cooper said, reaching the top of her deck steps a short sandy path away from his own, *"un peu de café pour toi."* As he filled her cup, he leaned in close enough for her to notice he smelled good. She thought he probably looked as good in his T-shirt and shorts as he did in a tux.

"Ah, *Monsieur, merci*! Gotta say, it's nice to be served. And French press no less, you take your coffee seriously, I'm guessing? My dad was the coffee guy around here, the gene skipped right over me."

"Don't tell me, Keurig?" He said it with the cutest wince.

"Guilty."

He smiled over the cup he raised to his mouth and it made his eyes crinkle at the corners. "I'm sure you're good at other things." If Tommy had said those words they'd have sounded sexual and come with a waggling of his eyebrows. It struck her how tiresome that actually was. Cooper's sincerity was pure. He took a seat next to her and they both looked out at the water as it changed color the higher the sun rose.

"So, the girls want to go out for breakfast – of course they haven't actually agreed on a spot – so I'm thinking we should try Lemon Press, I know they'll love it. I'm just not too psyched about the size of the crowd I always notice standing outside on the sidewalk ... waiting in line to eat is not something I have any patience for, unfortunately."

"I hear you, and I felt the same exact way about trying that place out *but* as it turns out, most of those people you see waiting have ordered theirs *to go*, believe it or not."

"Really? You just made my morning!"

"Well, you're easy," he said with a quick laugh, "tell me something, have you done much paddleboarding? I noticed a couple boards in the shed and it looks like this stretch of water might be a good spot?"

"I have done some paddleboarding and, yes, on a calm day when the water is smooth, this is the best spot for it. You wouldn't want to go out if you see whitecaps though – it isn't much fun getting dumped every time you get back up on the board, believe me."

"Excellent. I've never done it before but it looks like something I can handle. Or am I deluding myself – is it harder than it looks?" He was earnest and adorable with that hint of worry in his golden-brown eyes that he might not be good at it after all.

"That depends. On flat water it's not too hard – but I've tried it out at Nobadeer – south shore, where the waves live, and let me tell you, the guys doing that are making it look *way* easier than it is. I spent more time in the water than on the board, that's for sure. This I'm certain you can handle. You know, starting up on your knees maybe at first to get a feel for your balance, does that make sense?" Sheri was enjoying being the one in the know, it gave her a shot of confidence she didn't know she needed.

"In theory a lot of things make sense," Cooper said with a chuckle, "we'll see if I can put it into practice successfully."

He really had a disarming way about him that made Sheri feel comfortable and happy to be in his company. "How about we go out together one of these days?" She'd surprised herself with the offer but it felt good and like a perfectly natural thing to do.

"Aren't you busy with your daughters? I wasn't trying to worm my way into your schedule, I –"

"Please. They'd kill me if I tried to spend every single minute with them – which is of course a huge temptation for me, and maybe an actual problem, if I'm being honest."

"You're hard on yourself, I can tell. You seem like a terrific mom and they should feel lucky to have you want to spend so much time with them."

"Oh, they do. But Wyn will want to surf, like, a *lot*, and I'm sure Tia will want to show Jackson around without me tagging along – so I bet we can find some time to get out on the water, I'm excited – it's been awhile …"

∞

The sound of sneaker-clad feet running up the fifty-seven steps from the beach captured their collective attention. Wyn. Sheri should have known her youngest, equally wheeling-minded daughter, would not have been able to sleep through a Nantucket sunrise either and would be drawn outside for a good hard run along the water's edge.

"Morning, honey! I would have gone with you," Sheri said without thinking, maybe that's exactly what Wyn wouldn't want. "Was it amazing? And this is Cooper, our next-door neighbor – renting Stan and Ida's for the month."

"It's nice to meet you," Wyn said, with a friendly smile but also with a hint of polite distance. "Mom, you know my relationship with running – *amazing* isn't even in the top five things I feel about it. The view, *yes*, amazing, but *this* is the best part, the part about being done," she said, pulling one heel at a time to her butt to stretch her quads.

"Understood, absolutely," Sheri said, drinking in the view of her daughter, trying not to stare but also trying to memorize every inch of her. "Well, you look fantastic, Wyn, whatever you're doing, it's working for you."

Wyn rolled her eyes and changed the subject. "So, no Stan and Ida this summer either? Wait – don't tell me if it's something sad, I don't want to know."

"Not sad, really, they're just dealing with some health stuff – it happens, you know, when you get old, can't stop that, kiddo, they're no spring chickens." Sheri tried to measure the emotion in Wyn's light eyes before rambling on. She didn't want her to start the day feeling like everyone around them was old and dying. "So their son convinced them to rent the place out, for the summer anyway. Hey – Cooper has a son, Leo – your age – maybe you guys could—"

"Stop, Mom, no matchmaking. You do not have a strong record. No offense, Cooper." Looking at her mother's surprised expression, Wyn felt compelled to explain. "You really don't remember? Setting me up with the son of one of your co-workers, Mom? That dude, Mitchell? Oh, this is rich," Wyn looked from Cooper to her mother and told the story. "So, there we were, at a pretty decent restaurant, Italian, I forget the name. All my favorite pasta dishes on the menu, I was psyched, and he even sprung for a nice bottle of Montepulciano. He was back and forth from the bathroom more than seemed healthy but, you know, whatever, in between he seemed fine. And then he was texting and I was like *what the hell*? Then the waiter came over to me and said, *you know he's at a table in the other room on another date with a redhead, right?*"

"I must have repressed that, sorry, but this isn't matchmaking! Just saying, Leo is a surfer too – might be fun to have company."

"Sure," Wyn said to her mother. "It was nice meeting you," she said turning to Cooper, "now if you'll both excuse me, I'm starving and need a shower."

"Thanks for the coffee, Cooper," Sheri said, feeling a little indulgent keeping Cooper's company over her daughter's, "We'll figure out a paddleboarding day. Hey, how about we exchange numbers, that might make it easier."

"Great idea," he said, reaching into his pocket for his phone for Sheri to put her number in, "and thanks for a lovely morning." A slow smile curled on his face making Sheri feel like she'd arranged the morning's sorbet sky just for him. Her heart galloped for a few beats and she smiled up at him as he turned to go, hustling down the steps with his empty French press pot disappearing from view.

"Oh my God, I always forget how beautiful this is," Tia said, stepping outside, "what do you think, Jackson, insane, right?"

"Gorgeous," Jackson said, stretching his arms overhead then shielding his eyes from the sun, "is that the steamship way out there?"

"It is," Sheri said, "do you guys want me to make coffee or should we just get going to breakfast? I decided we're going to Lemon Press, if that suits?"

"YES!" Tia said. Which made Sheri smile, her oldest was a tough customer when it came to food. "I've been dying to check that place out, yay! Let's get dressed and skip the coffee."

"Speak for yourself, I'm having coffee," Wyn said, joining them outside, cradling her mug, still in running gear.

Tia and Jackson made themselves comfortable in the chaise lounges while Tia pulled up the breakfast menu for Lemon Press on her phone. That was so like her, Sheri thought, *fail to plan and plan to fail*, she'd always say with regard to her meals. She wondered if Tia would always be tracking her calories and her macronutrients, if she'd have to plan everything all the time. Sheri supposed her daughter would learn sooner or later what can become of even the best-laid plans ...

"Ooh, listen to this," Tia read from her phone, "*Lemon Press has such a great selection of specialty drinks and breakfast items. The line was definitely worth it. I got the mocha latte and the breakfast burrito. Although it's on the pricier side, the burrito was huge and filled with cheese, egg, potatoes, and avocado.* That all sounds so good, right? And you love breakfast burritos, Jax." And without giving Jackson time to respond she continued with her usual animation reserved for food, "Here's another great review: *Lemon Press might just be the hottest breakfast place in Nantucket – awesome no matter what you order! The place was very cute with a strong Mediterranean influence – maybe Persian – highly recommend.* We are definitely going here! Great choice, Mom."

"Okay, first of all, Persia is not in the Mediterranean," Jackson said, "it's more like Iran. And second of all, let me see that menu. Whoa – look at some of the coffees – they've got lavender-infused espresso with local honey and bee pollen, and vanilla and cinnamon-brown-sugar espresso, and something called the *Brainy ACK* – what the hell even is some of this: Chaga, reishi, lion's mane, cordyceps, cacao, agave, fiber, and stevia – are you kidding me?"

"Lion's mane? Are they serious?" Wyn said.

"Oh they have all the regular stuff too, even cold brew and teas – looks like something for everyone for sure," Jackson said.

"Well, I'm down for anything. Except waiting in some stupid line," Wyn said, echoing Sheri's thoughts."

"You're the one who needs a shower," Tia said, rising from her chair and holding her nose as she walked past her sister to go get dressed."

"What are you, in sixth grade?" Wyn said, and to Jackson, "my advance apologies for having to spend time with my sister."

"Okay, okay, that's quite enough, I think you two have regressed," Sheri said, rising up from her chair to go inside. She would not let herself feed into the bickering. "Wyn, the outside shower is stocked, chop-chop, let's be in the Bronco in no more than fifteen minutes."

Chapter Twenty-Three

It was a sunny summer Saturday on Nantucket and town was bustling with people in their cars, bikes, and on foot. You couldn't be angry about it or feel put out – it was part of the scene. Sheri used to feel impatient with the crowds but she'd learned to appreciate so many happy people in one place. Once they'd found a coveted parking spot, that is – circling the entire downtown multiple times wore on a person's good cheer.

"I can't believe we're here," Wyn said, as they walked from their spot on Broad Street to Main. "These lumpy old brick sidewalks and cobblestones are so familiar it's almost like we never left – like every summer melts into the next."

"Wait 'til you're my age," Sheri said, "time plays tricks on you for sure. You want to remember every day here, every minute, but it gets hard to separate the years – like how old you guys were when we saw this or did that."

"That's what photos are for," Tia added, "you guys are always making fun of me for documenting instead of being in the moment but there you go." And as if to prove her point she held her phone high focusing down for a selfie to post on Instagram.

"Preservation is one thing, but posting every single thing on Instagram is another issue," Wyn said.

"I don't post every single thing," Tia said, "and what's it to you anyway? Hey, look! The farmer's market! We totally need to go after breakfast."

"Definitely," Wyn said, "there's a kick-ass surf photographer I've seen on Instagram I want to check out. Let's Google the hours, I feel like we're never downtown on Saturdays."

As they rounded the corner from Federal onto Main, the throng of people thickened. "And this is why," Sheri said.

"Aw, c'mon, Mom, we got this," Tia said, taking charge of getting their names in for a table at Lemon Press, "remember, there's a whole upstairs and half these people are doing takeout."

"Do you guys remember when this was Arno's? I loved that place," Sheri said.

"Yes!" Wyn said, "they'd seat us upstairs usually with the other people with kids – it always looked so much cooler downstairs."

"I loved the giant Molly Dee paintings," Sheri said, "do you guys remember them? Those five-foot tall sepia-toned canvases of beachgoers, larger than life, from the twenties in their bathing costumes under striped umbrellas at the beach – I wanted to step right into the scene."

The four of them stood on the sidewalk taking it all in, looking to see if their favorite shops were still there, wondering what was new or gone forever.

"Aw, hello, Hub," Wyn said, "we'll hit you up for lattes some other day. And Mitchell's! We def need to go into Mitchell's after we eat, I need a new book."

"Me too," Tia said, "and we should check out their author signings coming up, they do such a good job with that. Hey, Mom, why hasn't Trudy ever done a signing there, or has she?"

"She has, but you guys had other priorities and don't remember. And I believe her new book comes out this fall so maybe she'll do a signing at Stroll in December."

"Oh, Christmas Stroll, we should do that this year!" Wyn said, just as their party of four was being called. Sheri wasn't disappointed to be seated upstairs, quieter and with the same exposed brick, funky lights, and giant windows. She was hoping the girls wouldn't be disappointed to be out of the fray and that the menu and experience would meet their expectations. *She really had to stop doing that to herself.*

"Wow, this place really does seem to do it all," Tia said, taking in the décor and the extensive menu. "I love the description, *airy all-day café* and *a little slice of L.A. on Nantucket*. And they seem to have everything from avocado toasts, chia puddings, sandwiches, and cold-pressed juices you can order with alcohol – how have we not come here before?"

"Not sure Dad would dig it here though – he likes such basic stuff, and don't even get me started on the Middle East vibe," Wyn said, as if she'd just remembered their tentative plans to have breakfast as a family. "Wait, weren't we supposed to text him or something?"

Sheri was wondering when it would come up. She'd half-hoped the girls had forgotten about it and that they hadn't noticed Tommy trying too hard to make last night just like old times – all snuggled under blankets together watching *Jaws*. God, she really didn't want to get into it all, especially with Jackson sitting there. What was he thinking about everything, what had Tia told him? Sheri felt the pressure of her blood actually pulsing through her veins. Jesus.

"What the f—" Wyn didn't need to finish her comment as they all looked out the window to see what she saw. Tommy. Crossing Main Street beside Stephanie and Aaro before disappearing into Breezin' Up. "Are you *friggin'* kidding me, what the *hell*." It wasn't a question, but aimed at Sheri anyway. What could she say? She sure as shit did not want to dissect the state of their relationship right there at breakfast. God, how she wished that she'd never seen Tommy that day at the beach, that he'd never run into her at Straight Wharf and a hundred other things. But she couldn't undo any of it.

"Look, girls, you know your dad is not here on Nantucket to be with me, or with you either for that matter – I'm sorry if that sounds harsh, if it feels harsh – but the fact is he came here with Stephanie and her son and is a guest in her father's home, you knew that, right?" Sheri watched the light fade from Tia's eyes while Wyn's grew darker with something closer to anger than sadness.

"But last night ..." Tia said, "I thought, I mean, it really felt like he wanted to be a part of this family again, didn't it? Mom?" Sheri recognized the pleading look in her oldest daughter's eyes, the set of her mouth, that turned her from twenty-five years old to nine. When did the disappointment end? When would it lose its power over them?

"Oh, grow up, Tia, seriously? Do you know Dad at *all*?" Wyn said, looking back out the window, scanning the intermittent crush of people walking in and out of shops for possibly another glimpse of her father and the young woman and child he'd left the family for. Sheri was rendered as powerless by what she saw in Wyn's eyes as Tia's. And as usual, Sheri felt torn between defending Tommy and encouraging them both to let it go.

Is that what life boiled down to? The letting go of so much in order to be able to move on at all? The looking ahead instead of back?

"Good morning, I'm Meshia and I'll be taking care of you. Have you been to Lemon Press before?"

∞

"That was the best egg sandwich I think I've ever had," Jackson said as they were finishing up their breakfast.

"And that's saying a lot for a New Yorker," Tia added, "I'm stuffed – that was so good. I need to walk around – what time did you say the farmer's market ends, Wyn?"

"Twelve thirty. But let's do that now, looks like some decent swell coming in later and I really need to get in the water."

"And there it is – revolving our days around Wyn's surf schedule."

"You're so predictable, Tia, Jesus, you could surf too. Jackson, how 'bout you?"

"He doesn't sur—" Tia started to say before Jackson spoke for himself.

"Sure, I could give it a shot, see what all the fuss is about." Tia looked at her boyfriend in surprise and Sheri thought, *good for him*.

"Awesome," Wyn said, "we have a longboard in the shed back at the house, that will be perfect. I mean I'm assuming it's still in decent condition. The shed is weather-tight, right, Mom?"

"As far as I know," Sheri was already starting to worry about the condition of the longboard – unless there'd been any cracks where water had gotten in, frozen and expanded in the cold, it should be fine. But if not, maybe their neighbor, Leo, had a spare board? Insane the somersaults her brain was already doing in the name of keeping the peace and keeping everyone happy. She was glad to be back outside and moving her body – stuffed after so much food and jittery from her macchiato.

"What gorgeous weather for our first day, right? How lucky are we?" Wyn said as they made their way to Cambridge Street, a concrete plan to surf already raising her up. "I hope there are some cool artisans at the farmer's market too – we haven't been to that in years."

"Wow, I had no idea how big it's gotten," Sheri said, blown away by all the vendors packed into the little street, "they have everything here!" There were native growers, visual arts including fish prints, photography, other original art, jewelry, bath and body products, woodwork, metalwork, ceramics, and textiles.

She watched as her girls meandered, Tia checking out the organic lotions and potions and island-inspired jewelry, while Wyn went straight for the massive prints of the inside and underbellies of waves. Sheri loved the woven blankets and linens and thought how her mother would linger over the handmade ceramic bowls and mugs – surely she'd have found one to add to her collection. Watching Jackson admiring the wooden whale sculptures and quarter boards, Sheri wondered how handy he was – if anybody was anymore – or if it had become just easier to pay people to do things for you.

Sheri was tempted to offer to buy her daughters something they might like, she had to resist the urge to do and want everything for them. They were grown women who could afford things, well, Tia more than Wyn, and she was never sure if she would insult them by putting her money down. Tia had her hands on a small bottle of Pure Body Nantucket nighttime face oil and an aloe, honey, and oats cleansing bar that she would treat herself to. But Sheri knew Wyn could never afford the Dan LeMaitre print she was admiring. But maybe she was thinking it would inspire her own photography. Sheri wouldn't step in to buy something so pricey.

The ceramic mug Wyn was holding with a seafoam glaze tugged at Sheri's heart – she was so much like her grandmother. Rose would have chosen that mug for her chamomile tea, would have pictured her own hands wrapped around it as she sipped from it on a chilly day and would have had to have it. Sheri pressed a tear from the corner of her eye before allowing it to fall. She would buy the mug for Wyn.

The sun was climbing higher in the sky practically begging them to get to the beach. Sheri could see that her gang had arrived at the same conclusion as they gathered with their packages at the corner of Cambridge and Federal Streets ready to head to the car.

"Daddy!" Tia yelled, spotting her father across the street.

Chapter Twenty-Four

M*AKE IT STOP*, **S**HERI thought, couldn't he and Stephanie just get off the island already? She didn't think she could bear any more iterations of her feelings about him, enough was enough. Sheri could see that Tommy was conflicted, standing there with his lover and her son – did Stephanie even know they were all on the island? Not Sheri's problem, she told herself, she wished she could turn the clock back. But how far back would she go?

Sheri would have been happy if the sidewalk opened up and swallowed team Stephanie whole. And she's pretty sure that would include Tommy.

"We missed you at breakfast, Daddy, we were at Lemon Press," Tia said, "have you tried it? Nothing like Downyflake but ..." she couldn't seem to stop rambling, Sheri recognized it as her unconscious way of filling the awkward space. If nothing else, Tommy was good on his feet, a sweet-talker if ever there was one, but Sheri was curious how he'd handle standing with his whole family there on the sidewalk while his new family looked less than pleased.

Aaro was making a scene, pulling on his mother's arm whining, "Let's *goooo*, Mom, you *said* I could get a new toy at Sunken Ship and I want to go *now*!"

Sheri studied the look Stephanie gave Tommy, who looked both embarrassed by Aaro and adoring of his daughters at the same time. The beseeching look he aimed at Sheri had her heart crumpling and she thought how easy it would be to save him, to pull him back into their fold and walk off into the sunset as though Stephanie had never existed. It almost seemed like there was a silent plea in Tommy's eyes begging her to do just that. Coward!

Stephanie seemed to see it all, looking from Tommy to Sheri and the rest of their group. When she pushed her Chanel cat-eye sunglasses on top of her head, Sheri saw the fatigue and disenchantment pooling there.

"When you figure your shit out, Steele, you know where to find me," she spat out, turning on her heel and yanking her son down the street in the direction of Sunken Ship.

This was neither the time nor the place for a scene and Tommy being Tommy simply brushed off Stephanie's little outburst and swooped in with an arm around each daughter, peeking into their little bags to see what they'd bought and asking them what was on tap for the rest of the day. How did he do that, Sheri wondered, shift gears so seamlessly and with a smile that kept all the unpleasant things away, all the while letting the women around him sweep away his bad behavior.

"We're going to the beach and we're going *now* before the wind shifts and trashes the surf," Wyn said, steering them all in the direction of the car. "If you're joining, Dad, we're leaving now and not dicking around."

"You kiss your mother with that mouth?" Tommy joked, buying time. "Hey, listen, tell me where you'll be and I'll try to meet you, okay? Nobadeer? Cisco?"

Sheri glared at him, knowing there was a 97 percent chance he wouldn't show. She wanted to say, *don't do that, don't get their hopes up like that only to let them down*. But what would be the point? Tommy would have an excuse for everything, the carnival ride was his MO.

∞

Sheri went to work packing a quick lunch for the beach out of habit – she couldn't imagine anyone being hungry any time soon after the size of their breakfast, but still. She crossed her fingers that the longboard in the shed had survived the winter and mentally patted herself on the back for getting the hard top on the Bronco with a roof rack. (The poor two-door decision notwithstanding.)

"Hey, Mom, keep it light – remember we're not driving on Nobadeer. I know hauling the coolers and chairs at Cisco is a pain but it looks like that's where the best swell is right now."

"Oh, don't worry about me, Wyn, I'm not a feeble old lady yet."

"I know, I know, just sayin'. Okay, people, let's goooo!"

Packed into the Bronco with the surfboards strapped to the roof, it took them less than twenty minutes to get to Cisco Beach's sand parking lot off Hummock Pond Road. The lot was packed, as expected, but they squeezed into an end space near a giant puddle. Sheri started to relax knowing she'd done all she could do to get the girls' first Nantucket beach day off the ground, the rest was up to them.

Wyn stood at the top of the steep drop-off leading down to the beach looking out at the lineup, every cylinder firing, her eyes an electric blue with anticipation. To feel that way about a thing was truly a gift, Sheri thought, although there was a backside too, like when the sea was flat for too long, or God forbid she found herself in Kansas for work. Knowing exactly where she wanted to be out there in the lineup, Wyn grabbed her board, backpack, and Rip Curl wetsuit and scrambled down the slope to wax her board and get in the water.

"Yeah, great, Wyn, catch ya later," Tia said with no small amount of sarcasm as her sister took off. Then to Jackson, she said, "she has to get a good sesh in before she can do anything else, don't mind her, she'll get you up on the longboard."

"Not worried," Jackson said good-naturedly as he lifted the board from the rack, "looks like we'll be making a couple trips, I can come back for the cooler," he offered as they each grabbed a chair and their totes and navigated the steep, sandy slant to the spot Wyn had dropped her backpack to set up their camp for the afternoon. Sheri admired his go-with-the-flow attitude and hoped it wasn't an act and that it would last – Tia and her sister were a handful.

Jackson's dark hair was short and coiffed, the way Tia preferred, product and all, and his T-shirt looked crisp and new over short Vineyard Vines swim trunks. So different from Wyn who liked her men a bit messier with long mops of hair they had to shake out of their eyes, worn T-shirts frayed at the neck with favorite bands or surf gear logos, and faded board shorts.

Sheri always planned to just sit back and read after sun-blocking her skin from top to bottom, but with a kid in the water, she never found it possible. It didn't matter how old the kid was. Wyn was her baby and nothing would ever change that. She was easy enough to spot out there with her sunny hair and Rip Curl springsuit. It had long sleeves but with a cheeky bottom – unlike colder days when everyone was in head-to-toe black neoprene. Sheri watched with equal parts wild excitement and nervous energy as her daughter paddled out to ride her share of the five-foot waves, duck-diving her way out until she got where she wanted to be.

Shark sightings were on the increase, hardly big news there with rising sea temps and the whole climate change mess, but what Sheri feared more was her daughter getting bonked on the head by her own board and getting tumbled and wrecked by crashing waves. As often as Wyn told her she surfed alone all the time, *you don't have to watch me every minute, Mom*, it was impossible for Sheri to tear her eyes away. That's just the way it was. Having children was having your heart running around outside your body – plain and simple.

"Those look pretty big," Jackson said, staring out at the yawning blue-green waves rising up and crashing down. "I'm thinking maybe a raincheck on the surf lesson." Smart man, Sheri thought, admiring his measured calm and awareness of his limits.

"Aw, Babe, don't sweat it, it'll change, you watch. Or if it doesn't, no big deal, you have a few days. I'm not going out in those either, three-footers are my limit. Besides, it's way too crowded out there. Wyn must be losing her shit with all those noobs dropping in."

"Yikes! Do they ever collide? Or mow down boogie-boarders?" Jackson asked.

"I've only seen that on @kookslams but I'm sure it happens. I wouldn't want to be a lifeguard here, that's for sure. Between the sharks and the rip and stupid people, no thanks!"

"Wyn's really good, isn't she, she must surf a lot," Jackson said, watching Wyn shred.

"She is good – she surfs all year round in Santa Cruz – she's obsessed. And she is ballsy, I'll give her that."

Sheri was enjoying the sun on her skin, it was the perfect temperature with the off-shore wind, and she liked sitting back and catching bits of Tia's and Jackson's observations and conversations. Tia really did love her sister even though she spent a needless amount of energy making it seem otherwise. Did Tia still compete with Wyn? When did that stop? *Would it?* They were pretty good friends, when they weren't performing for their mother. They'd be okay if anything ever happened to Sheri, right? They'd take care of each other?

Ah, Rose, where'd you go ... Sheri's heart started to crumple at the possibility of never hearing her mother's golden bits of wisdom again, all the momisms she'd come to rely on, her mother's unflinching confidence in the journey. The way she saw the world, the light she'd grasp from the simplest things and shine it back.

"Does Wyn know those guys out there?" Jackson asked, "looks like she's chatting it up with one dude anyway." Jackson's question brought her back.

"Nah, surfers are all just bros, know what I mean?" Tia said.

"Well, your sister hardly looks like just one of the guys ..."

"Aaand you're wondering why they're chatting her up, ha!" Tia said, "but seriously, surfing is like its own subculture I guess you'd say, a lifestyle, and they all kinda recognize that in each other, they look out for each other out there, it's pretty cool."

"Whoa, did you catch that? She just got wrecked! Seems like she was under a while – isn't that terrifying?"

"Yup. Why do you think I'm sitting here instead of out there?"

"Are the waves getting bigger or am I imagining it?" Sheri said, leaning forward in her chair.

"Not imagining it, Mom. And there are way too many people out there," Tia said looking over at her mother, "come on, Mom, she can handle herself, don't make yourself nuts, you always do that."

"Thanks, Kid – just wait until you're a mother."

"Who says I'm gonna be? Who can afford kids these days, Mom? Not to mention –"

"Stop. I can't hear any more about the dying planet and that you guys think you'll never be able to afford a life ..."

"Well, whether you want to hear it or not, it's true. Our generation is doomed."

"Oh, thank God she's coming out," Sheri said, noticing Wyn paddling in."

"And it looks like she has a new friend," Tia said, watching the tall dark-haired skinny dude in a full wetsuit walk beside her out of the water.

"Wait," Sheri said, tipping her sunglasses down to get a closer look, "is that Leo? What are the chances?"

"What? Do you know him or something, Mom?" Tia said.

Sheri slid her sunglasses back on to make staring less conspicuous. Of all the surfers on the island, Wyn is coming toward them with Leo Madden. The closer they got, the more Sheri saw how he resembled Cooper – same amber eyes but Leo's a shade darker - and he was taller and leaner than his dad. Wyn was playing it cool – didn't have that flirty look in her eyes but appeared genuinely interested in whatever Leo was saying. How perfectly convenient – she'd met Leo Madden all on her own.

"Did you guys catch my last wave?" Wyn was saying with a big smile, "that barrel? Well, for a hot second anyway, *so* fun."

"Mrs. Steele?" Leo said, then to Wyn, "wait, are you, is she –"

"Wait – you're *that* Leo? From next door? Unreal." Wyn said, setting her board down in the sand and peeling off her wetsuit looking from Leo to her mother.

"Small world," Cooper said coming up beside the group.

"Smaller island," Sheri laughed, standing up, "I don't know about you but I'm glad they're out of the water."

"Just taking a break, Mom, def going back out," Wyn said, "the waves are *firing* out there."

"I can see that," Sheri said, then turning to Cooper, "Do you ever get used to it? Your child out in that," she said, fanning an arm over the heaving sea. Cooper shook his head while Leo and Wyn offered a collective eye roll.

"They just don't get it, do they," Sheri said to Cooper, "when do you think this invincibility thing starts to wear off?"

"Either when they're parents themselves or when something unexpected and bad happens to them – whichever comes first, I suppose," Cooper said.

"I don't like the sound of that at all," Sheri said.

"Then can we please stop talking about my mortality again, Mom, and what did we bring to eat?" Wyn asked.

"We? You're hilarious, Wyn, as if you contributed anything ..."

"Leo, meet my sister, Tia."

Tia stood up from her beach chair to shake Leo's hand and had the decency to look contrite. Sheri could tell Tia knew she sounded childish and would take it back if she could. Growing pains.

After introductions had been made all around, Sheri asked Cooper and Leo if they'd like to join them, "I'm sure I made too many sandwiches and I threw in some beers and those Nantucket craft cocktails the kids like, there's plenty to go around. And no booze for either of you two," she said to Leo and Wyn, "until you're out of the water for the day, got it?"

"Yeah, yeah, yeah," Wyn muttered, already elbow-deep in the cooler, "turkey or ham?" she said turning to Leo.

"Really? Thanks! Ham would be great, are you sure? *Mmm*," he said, without waiting for a response, "this Portuguese bread, *yes*."

"Leo," Cooper interrupted, "we have food – I apologize for my Neanderthal son, Sheri."

"Not at all! I offered," she said, "now, what can I get you to drink? Why don't you come sit over here," Sheri was saying for the second time that day. Was she paying attention to the right signs?

The sun hung in the cloudless sky for the whole day as if to say*, give me all you got, live large and enjoy.* Leo and Wyn took to the waves again while Jackson and Tia went for a long walk. And instead of worrying about sitting there alone with just Cooper and feeling awkward or abandoned, Sheri felt a lightness she almost didn't recognize. Whatever preconceived judgments she'd harbored about him dissolved with the heat waves that shimmered over the hot sand. He was smart and funny and he listened when Sheri spoke – not just waiting for her to be finished so he could speak his piece. That, Sheri had come to appreciate, was a great gift. Other people Sheri had known in the medical profession came off as far more self-important, a challenge to talk with and get a word in. But not Cooper.

He'd explained in more detail how he got into medicine, cardiothoracic surgery specifically, when as a child visiting his Gran in Scotland he couldn't bear to see her sick.

"She was the toughest lady I ever knew, playing hide-and-seek with us, working in her gardens, until one summer she just wasn't the same. As it turned out, she had an undiagnosed congenital heart defect. A hole between the upper heart chambers that, left untreated, over time increased the amount of blood going through the lungs. All I wanted was for her to be the same, I wanted to be able to fix her and make her better."

Sheri couldn't help but be impressed. She thought people became doctors for the money, the prestige. The more she learned about Cooper, the more things she found to admire.

∞

The calm of the afternoon was ripped open by lifeguards speeding past them on ATVs hauling rescue equipment. People had started to gather down by the water pointing and Sheri and Cooper rose to their feet to follow as if in a trance. Fragmented speculations rode on the wind over to them: *Is it a shark? Did a swimmer get taken out in the rip? Is a surfer down?*

Time stopped and careened around Sheri as her blood turned to cold syrup. Her heart dropped like a stone as she scanned the open water wordlessly for Wyn's blond head. *How had she stopped paying attention* – how had she been so engrossed in a conversation that she hadn't been watching her daughter? "Do you see them?" she asked Cooper, grabbing his shoulder, with a voice she didn't recognize as her own. "When was the last time we saw them – are they still out there? I can't believe I—"

"Sheri, don't panic, please, I'm sure—"

"You're sure? You're sure of *what*? I don't see Wyn! Do you see your son? Did we miss them getting out of the water – what's going on, Cooper, something's obviously not right!"

A woman came running toward them, screaming in terror and with a heavy accent about her daughter, "Somebody! Get lifeguard! My daughter PLEASE! HELP ME PLEASE, she's not good swimmer, HELP!"

It was all so disorienting, this woman's blood-curdling pleas, and then, unbelievably, her turning away from the water to face the dunes, bending over with her hands on her knees. Sheri was trying to understand – if it had been Wyn or Tia in trouble out in the water, the last thing she would have done would be to turn her back on the ocean, take her eyes from the spot she'd last seen them. Questions pummeled in as Sheri looked out at the massive waves building and breaking then getting sucked out with a chilling force.

"Where is she? How old is she?" Sheri yelled to the hysterical woman, imploring her to look out and point in some direction, to give any information to help rescuers help her. Too many things raced through Sheri's mind – guiltily she'd be relieved if it were this woman's daughter in trouble instead of her own. It was surreal that this woman wouldn't look out at the water. Sheri was terrified for the woman as she trained her own eyes on the water for the little girl. There were so many people in the water. A couple looked like they were out too far, but were they in trouble? Were the lifeguards getting as confused – could they see who they were trying to rescue? Were those surfers trying to reach someone? *What was happening?*

Then Sheri could have sworn she saw a head go under and not resurface. The woman was still hysterical and looking away – *HOW do you turn your back – what is wrong with you?* Was that even a head she'd seen go under? Or a seal? No one seemed to know what was going on! Sheri turned and started to jog up the beach in the opposite direction, scanning land and sea for Wyn and Leo, hoping to see them out of the water and walking toward them. But she didn't see them anywhere.

Then the lifeguards rode by her heading back to their stand – no urgency, no one on the backboard? Sheri picked up her pace breaking into a jog back to where the crowd had gathered but was now dispersing. Through the throng of people she saw the retreating form of the lady with her arm around her young daughter, maybe eight years old, pulling her daughter's small body against her own as they walked side-by-side. And then behind them, walking toward Sheri, were Leo and Wyn, boards under their arms.

Sheri stopped and felt a wave of relieved nausea roll through her.

Cooper caught up to her and she startled at his hand on her low back. "She's alright," Sheri said, catching her breath, "they're okay, everyone's okay," she found herself repeating the words to herself as much as to Cooper, "so the lifeguards found her? I was afraid that –"

"No," Cooper said, holding Sheri's gaze, "the lifeguards were too late – it was Wyn who saw the girl go under, Wyn got to her first. Wyn saved that little girl's life, Sheri."

Chapter Twenty-Five

SHERI FELT FATIGUE SETTLE over her like a blanket of marbles as they unloaded her truck back at the house. They'd lingered at the beach with the Maddens until six o'clock and all the coolers were empty. No one seemed to want the day to end. She was beat. The gamut of emotions did her in more than if she'd run ten tideline miles. But something about it buoyed her too. She took a beat to acknowledge her brave girl, her strong, incredible daughter, and how the events of the day had bonded their small group in their gratitude.

The kids were amped and ready to keep the party going, anxious to shower and head downtown for the night. Sheri wanted nothing more than to curl up with a book and indulge in an early bedtime, secretly relieved their plan didn't include her. She'd be up with the sun and would rather burn her candle at that end.

Their bare feet padding up and down the stairs and their music playing as they got ready breathed life back into the house. The sweet smells of their lotions and hair products wafted down to her along with their jokes and easy conviviality – it was everything. It soothed the tumult she'd been hauling around. And she was pleased they'd included Leo in their plan, especially for Jackson, two Steele women could be one too many.

Just before drifting off to sleep, Sheri heard the low buzz of a text vibrating her phone on the night table. It startled her awake. It was an unknown number.

> Sheri, it's Cooper – it occurred to me that I have your number but you don't have mine. I hope this doesn't wake you! I'm feeling equal parts tired and wired – not a recipe for sleep. I just wanted to say thanks for including Leo and me in your beach day today, I haven't seen Leo that relaxed in a while. I hope we aren't imposing on family time with your daughters – don't be shy about letting me know if we are! Good night.

Sheri sat up in the bed as a smile curled on her face and a warmth bloomed inside her. She tucked herself back under the covers and closed her eyes, a soft, full joy settling over her like a nap under her grandmother's quilt.

Sheri was long asleep before the kids came home at midnight and awake at the first blush of dawn. Wrapping herself in her new fringed throw, she made her way out to a lounge chair on the deck to watch the glow rise up from the east. She stared out as the pinks and golds of the sun melted across everything until the water was a sheet of light, replaced unhurriedly by an unrippled blanket of amethyst. A new canvas every morning, never the same sweep of color. Deep swaths of paint streaked the sky, fading to blue as the sun rode higher on the horizon until it was a yellow ball sitting there, its rays not yet reaching her with summer warmth.

Sheri panned her eyes across her 180-degree ocean view to the west where the sun would set over Eel Point at eight fifteen that night, in fifteen hours, and wondered what the day would hold.

"Another remarkable beginning," Cooper said, startling her, from his chair on his deck beside hers, "makes you want to live up to it, doesn't it?"

"Then let's," she said, as if she felt he was there all along, "looks good for paddleboarding – you up for it?"

"We'll see if I can *stay* up for it," he kidded, "as long the wind doesn't pick up and start tossing those waves around ..."

"No guarantees! And you *will* fall, over and over, let's just get that out there." Sheri said with a sense of adventure bubbling up inside her.

"I'm fine with that. I'm expecting a short, steep learning curve."

"Not that steep, really," she said, at ease with their banter, "why don't you bring some of that Italian roast over here while the sun gets a little higher and warmer."

"I love a girl with a plan – be right over."

And I love having someone so easy to be around, Sheri thought, tucking deeper into her blanket, getting to witness the sweeping start of a brand new day.

∞

They were out on the water by nine o'clock – all the kids still in bed. It felt like a secret and Sheri's insides popped like prosecco. She was relieved to see he had a wide, thick board and not some fancy touring board that would be harder to balance on. She helped him set the paddle height for ten inches above his own so he wouldn't be bent over when he paddled, then they secured the leashes to their ankles and waded into the water of Dionis Beach right at the bottom of their respective staircases.

"This spot is perfect not only for its lake-like sheen but also because it stays shallow for a little ways. You don't need deep water to do standup paddle," Sheri said as they waded out to just above their knees. She was enjoying being the teacher and had to admit to feeling better about herself than she had in a while. Buoyed by her confidence she forgot to be self-conscious about her body in a bathing suit as she showed him the correct place on the board to center his weight as they started out kneeling to get a feel for balancing the board on the water.

"You'll start to feel that this is all about your core – keep it engaged." Sheri tried not to get preoccupied by the sight of his muscled form in just swim trunks. The man was in fine shape. The cut of his delts as he pulled through the water, the curve of his biceps in their exertion, and the way his suit sat low on his hips. He looked better than any man in the neighborhood of fifty had a right to. "Okay, you look like you're having an easy time balancing the board – let's try it at a stand."

"If you say so, coach," he said, wobbling as he rose to a stand in the middle of the board. A boat was ripping by in the distance and its wake sending ripples their way. He hung onto his stance for a heroic amount of time before getting dumped. He was still smiling. A good sport.

"Don't worry about it!" Sheri shouted, letting her laugh out, knowing he wouldn't mind at all, "but for the love of God, hold on to your paddle!" He was laughing too, which was a relief. He could easily have been some crazy perfectionist who'd want zero part of a thing he couldn't immediately dominate.

"Okay, so, keep your core engaged and your arms straight – think torso twist," Sheri coached, fully appreciating his sinewy muscled trunk, "and instead of pulling the paddle through the water, pull the board in front of the paddle, does that make sense? Reach out about two feet in front to paddle forward and switch sides to stay straight." She watched as he followed her every direction, of course he'd be an excellent student. "Keep the paddle vertical to hold the board in a straight line, that'll lessen the number of times you need to switch stroke sides, which can be tiresome, I know, especially out on the ocean." She loved his concentration and good humor, even as he fell again and again.

"Am I the worst student you've ever had?" he said, with a self-deprecating smile, shaking the water from his hair.

"No! Cooper, you're doing great. It's kind of like when you're riding a bike – it's easier when you're in motion. So as soon as possible after you stand up, get your paddle in the water and start moving. Then keep moving!"

And he was off. She had to work hard to keep pace with him once he got going. He was strong and fluid as he pulled through the water and she felt pride at being the one to have taught him that. She was feeling so good as the one with more knowledge and skill that she wasn't worried about the parts of her body that may be dimpled and jiggling in her bikini. "By George, I think he's got it!" She shouted over the water. He raised his paddle overhead in a playful victory stab and turned to smile back at her. God, he was hot. Which made her feel hot too.

Catching up to him, she showed him how to turn the board and reverse direction before they ended up at Smith's Point. "Hey, slow down, tiger! We need to turn around," she called out as he slowed. "It's simple enough – just reach back behind you and plant the paddle in the water near the tail of your board and make sure the blade is all the way under the surface of the water. Then, like with the forward stroke, you keep your arms straight and twist from your torso rather than pulling the blade forward with your arms. Are you with me?"

"Like this?" he asked as he followed her direction.

"Exactly. And doing the reverse stroke on the right side of your board will cause the nose of your board to turn to the right and vice versa. Easy, right? Now, since we flew out here it'll be tougher going on the way back, with the current – just be prepared for that."

"I'll be feeling this tomorrow," he said.

"Good, you should! Look at you go, you're a natural. Let's stay in tight to the shore – it's easy to get pulled out without realizing it."

They stayed shallow and paddled parallel to the shore taking in the sights from out on the water, appreciating the homes set way back in the dunes that weren't visible from the beach. "This is really special," Cooper said, angling his board close to hers, "I can't thank you enough, Sheri, I might not have attempted it alone." He was so appreciative it made her wonder if he'd been feeling as lonesome and flawed as she had. All she knew for certain was that it felt so deeply good to be in the company of someone so genuine and on the same wavelength.

As they coasted into the shallows just before the beach, Sheri dropped to sit, straddling her board. Cooper did the same. She'd become intensely aware of every move her body made. "It's entirely my pleasure, Cooper. And, y'know, I might not have taken the time for myself, so I should be thanking *you*. It's so cool being out on the water under your own steam …"

"A whole different perspective out here," he said as they sat with their legs dangling in the water, swirling them slowly for balance, taking in the 360-degree view from their spot in the water. Teenager thoughts wheeled in and Sheri thought about reaching her foot out to touch his underwater. Instead, she laid all the way back on her board to feel the full strength of the sun on her body.

"I'm afraid I'd roll off if I tried that," he said.

"You might," she said with a small smile, opening one eye to see if he might be checking her out. She felt an immediate drumbeat of desire. The sky filled her view and she breathed it in, the blue of it. "Do you think anyone's missing us yet?" She wasn't sure how much longer she could hold off her sense of duty – it felt so decadent just lying there under the sun on a board in the ocean with Cooper. While she wanted to preserve their simple peace and lack of conversational depth, she also found herself wanting to know everything about him.

Her hand traced small circles in the water and the air crackled around them as their boards bumped and rocked. He reached for her to steady them and the strength and heat of his grip spread through her body. A wistful hum folded over her like sunshine.

"Sorry," he said, "can't have you tipping over." She held on to his hand and pulled herself up to straddle her board again. That hand that held beating hearts. It was cold when he let go.

"We can head back if you'd like," he said, "what's your gang up to today?"

Trying not to look disappointed, trying not to *be* disappointed, she said, "You know, I'm not really sure. I was long asleep when they got home last night, but I'm sure they'll fill me in!"

He laughed and his golden-brown eyes caught and kept hers. "Well, I'd like to have you all over for a pizza night – there's this state-of-the-art firepit at our place – does that sound like something your kids would be into at all?"

"I didn't know firepits could *be* state-of-the-art, now I'm curious! Stan and Ida never spent much time out there. Are you sure you want us all over? You don't have to do that."

"I want to. It gets lonely over there just the two of us – and now it looks like you might be seeing Leo more than I do. Seriously though, I'm thrilled he and Wyn have been surfing and hanging out."

Sheri thought how lonely it probably got for Cooper to have his son choosing her gang's company over his and she felt a stab of compassion. "I'm sure they'd love it, I would too. I'm sure they're all rising from the dead – let's head back." She felt a stab of withdrawal at ending their time together as they paddled at a leisurely pace back to their beachfront. "We can leave the boards down here," she said as they dismounted and carried the boards up onto the sand, "the kids might want to go out on them today with the water so still."

Leaning in for a hug felt like the most natural thing in the world. As did Cooper's soft kiss on her cheek before they stepped apart. Sheri was suddenly aware of how little she was wearing and anxious to be alone with her thoughts and tingling body. She felt something move in – like weather she was helpless to control.

"Thanks again, coach," he said, smoothing out their goodbye and holding her gaze several beats longer. "That was amazing. And let me know about tonight, okay? Shoot me a text or whatever works." And with a two-finger salute and his wide smile, he jogged up the steps to the house.

Her legs were jelly. And it wasn't from the paddle. Sheri stared after him, taking in the view of his bronzed back and finely tapered calf muscles as he bounded up the winding staircase, then blew out the breath she didn't know she'd been holding.

∞

As it turned out, the water was quiet all over the island, no surf to speak of, and the kids decided to spend a chill day on their own beach. It was one of those planless days that sneak into the rotation of must-dos that you didn't know how much you needed. Sheri loved looking out at her daughters and Jackson, and eventually Leo down on the beach, comfortable doing their own things – alternately reading, napping, beachcombing, paddling, kayaking, and playing frisbee. Jackson and Leo had both played Ultimate in college and watching them dive in the sand for the frisbee had become a spectator sport.

And there was Sheri, with her full heart brimming, having the time of her life. It was all she could do to shut down the other part of her that was already missing it, the part of her that was watching it all happen from some point in the future.

There was just something spellbinding about their summer vacations on Nantucket that separated that time from the rest of the year. Maybe it was the fact that it was always a finite number of days that made them so special? Or the way they let the place and time into their hearts so fully, letting it change them. Whatever it was seemed to be happening on some grander scale for Sheri this year more than any other. Change was underfoot and she could feel herself begin to embrace it rather than run from it. Taking ownership of the house, her decisions, and her response to things was a big start.

And then there was Cooper. She let thoughts of him drift lazily in, like the shimmering waves of heat on the horizon of a perfect summer day, and let possibility tiptoe right on in after.

Chapter Twenty-Six

THE PIZZA/FIREPIT NIGHT was on but Tia only wanted to join for a drink or two having already made plans to take Jackson into town for dinner, and then maybe they'd all meet up at Gaslight if there was a good band or possibly the Chicken Box. That worked out well since Leo wanted to invite a couple of surfers he and Wyn had met the other day.

Sheri found herself looking forward to being a guest instead of a hostess and not being a slave to her phone. Tommy wasn't the first or even the fifth thing on her mind for a change and she planned to take that ball and run with it.

She allowed herself a longer-than-usual shower outside. The sky was the deepest blue before black and a faint spray of diamond-stars glowed brighter with each passing minute. As hot water sluiced over her body, she looked up to see what she remembered of the constellations her father had taught her. After the Big Dipper, Cassiopeia was the most recognizable one to her and she thought back to what he'd taught her from Greek mythology.

Cassiopeia was a constellation opposite the Big Dipper in the northern sky in the spiral arm of the Milky Way. It was named after the queen in ancient Greek mythology, Cassiopeia, and easily recognizable because of its distinctive *W* shape formed by five bright stars. As the story went, Cassiopeia had angered the gods by bragging too much about her own beauty and that of her daughter, Andromeda, claiming to be even more beautiful than the sea nymphs, the daughters of the sea god Poseidon. To punish Cassiopeia for her vanity, Poseidon chained Andromeda to a rock to be devoured by a sea monster while Cassiopeia was condemned to the zig-zag constellation to represent the vain queen chained to her throne.

Sheri wondered about a world where gods and humans had such a strong relationship, – where mythology was interwoven with every aspect of life. How the Greeks worshipped many gods and goddesses, each representing either some part of the universe or love or war, how they were revered and looked to for revelation.

As almost silly as that seemed in the current world culture, something about it was comforting. If not comforting, then at least like there was something more, something bigger, something *after*.

It felt like no one believed in anything anymore. At least nothing that couldn't be seen, touched, proven, and measured by science. Were they better off for it? People seemed so cynical, angry, divisive – what was the endgame? She sighed and took a last long look at the sky – the brilliant bright stars blanketing it on the clear night.

She'd read once that looking up at the stars, was actually looking into the past. That many of the stars you saw at night have already died. Was it true? She just wanted to look up at them and get lost in their winking magic. She was dizzy with it. Her problems were less than a speck's speck in the vastness that was the universe. It seemed beyond ridiculous to be stressing about what she was going to wear to Cooper's, would she straighten her hair?

∞

Sheri didn't want to show up empty-handed, so she grabbed a cabernet sauvignon from her father's wine rack. Not being a big red wine lover, she didn't know as much about them as she should, she hoped the 2016 Château Pape Clément was decent.

"Wyn – what's your time-frame up there?" she called upstairs. Tia was still getting ready and Sheri could hear Slightly Stoopid blasting reggae from Wyn's JBL speaker in the bathroom. Almost nothing made Sheri happier than picturing them up there doing their hair and putting on makeup together. Jackson was a good sport and Sheri wondered if he was sitting in there with them or on his phone in the bedroom. She was glad that Wyn liked Jackson – that was always a good test.

"*Coming*," Wyn yelled down, "two secs!" Wyn and Leo had struck up an easy friendship – which would make things easier all around – but she was hoping it was casual and just for fun. No good could come of *another* attempt at a long-distance relationship for Wyn. *Jesus – what was she even thinking?* Leo and Wyn barely knew each other, and most of that was bonding over surfing and the heady trip of rescuing a little girl from the big waves. Wyn's running flip-flop-clad feet on the hardwood stairs pulled her from her spiraling thoughts. "You look more beautiful than usual," she said to her daughter, taking in the precisely applied barely-there effect of eyeliner and mascara.

"Mom."

"You're right, I'll stop talking. You look lovely. Leo doesn't stand a chance."

"MOM!"

"Sorry!"

"And, seriously?" Wyn added, looking her mother up and down at her super-cute frayed khaki cutoffs and adorable diaphanous bell-sleeved top, "what about you – is there something you want to tell me about your friend Coop? I mean ..."

"Wyn!"

"How does it feel? Now let's go." And with that they were off to the house next door, weighing the merits of Sophie T's pizza over the Muse's. They heard the music before they made it up the front steps and Sheri had a déjà vu moment.

"Ladies, Jackson," Cooper greeted them, "come in, come in! Hope you don't mind us starting without you – Leo's buddies are already here."

"More the merrier," Wyn said, and Sheri wasn't 100 percent certain she meant it."

"He says you met them out there in the water the other day – Brayden and Quinn? Anyway, they're outside by the fire," Cooper said, "what can I get everyone to drink? I'm pretty sure they have a cooler out there – but it might just be beer."

"Thanks, we'll go check it out," Wyn spoke for the group as she, Tia, and Jackson headed out back.

From the living room windows, Sheri could see the bluestone patio at the base of the sprawling deck with the gorgeous stone fire pit rising up out of the center of the space and the six of them in the seating all around it. "Wow, you weren't kidding. Such a manicured space – it's beautiful though." While Sheri could appreciate finely designed homes and properties, she still preferred more rustic, less curation. The huge sky and sea were gift enough for her.

"It's a bit extravagant for me," Cooper said, to Sheri's relief, "but it is nice to have that separate outside space that's like a second living room."

"Don't you mean third or fourth? Ha! This place is bigger than I'd imagined. Okay, make me a drink – one of those gin and tonics you made the last time I was here, that was amazing," Sheri said, feeling like one of the kids.

Sheri climbed up onto a high stool while Cooper went behind the bar to make their drinks. "All We Ever Knew" was playing at just the right volume from invisible speakers. "Ah, Head and the Heart, I love this band."

"Leo has pretty good taste, he's DJ tonight," Cooper said, his eyes catching the amber lighting from the pendants over the bar making them more gold than hazel. A ping of excited thirst hit the back of her throat anticipating Cooper's herbaceous concoction. She found herself watching his skilled hands adding the gin to the highball glasses of ice, topping with tonic, then stirring, then slicing the lime wheels to add. The same hands that repaired valves and closed holes in the hearts of humans.

"Don't cut yourself!" she blurted. Then felt ridiculous for it. "I'm sorry, it just hit me how important your hands are and –"

"If I worried about every little thing I did potentially ending my career, where would I be?" he said with a low chuckle. *He was so f*cking sexy.*

"Right, but how do you know where to draw the line? I mean, what kinds of things are off-limits for you? You know, like they sure didn't want Tom Brady skiing back in the day or climbing in the Himalayas – are there contract stipulations like that for surgeons?"

Cooper took long sip of his drink never losing eye contact with her over the rim of his glass. "The way I look at it is, ultimately, you have to live your life and be happy. If I let it, my career would control my life, prevent me from pursuing most kinds of recreation, and become suffocating. And while I have excellent disability insurance, I personally prefer low-risk stuff anyway. I run rather than mountain bike, do yoga instead of Krav Maga, and honestly the closest thing to a debilitating injury I've suffered was a broken ankle a couple years ago playing softball for our department team championships."

"Wait – the cardiology department, the heart surgeons have a softball team?"

"Sure they do. Surgery would consume every minute of our time and energy if we let it, and like anything else – *anyone* else – we'd come to resent it if we let it deplete what few outside passions we allow ourselves." Sheri couldn't have agreed more.

"That actually makes a lot of sense, good for you. I personally think I'd always be worried about hurting myself," Sheri said, "like if these hands were due to scrub in on Monday morning, I'd be the one to slice my finger cutting potatoes for Sunday dinner."

"I don't think you would. You can't live like that, think like that. The ol' self-fulfilling-prophecy business. Exactly what you're trying so hard *not to do* will be the thing that ends up happening. Because that's where you'd be focusing your energy and thoughts."

"Ah, a philosopher too, I like that," Sheri said, as Cooper came around to sit beside her. "Cheers to harnessing the vibrations of the universe," she said, clinking her glass to his. She found herself wanting some part of her body to be touching his, leaning into the way his bare thigh was near enough for her to feel his heat. She let her leg rest there against his as he looked down from a text from his son. *Hot*.

"Sorry," he said, "damn kids have to text you from the same house – I'll never get used to that. Looks like Sophie T's has too long a wait so they put in an order at the Muse. Oh shoot – I didn't ask you what you like?"

"Oh, I like everything – as long as there are mushrooms in there somewhere?"

"Ah, let me see," he said scrolling back the texts, "there are indeed, are you sure that's all you require, Milady?" He looked over at her with an ingratiating grin and she wondered if he had any flaws at all.

"That and for you to keep our glasses filled ... and maybe a chance for us to sit around that bougie fire pit?"

"I like your style, Sheri, and you got it. As soon as they head out to pick up the pizza, it's our turn out there.

∞

Cooper gave her the fifty-cent tour and Sheri tried to imagine Stan and Ida there, wondering just how much renovating had been done by their son, Phillip. And it occurred to her that, like her own parents, maybe Stan and Ida would never be back. It was too upsetting to think about.

Sheri was eager to get outside when Tia and Jackson took off for downtown and the rest of the gang went to get the pizza. The night was just cool enough at the edges for Cooper and her to lean into the warmth of the fire. "Lava rocks? Well, look at that – no messy wood, stray sparks, or ashy-smelling hair, very nice."

"Natural volcanic lava rock," Cooper said, "but if we were really posh, it'd be that blue glass, right?" he said, leaning forward in the chair, nudging Sheri's whole body with his, the drink having loosened his more conservative way. "Do you think this was Stan and Ida's doing?"

"I think definitely *no*, this has to be their son's idea of classing up the place. No, that's the wrong word – it was plenty classy. Now it's just next-level I guess? And in my opinion, this was Phillip's impression of what pretentious people looking to rent on Nantucket would want. *Oh!* That came out wrong – I didn't mean you! You know what I mean – of course there are plenty of regular people who want to come to Nantucket, if for no other reason than to see what the fuss is all about. *Not that you're not a regular person* – okay, I should stop talking ..."

"You're cute when you're rambling," he said with his arm on the arm of her chair, "And I'm confused – is being a regular person a good thing or a bad thing?" His smile turned into a laugh and all Sheri could think was that she wanted to keep being the reason for its soothing sound.

She slid all the way back in her Adirondack, the only comfortable way to be in one, and looked up at the stars. "Have you ever in your life seen so many stars? I mean just look at them all ..."

"Well, Vermont nights get pretty clear too, maybe not thirty-miles-out-to-sea clear but ..."

"Vermont nights?" Sheri asked, confused, "You have New York plates on your car, don't you? I'm so confused." How did she know so much and yet so little about this man?

Sheri sat with her heart knocking around in her chest as Cooper explained his transfer to the UVM Medical Center from a New York hospital and his for-now commute on the ferry from Plattsburg to Grand Isle, Vermont. Thoughts ricocheted off the walls of her drink-loose mind ...

She'd been flirting with him and enjoying it. It was easy and fun because it was all vacation-mode with no rules, no consequences, really. Why did this new information change anything? Did it? How had she not known he worked at a Vermont hospital? Did he know she lived in Vermont – just outside Burlington? Had they talked about anything real?

"Sheri? Are you with me? You look like you've seen a ghost, you alright?"

"What? Sure, I mean, yes, I'm fine, no ghost," she said, thinking unless he meant a ghost of the future. "How is it that we haven't talked about this?"

"About what specifically?"

"About the fact that you work less than ten miles from where I live? But somehow you live in New York?"

"It's complicated ..."

"It always is," Sheri said, thinking of her own mess and wondering just how divorced Cooper was, with one foot in New York and the other in Vermont. She had so many questions.

The kids returned with the pizzas and everyone pulled a chair up to the fire to dig in. Sheri would have to bask a while longer in the mystery, which, she decided, she didn't mind at all.

Chapter Twenty-Seven

SHERI COULD HAVE SWORN a whiff of weed rode in on the air around the four kids. And they devoured the pizza like they hadn't eaten in days. Marijuana was legal in Massachusetts so it really wasn't a huge deal, but weren't they headed out after? Who was driving? How were you supposed to parent adult children anyway – where was that manual? "This is really good pizza," was what she ended up with, "was the Muse crowded? Was there a band?"

"Later probably," Leo said, "some dudes shooting pool – not too crowded."

"Not smoking in my car I hope," Cooper said to Leo. Sheri almost spit out her drink. She loved his candor, not even pretending there wasn't a skunky smell clinging to them.

"We took Brayden's Jeep, Dad, and no, no one was smoking and driving if that's what you're getting at."

Sheri could see Cooper weighing whether or not to pursue the matter and deciding to trust his son and let it go for now. After all, they were bouncing off twenty-four years old. Which, on one hand, seemed old enough to be married and starting a family – like she'd done – but on the other, *not*.

Once the pizza was gone, she and Cooper decided to head back inside. "It felt like the right time to leave the kids to themselves, you okay with that?" Cooper asked, as they moved up to the sprawling deck. "Besides, from here we can see the water *and* the stars. And with more comfortable seating."

"Ooh, don't mind if I do," Sheri said taking a seat beside him on the deeply cushioned loveseat. Cooper reached behind them to a teak storage bench and pulled out a luxurious blanket. "Do not even tell me this is cashmere," she said draping it across them, rubbing the fringed sage-green plaid softness to her cheek.

"What they can do with faux cashmere these days, totally machine washable. I really have to thank Stan and Ida's son for all these thoughtful touches."

"You're cute," she said nudging him, feeling a pull to keep some part of her body touching his. "But he probably has people – I can't see a dude, one who's never enjoyed Nantucket at all, go to the trouble," Sheri said, grateful for the soft weight of the blanket on her bare legs. It seemed so easy to sink into the pleasure of sitting so close to this man, under the stars on a clear summer night without a care in the world. To put reality and responsibilities on hold, push them to the back row of her thoughts. Her body was humming in a way that longed for more.

The warmth of their bodies mingled under the blanket as they sat, lulled by the rhythmic pulse of the sea beyond, his hand brushing over her skin as softly as moonlight. She wanted to ask him more about his ex-wife, how much was she still in his life, in Leo's. Where did Leo spend most of his time? With his mother, on his own? Was Cooper in the process of moving to Vermont permanently? That ferry commute was not sustainable – what was his hospital schedule? In the silence she wondered what questions he might be asking himself about her – if he was thinking about her at all. Jesus, just how much alcohol would it take for her brain to shut up?

"Could you live here year round?" he asked. She was glad to be rescued from the monologue inside her head.

"I used to think so as a kid, in that romantic way that let you believe it would always be summer. But now I don't know. I'm afraid it would feel lonely in the off-season, without the energy, color, and hum of summertime. Being immersed in the long, gray winters scares me a little I guess. How about you?" She could smell his shampoo and his spicy scent blending with the salty air and she let her leg lean against his and stay there. He stretched his arms across the back of the loveseat disturbing the pocket of heat between their bodies, but making room for her to be closer if she wanted. She wanted.

"I think rather than staying here all year it might be fun instead to celebrate Thanksgiving here or maybe Christmas ... if family members were willing to swing it." Cooper said.

She could see it, as if someone were holding up a magic snow globe with those holiday images swirling inside. A fire crackling in her parents' stone fireplace beneath the mantle draped in spruce garland woven with pinecones. Hurricane lanterns filled with cranberries from the bog and thick cream candles, and a big Frasier Fir in the corner by the slider with scallop-shell lights and gold-and-silver balls. "That sounds perfect actually ..."

Sheri felt Cooper's leg press into hers as if he shared the vision. And there in that moment it was a reachable thing – under that canopy of diamond stars on a perfect Nantucket summer night.

But then there was the part of her that shook the snow globe, whiting out the dream. Sheri had become bad at trusting the future.

∞

The kids left for downtown and a spiral of pleasure whirled at the thought of time alone with Cooper. She felt the whole side of her body against his, heat magnifying in the small space. She took her eyes away from the stars to steal a glance at his profile, his jaw smooth and clean-shaven. As if feeling her gaze on him he turned. Their eyes snagged and a warmth gathered at her core. His arm settled over her, cloaking her in his smell and his slight smile unzipped her vertebrae by vertebrae.

"You are beautiful out here," he said with a disarming tenderness, "your skin dewy with the sea air and kissed by the moonlight, your hair tangled and lovely and wild ..."

It seemed to take his mouth forever to reach hers, dragging his warm citrusy breath across her jaw then up to her lips. The slightest nibble on her bottom lip sent a slow purr of desire through her. Their mouths grazed slowly over each other's, the simplest but deepest pleasure. She felt his mouth curve into a smile and bump into her own as it sank hot and light against her lips, opening them to let him in. Heat rushed into her mouth, flooding through her like a brook baked by the sun.

He gathered her closer on the loveseat with her full breasts flush against him. She groaned softly into his mouth and deepened the kiss. It was a warm, slow drink of a kiss and she felt herself coming undone. All she knew in that moment was that she didn't want it to end, wanted to be devoured by this fire that smoldered in an unfamiliar way. Her whole body was begging him for more. She drew her leg across his lap to face him fully, settling deeply until there was no space between them. It was his turn to groan as he moved his hands from the sides of her face down to her hips pulling her tighter against him.

"Oh, Sheri ..." He spoke her name with wonder and respect, as if it was a beautiful name, as if she was a beautiful woman.

Hunger and need raced through her in one twisted braid as he explored under her top, her breasts spilling over his hands. Her legs squeezed tight as their hips rocked in a slow deliberate spiral. She felt his warm hands move to her bare legs leaving a hot trail before returning to her breasts and unhooking her bra. She cried out softly, tipping her head back before meeting his eyes as he looked into hers. Her hands were on his as he cupped her breasts and bent to take one at a time into his mouth. She felt the wave build inside her, the hard press of him pulsing through her shorts, the song crescendoed higher, faster, taking her breath, before erupting into a million little stars exploding inside her.

He stood to take Sheri inside, her legs slowly unfolding to stand on bare feet before him while the blanket dropped to the deck. Her body still locked against his, not wanting air to come between them. While she would feel embarrassed later about her promiscuity, the forcefield that bound them in that moment felt once-in-a-lifetime. All she wanted in the world was to be in Cooper's arms, in his bed, skin on skin.

The vibrating jangle of her phone on the teak table signaling a call instead of a text rented her from her trance. She wanted to ignore it more than she'd wanted anything in a long time, but seeing Tia's name lighting up the screen, she knew she could not.

"What's up, Tia?" she said, trying to level her breath and get to the point.

"Hi, Mrs. Steele, it's Jackson."

A thousand things would go through a mother's mind getting a call from someone else on her daughter's phone. *Was she hurt? Was there an accident? Was she dead? Was her sister in trouble, injured, arrested, in a ditch?* All within the seconds it took for the person to respond.

"It's Tia, she's really sick. I don't know what's wrong with her – she can't stop throwing up – we ate the same exact thing, I don't get it. I wouldn't have called but I'm starting to worry about her, it won't stop – she's like a rag doll, I'm afraid she's gonna pass out – she hasn't moved from the toilet –"

"Jackson, *Jackson,* where are you?" Sheri said, having to interrupt to gather information quickly while her mind spun. Cooper stood, running a hand through his hair to smooth it then turned to switch on the deck lights. "Okay, okay, take a breath, sit tight, I'm right next door. Be right there!"

∞

Sheri's heart was beating in her throat as she pushed her feet into her flip-flops. As they walked through the house and out the front door, she filled Cooper in on what she knew. "So it can't be food poisoning, right? Because they ate the same thing – but could a stomach bug be this violent?" Her thoughts raced off her tongue in a jumble while her mind jumped to uglier scenarios: was she drugged, did she have some horrible bacterial infection? Was there some funky new virus going around? You just never knew! She tripped running down Cooper's front steps but he was there to catch her before she fell all the way down.

Sheri ran up her own steps into the house and up to the second floor where Jackson sat on the edge of the tub trying to comfort Tia and hold back her hair as she dry-heaved into the toilet. "Tia, honey, look at me," Sheri said, crouching on the floor beside her, touching her face and forehead. "She's on fire and clammy at the same time," she said looking up at Cooper. "Tia, talk to me – she's not responding – is she fainting? Tell me what to do!" She couldn't care about the panic choking her voice or about the makeup that must be smudged and ghoulish in the fluorescent lighting of the bathroom.

Cooper switched places with Sheri on the floor supporting Tia's crumpled body as she came to. *"Mom, are you here? Mommy?"*

Relief flooded Sheri's body. But she tried to keep her voice level and alarm from it, "I'm right here, honey, with Doctor Madden – you know, our neighbor Cooper?" She had a million questions but she bit her tongue so Cooper could check out her daughter – her pulse, her pupils – Sheri felt an enormous relief just having him there. And then Tia was retching again, her body convulsing.

"Should I call 911? What should we do – she can't have anything left in her – she must be so dehydrated!" Jackson said, his hysteria rising seeing Tia that shade of green and in and out of consciousness.

"Listen to me, Son," Cooper said with reassuring authority, "I need you to grab a towel and head downstairs to the Bronco, can you do that? Sheri, are the keys on the table by the front door?"

"Yes," Sheri said, relieved to have an answer to something, and for Jackson to have an assignment.

"I'll drive us to Cottage Hospital, Sheri – Jackson up front with me navigating and you and Tia in the back – okay?"

"Yes, good, okay," she said, annoyed with herself *again* for not springing for the four-door.

"I'm going to carry her down and you're going to open the doors for us as we go, alright?"

He was talking to her like a child, slowly, plainly, and it was working. If Tia was really bad off, Sheri thought, Cooper would have called 911, there would be more urgency in his voice, his actions, right? *Everything was going to be okay, right?* Her daughter was going to be alright, there was no other option. Sheri's phone was pinging again, a text this time. It would have to wait, Sheri had to pay attention, they had to get Tia to the hospital. They had to find out what was wrong with her, they had to fix her.

The six-mile drive to the hospital on Prospect Street would take at least fifteen minutes along Madaket Road. Cooper got Jackson to talk about where they'd been, what they'd had to eat and drink while Tia was propped against Sheri upright in case she vomited again. Sheri wanted to believe Tia was just dozing instead of unconscious but she didn't honestly know. She followed Cooper's calm lead. Her phone pinged twice more and she reached for it in her back pocket.

It was Wyn's name illuminating the screen this time.

> Where's Tia? Supposed to meet at Gaslight – I've been here an hour she never showed – not answering texts or calls!

Sheri swept her thoughts together in a small pile in her brain. And instead of composing some perfectly worded response, she just tapped in the truth.

> Taking her to hospital – won't stop throwing up – fever
> and worried about dehydration not sure what's going on

Sheri reread what she'd written then deleted it. The last thing she wanted to do was scare Wyn and have her driving to the hospital like a maniac, or driving *at all*, after drinking and who knew what else. But then what if Wyn got home to an empty house? So she hit *call* instead of trying to text. But then Tia bent forward to heave again and Sheri dropped her phone reaching for the towel and holding onto her daughter.

But Sheri hadn't actually deleted the text, and instead of calling Wyn, she accidentally hit *send*.

∞

They pulled up to the emergency entrance and Jackson jumped out to find a wheelchair. Sheri felt like they were playing their parts in every hospital drama there ever was. Which reminded her to grab her purse with her insurance information. Which would have been great if only it had been Tia's purse with *her* wallet and insurance card.

"Oh no," Sheri said, "I don't have any of Tia's insurance information!"

"Don't worry about that," Cooper said, helping Tia out of the Bronco and into the wheelchair, "Emergency rooms have to provide treatment without requiring payment or proof of insurance. You can figure that all out later, just get her inside while I park."

The place was quiet for a Saturday night – but then it wasn't exactly Chicago Hope. Jackson was sitting in the waiting room with Tia while Sheri did her best at the front desk with the paperwork when Cooper returned. A triage nurse appeared once they were checked in to assess Tia's condition, taking her pulse, blood pressure, temperature, respiratory rate, and other vital signs as well as testing her ability to follow commands. She had a grandmotherly way about her with her raspberry scrub pants and flowered top to match, a neat platinum bun that was either the whitest white or the blondest blond. Rimless glasses rode the tip of her nose as she went about her work carrying a waft of baby powder and Jean Naté.

"Hey, Darlin', my name's Eileen, not where you want to be on a Saturday night, huh? Well, don't you worry – you're in good hands and we'll have you feelin' right as rain soon enough, okay? Now keep those pretty blue eyes open for me and see if you can follow my finger. That's a girl, now are you feeling any pain?"

Tia could barely communicate and clutched at her stomach in response, which Eileen asked her to rate on a pain scale of one to ten. Then Tia bent over and retched into the plastic vomit basin that had been placed in her lap. "Well, now I'm sure glad you have all this beautiful hair tied back," Eileen said, taking it all in stride, treating it all like business as usual, which had a comforting effect on Sheri. "Now, you just sit tight and I'll be right back."

While they waited for Eileen to return, Cooper explained that while it was scary to see her daughter like that, Tia hadn't been vomiting for a concerning number of hours and wasn't presenting with any other symptoms other than a low-grade fever and probably dehydration. "My guess is that it's some type of food poisoning – even though she and Jackson ate the same thing, Tia could have had a drink with tainted ice or a contaminated lemon slice – it happens, you can't always pinpoint it. They'll treat the nausea with medication, probably promethazine, which blocks those receptors in the brain that cause nausea and vomiting. They'll also administer fluids intravenously to replace her electrolytes and rehydrate."

Sheri listened and was lulled by his self-possession and composed demeanor. The way his eyes held hers slowed her wayward pulse and made her feel like she could lean into his confidence. Her instinct was to reach for his hand to feel its strength and warmth wrapped around hers, but she shook off the displaced thought. "Will she have to be admitted?" Sheri asked Cooper.

"My guess is no, not unless they find some kind of intestinal blockage or her fever spikes or –"

"Okay, okay, I don't think I really want to know the worst-case scenario." As Tia was being moved to an exam room to wait for an emergency doctor to examine her, Sheri told Cooper over her shoulder that she was going in with her. She noticed Jackson looking a bit pale in the plastic chair under the bright lights and was grateful Cooper was there to keep him company. "Hey, thanks for being here. Both of you."

As the doors swung closed behind Eileen, Tia, and Sheri, Wyn and Leo rushed in through the emergency entrance. Jackson got to his feet and met them halfway, "Wow – it's so good to see you guys," Looking more closely from Leo to Wyn and back again, he said, "wait – are you high? Are you kidding me right now?"

"Bro, calm down," Wyn said, "How the hell is my sister – *what* is going on, Dude?" Before Jackson could answer, Cooper had materialized, looking from Wyn's red-rimmed eyes to his son's and back to Wyn's.

To Wyn, Cooper said, "Your sister is going to be fine, it looks like she's got a bit of food poisoning. She's not presenting with a high fever or other concerning symptoms and my guess is she'll be feeling like her old self within a day or so. Your mother is with her while the ER doctor examines her – they'll get some fluids in her and I'm sure she'll be sent home." Then to his son, he said, "Could I speak with you privately, Leo?" It wasn't a question.

Beside Tia's bed, Sheri stood wringing her hands behind her back as the ER doctor examined her daughter. Tia's complexion was ashy and her hair was dull and limp with perspiration. Her lifeless appearance made Sheri's stomach churn and she thought how brutal it was to not be able to trade places with her child. Clumsy prayers marched back and forth in her brain and she wondered how in the hell parents of critically ill children survived any of it. She felt weak and afraid. They would *wait and watch*, the doctor told her.

Sitting under the harsh lighting of a hospital emergency room in the middle of the night while your daughter received intravenous medication and fluids was a perspective slap. Sheri would always ever be a mother first and last, her children were all that mattered. And it occurred to her that every single decision she made about her own life would impact her daughters in some way. How Cooper might fit into all that was a background question at best.

∞

It was a long night in the ER but Tia didn't need to be admitted and everyone got to sleep in their own beds. Tia responded well to the anti-nausea medication and intravenous fluids. Blood and urine tests showed no sign of infection, and there had been no need for an MRI or CT scan. The doctor told her she may continue to have diarrhea for another twelve to twenty-four hours, that it was normal and not cause for alarm and that, most importantly, she needed to stay hydrated.

They were "lucky." That always sounded like the weirdest thing to say when you actually had to be rushed to the hospital on your vacation. *Lucky*. But, of course, they *were* lucky.

Tia, Jackson, and Wyn rode back home with Sheri at nearly two o'clock in the morning – Cooper and Leo having left hours earlier. Cooper was the MVP across the categories of neighbor, doctor, and friend, but he was pissed that his son had shown up baked. Sheri hadn't been ecstatic about Wyn's bloodshot eyes and flaky behavior either but they were adults. And they got points for Ubering to the hospital instead of driving Cooper's Range, the current location of which wasn't crystal clear.

A herculean task, parenting adult children.

Sheri was asleep before she had to worry about her cyclone of thoughts. And blissfully, for a change, she slept past sunrise. When she finally woke up, it took a minute to remember what day it was and where she was in the family flow of summer vacation.

The house was quiet, she couldn't imagine anyone waking up before noon. Adding a second pillow under her head, she stared up at the ceiling, reluctant to start the day. She was still shaken by the night's events but relieved beyond measure that Tia was fine. Exhaustion pinned her in place and she could feel her nerves rev as a vortex of thoughts piled in, each pushing to the front for attention. Too tired to organize them, she let them rush in and have their way in whatever order they showed up.

Was Tommy still on-island? Had he been in contact with his daughters? Did he understand that she and him would not be getting back together as they'd fooled themselves into thinking? Did he understand that there would be no more chapters starring Sheri and Tommy? *Did she?* They'd be bound by their children ever after. But that story, moving forward, would only, could only, ever be about their daughters.

Her daughters ... whose lives she could not manage to distance herself from, no matter how old they got. Sheri had to find a way to stop worrying about the choices they made, their futures. Would they be reckless with their hearts, their decisions? They had to live their lives. Which meant she had to live hers too. And she had to move forward instead of back. And she had to grow up and face the hard things.

Her mom ... Was she still mourning Rose's diagnosis? Grieving current *and* future losses? How would they keep up with the "new normal"? And wouldn't that keep changing? Sheri felt a single hot tear roll into her ear. Her beautiful mom, losing her identity by degrees. It was irreconcilable. And while George described the challenge of Rose asking herself *who am I now?* Selfishly, Sheri was more worried about the day her mother looked at her and said, *who are you?*

Cooper ... There *he* was, leaning patiently at the edges of her mind, with that half-smile and those harvest-gold-rimmed eyes. What was he doing there? She hadn't invited him in. But she liked him there, wanted him to stay. Heat spread through her and she didn't know what to make of that. It felt good. And her body was taking her back to his lap, the warm smell of him rising up out of the collar of his shirt, his mouth teasing her lips open, his hands on her, coaxing her body and her mind.

She slid her hand down under the sheet to find that silky song again, that would drown out the other rain of thoughts, and pretended her fingers were his.

Chapter Twenty-Eight

As the days passed with her full house, Sheri settled into their routine and started to feel more optimistic about things than she had since arriving on the island.

As ever, Wyn was trying to get as much surfing in as possible while remaining mindful of not neglecting family time in the process. It wasn't easy accommodating everyone's schedules and desires but meeting up at Cisco Brewery with Trudy and Griff's son, Oliver, was non-negotiable. Sheri lost track of when Trudy's husband was on or off the island but it was always a bonus when Griffin joined them. Sheri thought back to the sunset sail on *Fantasea* and it seemed almost strange remembering that Cooper had been there. She'd barely known him. *How much better did she know him now?* He'd been radio silent since making sure Tia was alright after the hospital scare

Her parents had sounded good! She'd called them from the sunny deck while she had her coffee, describing the bright beach towels lifting off the railing in the breeze with the misty ocean booming in the background. She told her dad that she missed his coffee – that no one made it quite like he did. He sounded so pleased – sometimes the simplest things had the biggest impact – those little things you didn't think to say.

Her mom asked how the grasses looked, did they need thinning? And was the Rosa Rugosa still in bloom or had it gone already to seed?

You know, dear, you can simply cut off both ends of the rose hip, slice the fruit open, and remove that seedy, hairy inside to make a great jelly. It was a profound comfort to have her mother planted firmly in the moment. They talked about the girls with Rose expressing her concern over the uptick in sharks she'd been reading about – was Wyn being careful? Was Tia spending all her money on fancy things? Rose was there, 100 percent. Sheri's heart was a helium balloon.

"Your father tells me that Stan and Ida have the house rented out this summer, is that right?" Rose said, continuing on without letting Sheri answer right away, "That son of theirs, too good for Nantucket, I mean *really* now. They'd better be careful he doesn't sell it right out from under them, I'll tell you that."

Sheri couldn't suppress the grin on her face listening to the familiar cadence of her mother's voice and opinions. "There is a very nice father and son renting, Mom, Cooper and Leo Madden. You would approve. But you wouldn't believe the outside living room over there now – bluestone patio under a big pergola, a raised circular stone firepit with lava rocks, teak furniture with deep cushions, it's really –"

"What on earth are you talking about, dear, a living room *outside*? I'm sure I don't know what you're talking about. And two men living there you say? Where is the wife? That boy's mother?" Sheri realized she was biting her lip – had she talked too long? Had she confused her mother? Then her dad chimed in, helping Rose understand that it was probably just a fancy patio, and Sheri was glad they were on speaker.

"Dad, you're exactly right. And Mom, I don't have details about the renters but I do know they're here on a sort of reset after a difficult divorce. He's a doctor, at the UVM hospital if you can believe, and he's very nice. And his son, Leo, and Wyn have been surfing most days, which is good for me – you know how I get when she goes out alone."

"Stan and Ida *divorced*? Well that's awful news, no wonder they're selling, oh that's a *shame*," Rose said, clucking her tongue, "and where's that husband of yours? Put Tommy on …"

And just like that Sheri was back on the ground, her balloon-heart with a slow leak.

"Hey, Rosie," her dad said, "let's go see if they have those Belgian waffles you like today with the boysenberry syrup, how does that sound?" Her father was already so good at steering the conversation. He was the best man she knew and her insides ached for him.

"Oh, that sounds divine, George, yes, let's. Maybe Phyllis is already down there, oh, but I hope she's not with that Edith, you know I don't like her at *all* with that ghastly crumbly lipstick. She must have bought that before the war, oh *honestly*!"

"Well, I'll let you two go," Sheri said, infusing her voice with a cheer she was trying to hold on to, "Mom's already halfway to the door isn't she, Dad," Sheri said, picturing Rose already on to the next thing, hanging her big purse in the crook of her elbow.

"You know your mother," George said, with a smile in his voice that was always there – how did he do it? "Thanks for calling, Sweetheart, we love you, and let me know when you get that toilet in. I know it's still functional but I hope it hasn't been backing up too much on you. I'll feel better when it's been replaced."

"I love you so much too, Dad," she said, swallowing around the golf ball in her throat, "it's not the same here without you! And yup – Wes the plumber is my next call. You better catch up to Mom! Love you!"

Sheri set her phone on the little table next to her chair and sat back in the chair to stare out at the sea. She considered the timeless of it, its deep, infinite, lasting existence. The eternal presence of the sky overhead, how it endured all things. While human beings did not, how they could be plucked in an instant from the physical world leaving behind only their essence – if they left anything at all.

Was she meant to weigh the magnitude of everything in order to live fully and intentionally? It was too much. It made ordinary things too precious to enjoy with a light heart.

∞

The temptation to wallow was staring her down. And while she was at it, *why the hell hadn't she heard from Cooper since his quick check-in about Tia?* It had only been a few days, but still. She'd gotten used to sharing the sunrises with him and to the way she felt when he looked at her.

They'd almost gone to bed together, hadn't they? And she knew she wasn't the only one who'd wanted that. It had felt so pure, the only natural conclusion to that night until Jackson's phone call. Sheri was certain that Cooper's desire had matched hers, you don't just make up a thing like that. *Do you?* It had to be real, it couldn't just evaporate like that. *Could it?* Her phone pinged from the table and her heart galloped – it had to be Cooper, she'd conjured him.

Does tomorrow 9 a.m. work for toilet install?

Great, she'd manifested Wes instead. Damn universe listening to the wrong conversation.

Sure see you then

She shouldn't take it out on her plumber. She had to do something, maybe hit Ladies Beach with Trudy and a cooler of adult beverages. The perfect quiet spot in between Nobadeer and Cisco. They couldn't drive onto that beach and would have to carry all their stuff from the sandy parking lot, but the peace of Ladies would be worth it. She'd leave the Bronco for the kids and have her friend pick her up in her topless, doorless, cherry-red Jeep Wrangler. They'd hit Bartlett Farm for sandwiches then head just a bit more south to the Smooth Hummocks Coastal Preserve – it was just what she needed.

How lucky that Trudy needed it too. They had the eight miles on the way to Bartlett to get their collective gripes out in the open air set to their favorite 80s tunes. Of course "I Want to Know What Love Is" came on and Sheri thought how she felt like a *Foreigner* in her own skin. She toyed with the idea of coming clean about where she'd been headed with Tommy. But she was really more interested in filling Trudy in on Cooper. Over a glass or three of rosé on the beach.

"And you'd think Oliver would be out of bed on this gorgeous day, right? Drives me nuts – it's not like he's a teenager anymore, such a waste of time," Trudy shouted over the wind. "How about your gang – do they sleep in so late? Probably not, girls are so different. You know if his father were here, he'd be up, you could put money on that. And I swear to God, this summer it seems like Griffin is always somewhere else. I'm not digging it, I mean it's *Nantucket* – where else would you want to be?" Trudy's words came tumbling out over the loud songs and it helped get Sheri out of her own funk – even the happiest people had stuff. It was reassuring.

There was just the right onshore breeze to lift delicious summer heat from their skin as they reclined in Trudy's new deluxe beach chairs. They'd been a pain in the ass to haul from the Jeep but worth it with their massage-table-style face openings with actual arm slots for reading. "I honestly can't think of anyone else I know who'd pay two-hundred dollars for a beach chair from Hammacher Schlemmer, Trude, you are an original."

"Why, thank ya, not that we'll be doing much reading today, but it seemed like a good idea at the time."

"Speaking of," Sheri said, laying all the way back, "what books do I need to put on my list? You know, the good stuff, even if you think they're out of my wheelhouse. No horror or fantasy, please, or coming-of-age stuff – hit me with some literary fiction. Ooh, and maybe some historical fiction too."

"Let me think on that. My own to-be-read stack is a mountain, come over and see what moves you."

"So the writing's going good?" Sheri asked, eyes closed against the sun, "and which part do you like better – the composing part or the editing and rewrite part?"

"I hate them both equally," Trudy said, with a faraway voice as though she'd almost fallen asleep. "Nah, I'm kiddin'. But sitting my ass in a chair for five hours a day getting in my two thousand words can be a real bitch."

"I cannot even imagine ... sitting still that long for starters!"

"That's why I start the day with a long run, pound it out, you know?" Trudy said, splashing more wine in her cup. "And every day is different – you never know who's gonna show up on the page or what they're up to, where they're from, where they're going. That part's friggin' great. It's the blinking cursor on the blank page that sucks."

"But you're so disciplined, Tru, you're so lucky."

"Luck ain't got nothing to do with it, Sister."

"You're right ... I've always admired your work ethic. I feel all over the place half the time."

"Social worker and novelist – different stratospheres. But I don't want to talk about work. Let's talk orgasms, Botox, or, like, if you ran away with the circus, what would your job be?"

∞

After volleying the merits of edamame, nut butters, and bikinis at their age – and three cups of wine later, Sheri found the nerve to dish about Cooper. She was leaving the Tommy debacle in the vault.

"So, let me get this straight," Trudy said sitting up in her chair, the kids were down below around the fire while you were dry-humping the dad up on the deck?" Trudy's cup of wine was spilling over the sides with the vibration of her uncontrollable laughing.

"No! Well, yes, but the kids had left for downtown. I'm trying to share this thing I can't really explain and you think it's comedy, Trudy, come *on! What should I do?* I'm serious. You're drunk and I'm not drunk enough. Please don't ruin this for me, Tru, I've never felt like, I mean, it felt so, *ugh* – I can't put it into words. And sitting here trying to is making it sound so cheap and stupid. Do you think *he* thinks I'm cheap and stupid?" Sheri was startled by the hysteria she could hear in her own voice, not attractive. Her nerves were too close to the surface.

Being in Cooper's company was so much more fun than this childish worry about why she hadn't heard from him. She was getting sick of herself. *Why was everything so complicated?*

"What kind of a question is that, seriously, Sheri?" Trudy said, sitting forward in her chair and pushing her sunglasses to the top of her head to look into the eyes of her friend. "No. You are absolutely not cheap and not stupid. I'm sorry for laughing, sorry for saying dry-humping. I blame the wine. Maybe we should open a bar called *Pour Decisions* …"

Trudy couldn't stop her body from shaking with restrained laughter, leaning back again in her chair. "No, no, in all seriousness I think Cooper is a great catch – remember I'm the one who invited him on the boat, for *you*! Well, Griff did – per recommendation of their mutual buddy – Noah, but I was like hell, *yes*! He seems *amazing*, Sheri, and you deserve amazing after Tommy. Not that Tommy isn't, *wasn't* amazing, you know what I mean. Do I even know what I mean? We all loved Tommy, still love him, we love you, and it just sucks how it played out."

Sheri reached over to squeeze her friend's hand. Trudy was a lifeline, a bright buoy keeping Sheri's head above the water that rose and fell beneath her. "We've known each other for about twenty-five years, Tru, and almost all of those included Tommy. I appreciate you so much – especially your brutal honesty, even when I'm not ready to accept it. I just want you to know that, okay?"

Trudy squeezed right back. "Of course I know that. And that you'd do the same for me." Trudy took a long sip of her drink before saying, "So, do you think he's still here with Stephanie and what's his name – Axel?"

"*Aaro*," Sheri said, looking out on the lazy blue sea as if it had the answer, drumming her fingers on her tan thigh, "And I honestly don't know ... I've heard nothing." Sheri knew there was no way she was steering the conversation in *that* direction. There wasn't enough rosé in the cooler for that.

Chapter Twenty-Nine

SHERI DID FEEL BETTER after a day at the beach with Trudy, lighter. You don't realize how much the stuff you're hauling around weighs. How much it weighs you *down*. Perspective is everything, and you just don't get that from the view inside your head. She was also happy to have both girls home and everyone hanging out on the deck peaceably. Even if it was probably because they were all a little buzzed.

"Mommy's home!" Wyn said, in her little-girl voice that was reserved only for Sheri in moments of genuine Wyn-joy. The deck was drenched in the orange sunshine of late afternoon and everyone seemed happy "So, it feels like a Tavern night, don't you think? We haven't been yet and –"

"You don't have to talk me into it, kiddo – I'll just need a quick shower," Sheri said, pulling her youngest daughter in for a side hug, "Ladies Beach was supreme today – so peaceful. I forget what a nice alternative it is to crazy Nobadeer."

"I thought it was called Fat Ladies Beach? *Ooh* … probs not PC anymore, right? Ha! Anyway, you didn't have to keep combing the horizon to make sure I hadn't been swallowed by a wave – so I hear ya, Mom. How's Tru? And isn't Ollie on-island now? We keep talking about it but we really need to get a brewery day on the calendar."

"Let's talk at dinner. I'll get my shower so we can head out sooner than later."

"Wait," Wyn said, "the let's-talk-later thing – what gives? Who's dying?"

"Oh, Wyn, always so suspicious," Sheri said, cupping her daughter's chin and looking straight into her green-rimmed ocean eyes, "why do you jump to the worst possible thing – when did that happen to you? Everyone is fine."

"When did that happen to me? Well, It started when you sat us down to tell us Simba died – I loved that kitten more than life. And then when you and Dad were separating, you said we needed to all sit down and talk. And *again* when you'd decided divorce instead of reconciling. And *then* with Nanna. So yeah, I can't help it if my brain short-circuits and wants you to cut to the chase."

"Aw, honey. You're too young to be this cynical, and I'm sorry about it. All of it. And if it seems like I keep things from you for too long or you think I wait until the last minute to tell you things … it's only because I can't bear your pain. I know that probably makes no sense to you, *especially* you, who wants the straight deal from the get-go. But I can't resist a little sugar-coating, I can't help it. But – nothing is wrong now. Nothing new anyway."

Wyn did a full body shake, as if to literally shrug it all off, then put her smile back on and shoved her mother gently in the direction of the outdoor shower. "We leave in t-minus twenty minutes," she said.

∞

The Tavern and Gazebo were alive with tourists and regulars alike. Sometimes you could tell the difference. It didn't matter anyway. Smiling customers spilled out onto the cobblestones as more piled in – mouths watering for the chicken wings and boozy mudslides. They'd wait for however long it took to get a table outside. From there they could see everyone walking by: harried folks rushing to catch their ferry home, bags hanging from both arms, pulling suitcases, pushing strollers, or the lucky ones who'd just arrived, windblown and excited.

The characters coming off the pier from the yachts provided the most entertainment – who were they to have such enormous vessels with a full staff, and where were they going in expensive sport coats and flowing silk dresses that skimmed the ground with heels not meant for cobblestones? For as long as they'd been coming to Nantucket, they'd spun stories about the super-rich and what that would be like. Were they happier?

Looking out at the people coming and going, the ones holding hands embracing the moment, Sheri realized her eyes were darting over the wave of people, half afraid Tommy was among them. It was as if Tia had read her mind.

"Is Daddy still here? How do we not know that?"

Wasn't that a huge part of what was wrong? Sheri thought.

"Exactly," Wyn said, "how do we not know a ton of shit about Dad, like where the hell he is half the time?"

"I feel like it wouldn't be weird at all if he just popped up out of the crowd in a pink shirt and blue shorts maybe with some whales on them," Tia said, eyes searching.

Tia would run out and throw her arms around Tommy if she saw him, completely ignore Stephanie, literally not see her even if she were standing in front of her. How did she do that? Had she gotten so good at only seeing what she wanted? Denial was in such contrast with her otherwise matter-of-fact personality. Wyn, on the other hand, would always be guarded.

Self-preservation came in different packages. And Sheri was always somewhere in the middle – feeling like she was one shaky breath of wind away from switching sides.

Their meals came fast – Sheri was happy both for the change of subject and to see Tia back to her normal color -- if not her usual order of fish tacos. Wings for Wyn, the Tavern burger for Jackson, and Sheri's favorite, the Super Crunch Salad with grilled shrimp. She didn't want the evening to go by too fast. Even if the waitress was anxious to turn the table over, Sheri wasn't going to be rushed, so they ordered another round of drinks.

They could see a fog stealing in and the night hanging in a lavender mist. The amber lights of the yachts swaying in their slips rippled in the harbor. Sheri's breath caught as she thought she saw Cooper taking a left onto Old South Wharf – but it was too far to be certain. She felt her face redden, either for the foolishness of thinking it was him or the wanting it to be.

"Mom?" Wyn said, "What – do you see Dad or something? You look funny."

Everyone looked in the direction she'd been staring. But only strangers passed by. "No, no, I just thought I saw someone I recognized, that's all. How are those wings you've been dying for? As good as you remember?"

After dinner the four of them strolled around town, popping leisurely in and out of the shops that were still open. Sheri felt glad for their company and that unlike their teenaged selves, now they didn't always need to ditch her for grander plans to see and be seen. Was this when she appreciated them most, missed them most? Even though they were walking right beside her? It was hard not memorize every moment.

It surprised Sheri to see one or the other of her daughters pick something up in a shop, turn it over in her hands admiring it, only to put it back after seeing the price, saying, "that's crazy, it's just not worth that." While Sheri generally threw good sense to the wind, plunking down whatever unreasonable sum to purchase a Nantucket treasure.

How did they always have room for ice cream? At least they didn't need to stand for an hour in line at Juice Bar anymore– oh, they would at least once before they left – but frappes at the old-school soda fountain at the Nantucket Pharmacy were an equal or greater treat. And being a part of their joy tripled her own.

As Sheri sat on a bench outside the pharmacy waiting for the kids to get their frappes, she took out her phone and let her good mood take the reins. She pulled up Cooper's contact and tapped in a message before she could overthink it:

> Hi! What a gorgeous night, did you catch the sunset? I was picturing you out on your deck taking it all in. Having a great evening downtown with the girls and Jackson – he really is an easygoing guy – Tia's a lucky woman. We're at the ice cream portion of the evening now ☺ Anyway – just wanted to say I'm thinking of you.

She hit *send* before she could edit to achieve a more perfect lightness of tone or delete it altogether.

Sheri looked up to see Jackson trying to get his melting ice cream cone under control as the girls told him about their little-kid days and the sidewalk music man who'd play "Puff the Magic Dragon" for them on his guitar, how they'd dance on the lumpy brick sidewalk, twirling whichever dresses they'd chosen that night for special dinners out at Cioppino's or 56 Union. Both gone now, but as real as any of the memories that clunked into place in their kaleidoscope minds.

Sheri wondered where the girls' futures would take them – would their partners and families do Nantucket? Would they *have* children? Sheri couldn't imagine otherwise but the world was changing faster than it used to. Would *Moor to Sea* still belong to them? Or would it become a casualty of time and finances? Inconceivable to consider its surrender.

Why was it such a challenge to sit exactly in the moment, without mourning its loss while you were right there splashing around in it? Maybe divorce did that to you, or confronting your parents' mortality, or facing down your own midlife crises.

Sheri had done well to not keep checking her phone for a response from Cooper. She'd been in good company all day and night which made that easier. But it was still hanging there – the wondering, the wishing and hoping. And then the self-recrimination that followed for allowing anyone else to pull the strings of her happiness. Now that they were all back at the house for the night, ensconced in their own quiet things, there was wide-open opportunity for self-destructive behavior.

∞

Alone in her room after three games of Crazy Eights with the kids and two failed games of Solitaire, she felt almost giddy about checking her phone, so certain was she of some kind of communication from Cooper. She'd left her phone on the bed to prove she didn't need it *and* to demonstrate her confidence to the texting gods. She'd put her children and everyone else first, had given them her whole and present self, happily. Surely that was enough for a win.

The blank and silent screen of her iPhone mocked her and was a freefall from her summit of hope.

She lay back on the bed with force, stomping her feet on the mattress like a thwarted teenager. WHY? She screamed in her head, *what was going on?* She'd been so sure something good was starting, that she and Cooper were on the same page – their ease in each other's company over coffee and a sunrise, on a paddleboard in the middle of the ocean, and the easy mingling of their kids. Not to mention the heat between them that was *real*, she *knew* it was, and that she hadn't been alone in it. The trail of sparks his hands left on her body, the look in his eyes that felt like he was trying to show her something. She'd been able to see beyond the moment for a change, with a heart that had no edges. *Where did he go?*

Sheri leaned over to her mother's side of the bed reaching for tissues in the night table. But there was only a folded cloth handkerchief of her dad's. When she pulled it from the drawer, an envelope with her name on it fell to the floor. Her mother's swirly script more recognizable than her own. She held it tenderly as she crawled under her periwinkle blanket and leaned against her new fat pillows to read what was inside.

My dear Petal ~

You must think your old mother has really lost her mind tucking a note away for you like this. (I haven't lost it yet, but they tell me I will! Isn't that something?) Oh, honestly!

Your father and I are just back from the tailgate picnic in S'conset with Stan and Ida — you know how he gussies up that old Wagoneer for Daffodil Festival every year. It was brilliant sunshine for the parade but I must say I am chilled to the bone. This getting old business is for the birds.

Darling, I'm wondering how you are, reading this. (I'm wondering how I am ...) Is it very strange? When we speak, are you worried I've already gone round the bend? (Have I?) I'm so sorry about it, Honey, I know how sensitive you are and how tightly you hold onto things. Letting go is a tough customer. But there are times when we simply must.

Please don't worry so much about me, thinking I'm lost to you. My darling girl, you will never lose me. (I may lose me, but I'll be none the wiser!) That was a terrible joke, I apologize. Hear me laughing. Please don't forget about the laughing.

I am picturing you there in that old summer house alone, without your dad and me, and if my granddaughters have yet to arrive. I do hope you've found a way to enjoy your solitude, my sweet rose petal, instead of feeling imprisoned by your own nostalgia. But I know you! Wipe those tears away this instant, do you hear me?

Hear my voice when I've grown quiet. Keep talking to me. And when I no longer recognize your face, Petal, know that I still hold you in my heart.

And take care of your father. He'll need that - though he'll never let on. That George ... I got a good one!

I love you,
Mom

P.S. If I forget to tell you, remember that your happiness is as important as everyone else's!

Sheri laid there still as a stone pressing her mother's words to her chest, branding them upon her heart. She folded the letter and placed it back in the drawer of the night table, trading it for her father's hanky, before falling asleep with salty tears drying on her cheeks.

Chapter Thirty

SHERI WAS DRESSED AND on her second cup of coffee the next morning when Wes showed up to install the toilet. At least it was a distraction from her thoughts and it was almost satisfying that the gray day mirrored her mood. Wes was a charming guy who liked to talk – but Sheri wasn't feeling it. And she didn't really want to know why he carried a bucket filled with rags and sponges in along with a toolbox. But she made the mistake of walking back to the master bathroom with him anyway to hear him out on his job summary. Really all she wanted was to say, *do what you gotta – let me know when you're done.*

"First things first," he began, "I'll just turn off the water supply valve here and flush the toilet to empty the tank." Sheri responded only with *ahuh and mmhmm* catching every other phrase Wes offered, "remove the mounting nuts ... inspect the flange ... test-fit new toilet ... wax ring ..."

"That all sounds great, I'll leave you to it, Wes."

"Shame about your neighbor's water heater bursting like that – if you want, I could take a look at yours once I finish this up. That's the trouble with well water—"

"I'm sorry, what exactly are you talking about?" Sheri's insides betrayed her and were on high alert just at the mention of her neighbor, which she knew could only mean Cooper. Cooper who she hadn't heard from, Cooper who was apparently ghosting her.

"Damn thing burst – made quite a mess – and wouldn't you know it, just when the wife had gotten in."

Sheri's heart sank like a stone, tearing through her stomach and dive-bombing straight to her bowels. Wes couldn't see it and kept on talking.

"See, well water is generally hard because the water is coming directly from the ground, and absorbs minerals from the soil surrounding it over time. Scale and sediment result from repeatedly heating hard water, and if you let it accumulate without routine cleaning, well, you can imagine the corrosion …"

Yes, she could imagine the corrosion. The complete and utter decay of hope, the bubble of optimism she'd been allowing herself. She felt like her insides had been scooped out with a melon baller, one with serrated edges. She walked out onto the deck – her only thought was to get away from this news, this unacceptable information and its messenger. She hoped everyone slept in, her face was in no shape for company. She wasn't even in a space where she'd be capable of arranging her features into a pleasant expression. She let her coffee go cold in her hands as she just stared out into the thick gray sky, a low ceiling of pewter over a matching sea.

His *wife*? His *ex*-wife, *right*? She was there on Nantucket? Right *next door* to where she was in that exact moment? Scenarios unspooled in her brain. Leo could have reached out and begged his mother to come, although he didn't seem the type. Or maybe she just took it upon herself to get a piece of Nantucket and arrived uninvited and unwelcome? Or she just happened to be on-island with friends and popped over to Eel Point Road to see her son? It's not like Eel Point Road wasn't *the farthest northwestern point from town* – and not pop-in distance at all! There was no way Cooper invited his ex-wife to come to the place where he and his son were trying to reset from whatever post-divorce shit Cooper had only alluded to. No. Freakin'. Way.

Sheri could pump Wes for information! He seemed to be cut out for gossip, he'd be sure to dish. Who was this woman? Was she pretty? How old was she? How long were they married? At least twenty-five years. Her stomach bottomed out thinking of just what she and her own ex had been recently up to. *Was there always unfinished sexual tension between exes?* Could she ask Wes if they seemed chummy? Was there touching, smiling? Or was there yelling and fighting and *why in the world was she there?* Of course she could not ask any of those things.

Sheri was really losing it. She could go for a long run on the beach. Be swallowed by the fog. She couldn't sit there and fall apart. But even in her flight impulse, she wouldn't leave the girls to wake up to a strange man in her bathroom. She felt trapped, fogged in, a hostage of her own wheeling brain. It was way too early to start drinking – which was a repugnant thought anyway – and she wouldn't be able to concentrate on a book, or even enjoy a mind-numbing scroll through Instagram.

∞

"Knock-knock," came a familiar male voice on the deck railing below, followed by footsteps on the way up, "good morning." It was Leo looking for Wyn. Sheri felt foolish and chagrined for her nanosecond of hope. Leo's voice was a lot like his father's. "Sorry if I'm disturbing you, Mrs. Steele, but Wyn's not returning my texts and the waves are going off out at Cisco right now and, well, my dad took the Range somewhere this morning so I'm kinda stranded and was hoping …"

"Dude," Wyn said, appearing out onto the deck, "are you lost? What are you doing here?"

"Don't you read your texts? Come on, let's hit Cisco before the wind shifts, Bruh."

"One, I'm not your *bruh*, and two, I need food first. Oh, and Mom, can I take your car? Two hours max?" Then to Leo, Wyn said, "bagel?"

Sheri's mind was grinding and she was dying to ask Leo if his mother was there. Couldn't he just spare her and volunteer some information – any information at all? Sheri found herself studying Leo's face, his expression, for any sign of distress or unhappiness, but she didn't know his features well enough to tell. His only concern seemed to be hitting the waves. Or was he just anxious to get out of his house? Sheri couldn't stop her mind from reaching.

Trapped, was all Sheri could think as the two of them went back into the house for bagels and her keys. She couldn't even send herself to her room to sulk in private – how long did a toilet installation take anyway? And where was Cooper already off to that morning? At Black-Eyed Susan's for breakfast with his *wife*? Or having a romantic day for two? She felt her stomach go sour at the thought and a headache bloomed behind her eyes.

She had to get out of there and change the way her heart was beating. There were bikes in the shed – at least one had to be in decent enough shape and need only air in the tires. Just the thought of having a plan helped her blood start to move again, the congealing of it in her veins was making her lightheaded and nauseous.

She dragged herself out of the lounger feeling damp from the fog and took one last look at the sky for signs of it clearing before heading back into the house. With Wes still working in her bathroom, she had nowhere to hide. She couldn't busy herself in the kitchen making a big breakfast because Wyn already had her bagel and peanut butter to go and good luck to her if she should attempt to know what Tia wanted and how she'd want it.

She thought back to being a young mom with young kids – exhausting on multiple levels with all the stuff it came with: the cribs, highchairs, car seats, and toys, the diapers, the naps, snacks and sippy cups, the bad dreams and no sleep. But it all worked. She could control most of it, plan for it, rock away the sadness, kiss away the tears.

But this was next-level. The pit in her stomach of aloneness, of losing everyone from her days, from life as she'd known it. That balloon of basic joy that carried her, that she didn't know was everything, until so much went missing. Her husband, gone, her little girls grown up and gone, her parents vanishing in all the nameless ways things disappear.

She had Trudy. She'd change in Wyn's room then see about the bikes in the shed. She'd text her friend and ride to her house – they'd come up with something. Sheri heard her phone ping and let her hopes rise again, feeling rewarded for making plans, getting on with things rather than feeling sorry for herself. Although she still hated herself for the rise of hope that came. But it was Trudy. As if she'd summoned her.

> Griff's out fishing with his buddies – I'm not happy ☺ come play with me?!
>
> I was just about to hop on my bike and ride over ☺
>
> Bike?
>
> Wyn has my Bronco – maternal sacrifices never end
>
> Cu soon

Sheri was glad to hear Tia and Jackson awake and moving around so she could check in with them about Wes before she left. She knew they'd be happy to Uber anywhere they wanted to go if they weren't feeling the bikes in the shed as a desired mode of transportation.

They'd figure it out. As she was constantly being reminded. She found a small enough backpack to throw some essentials in and hoped Trudy didn't have a bougie day of shopping in mind.

She was grateful for her father's orderly racks in the shed and found the pump for the bike tires easily. Her heart tripped over itself choosing her mom's turquoise bike with the perfectly weathered basket on the handlebars. The seven-speed Chatham Beach Cruiser George had bought Rose years ago still looked new. Sheri remembered her mom wanting it so badly, even as a seventy-year-old lady, seeing herself as ever-young and able. Had Sheri ever even joined her mother on a bike ride? Maybe once? The girls would have been young teens and more than a handful – Sheri wouldn't have paid attention to much beyond keeping those two on the straight and narrow – especially summers on Nantucket where the rule of thumb always seemed to be *no rules!*

She walked it down the shell driveway before swinging her leg over to sit. Her first instinct was to hold her phone out and get a quick selfie to text her mom, but then she thought better of it, deciding it might either confuse Rose or maybe make her sad. Instead, she just put the phone in the basket and pedaled in the direction of Trudy's. At the bottom of Eel Point Road, Sheri triple-checked for cars before crossing Madaket Road onto the bike path.

Just before completely crossing to the path, Sheri caught Cooper's British Racing Green Range Rover turning right onto Eel Point. He wasn't alone. She missed the pedal, scraping her shin, and nearly spun out on a sandy patch before collecting herself and getting it together.

What a waste of one of the longest and most scenic sidepaths on Nantucket. Replaying her embarrassment and misery she'd missed most of the pond views and conservation land's rolling moors. Sweat prickled under her arms and beaded on her forehead – she would kill Trudy if she looked fresh and beautiful and wanted to take her to Topper's for lunch.

Chapter Thirty-One

STEPHANIE AND GRIFF LIVED in the highly coveted Cliff neighborhood of Nantucket, east of Eel Point and west of town. Sheri was grateful that the Madaket Road bike path connected seamlessly to Cliff and for the gorgeous views it allowed her. The grand homes and estates you saw first coming in on the ferry to the right of Brant Point Lighthouse were Cliff homes, quintessential summer houses in picturesque neighborhoods that seemed to have the best of Nantucket. It didn't have the booming surf of the south shore but Sheri could understand the allure of quieter white-sand north shore beaches, the calm of all that conservation land, plus its biking distance to town.

Trudy and Griff's house was to die for on a private shell lane off Cliff Road with its wrap-around porch behind a thick heirloom hedge of lavender-blue hydrangeas. Its cedar shingles had faded to the classic silver that on brighter days glinted like fish scales in the sun with white trim that popped and was the perfect contrast even on a foggy day. Every detail inside quietly claimed your attention – the wide-planked pine flooring, the white-washed shiplap walls and beamed ceilings were so like Trudy and Griffin – gorgeous, sophisticated, and categorically upscale yet perfectly casual and infinitely comfortable.

Sheri leaned her bike against the white porch, shrugged off her small pack, and wiped her forehead with the bottom of her tank top before taking the wide stairs two at a time. The sweat came fast without the breeze from riding to whisk the heat away and she was glad she'd had the foresight to pack her little sleeveless blue-and-white striped cotton dress for whatever the day held.

"Hello, Gorgeous," Trudy said to Sheri, who was feeling anything but.

"You stole my line, Tru, seriously, how do you manage to always look like the sun is trapped in your hair and the sky in your eyes? Even on this grey-lady day?" Just then, Ollie's Husky, Zuri, bounded into the room to greet her guest. Sheri got down on her knees to give the beautiful blue-eyed animal a proper hello. "Well, hello, *hello* there, Sweet Girl! Aren't you just the most lovely lady? And so polite ... Oh, Tru, she is just awesome, and these eyes are lethal ..." Sheri stood and scratched the top of Zuri's black and white head, then her silky ears while her tail seemed to curl even tighter in delight. "Don't tell me," Sheri said to the stunning animal sitting politely at her feet, "your daddy is still in bed."

"You got that right, which is exactly why we're going to steal her for a romp on Tupancy Links trail."

"Ooh, that sounds perfect. I love how dog friendly Nantucket is. And, hey, if we go for a swim later, I'll have done a triathlon today, ha!"

"If this fog ever lifts – I have my doubts about it today," Trudy said, without her usual light.

"Everything alright? Cloudy days don't usually get you down. You annoyed by Oliver sleeping in again or something?"

"Or something ... Griff's out with Noah and Mike doing some deep-sea fishing in Mike's new boat."

Sheri waited for more, but none was forthcoming. "And? It's not like it's their first rodeo. What am I missing?"

"I know. And you're right – I just have a weird feeling, you know?" Trudy said, brows furrowed and clouds scudding across her sky eyes.

"Have you been composing some new macabre tale? *Lost at Sea*? *Death Under Sail*? Come on, Tru. Let's go for that walk. Right, Zuri? *Who's a good girl*? Does she have a special water bowl I can tuck in my pack? Let's make tracks. No phones. And I can distract you with my own crap."

"Let me just leave a note for Oliver that we've kidnapped his dog."

∞

The trailhead was a short walk from Trudy's and the fog hung stubbornly over them. Sheri hoped it wouldn't completely swallow the day, that it might lift enough so they could enjoy the sweeping views from the Tupancy trails. It was crazy that just one mile from the bustle of town there was this seventy-four-acre chunk of conservation land sitting between Nantucket Harbor and Cliff Road. "What's the story behind this land again? I know it was a golf course but I forget the details."

"Right – it was called The Tupancy Links after Oswald Tupancy and was originally part of the Nantucket Golf Course as the first golf club on the island. It was only a nine-hole course that – get this – used to be mowed by two hundred sheep and fifty angora goats!"

"I love that. So organic, ha!"

"Right? So anyway, as golfing became more popular on the island, the course was expanded to eighteen holes. Then around 1950, Mr. Tupancy bought enough of the Nantucket Golf Course property to operate his own private nine-hole course. And by that time the rest of the course's original land was being converted to house lots. Mr. Tupancy ran his course for only a few years, then he and his wife, Sallie, donated the property to the Nantucket Conservation Foundation to prevent any more building. I mean, can you imagine if this was all built up and full of homes?"

"I'm glad at least some people back in the day had the foresight to preserve the precious landscape of this little island. Especially since people don't seem to be building just little summer cottages anymore. God, I just hate these showy properties with ten-thousand-square-foot main houses! And their multiple guest houses wrapped in multiple terraces, with their field-size lawns and flower beds, I can't!"

"Tell me how you really feel, Sher, ha! I hear you, of course, it's disgusting. But let's take a breath. Because we have *this*," Trudy said, stretching her arm over the expanse of pristine land. "Now I know we can't see much with this gray day but I can tell you what you're missing. They only mow once a year, early in the season, to allow all the native grasses and wildflowers to grow, flower, and seed all through the summer, fall, and early winter – how cool is that?"

"Sounds like the perfect way to maintain this unique habitat. I recognize the Queen Anne's lace and the sandplain grasses that look like what my mom planted, and of course the daisies ..."

"You got it, and the dominant grass in this area is called Little Bluestem – in late summer it'll have tall flowering stems that turn a gorgeous purplish-blue color in early fall. Then see that low ground cover over there? That explodes with bright-yellow flowers only in early summer, and then what's lost in the fog are thickets of bayberry, beach plum, and blueberry." Sheri was always blown away by her friend's knowledge of the natural world that surrounded her, the intimacy and sense of grandeur she felt for the smallest, simplest things. Sheri watched her as she piled her mane of strawberry blond curls on top of her head and whistled for Zuri who'd found a friend.

"So many doggies here," Sheri said, "they must love it so much – running free and with so many smells to investigate." Trudy seemed to be somewhere else and Sheri wondered why she was so worried about her husband – he was no stranger to being out on the water or deep-sea fishing, nor were the friends he was with – and fog was a given on Nantucket. "Okay, so tell me, on a super-clear day can you see Great Point Lighthouse from here?"

"On a crystal-clear day, yes. It's eight miles from where we're standing. I love the view of the church steeples from this perspective and the town clock ... and the way the whaling captains' mansions in town are silhouetted against the eastern horizon – it's just so timeless. But we certainly don't have that kind of clarity today."

"Clarity ... now there's a concept ..."

"Now you're the one being cryptic, what gives?"

Sheri took in a deep breath of the salty sweet heathland and sighed it out. "I just feel like my heart has been taking a beating lately I guess. Which sounds bratty and foolish even to my own ears. I mean look at where I am right now – it doesn't get any better than this. Well, if there were sun, that would be better, but I'm in my favorite place in the world, Tru, and my girls are here with me. Why can't I just be happy for that?"

"Aw, Sher, you *are* happy and grateful for those things, I *know* you. Maybe you don't realize what a toll your parents' situation is taking on you. I mean I know that even though we expect our parents to age at some point, and eventually leave us, it's an impossible thing to reconcile when you're in the crush of it. You remember when I lost my mom ... I couldn't get out of my own way, could barely see my own path anymore – it was like it didn't exist without her, like *I* didn't exist anymore. I know this is different, Sheri, that Alzheimer's is a hideous and cruel thing that will take her from you by degrees, that it's a brutally unfair thing. But I also know how strong you are."

"What if I'm tired of being strong, Trudy? What if my dad needs me and I just can't handle it? I've had to really force myself to call them some days, I'm so afraid of the progression of the disease. I hate myself for it. So weak. And then what if the one man I've opened up to since Tommy, the man who I was so certain felt the same way about me, is just opting out? Just gone? Even though he's right next door? Like literally. It just doesn't make sense. Because it made so much sense!"

"I feel like I missed something. I thought you two were getting close, that there was this simmering chemistry, did something happen? I mean your girls are here – he knows how important family is to you – maybe he's just giving you space?"

"I get that – but to completely ignore my text. I mean, it was just a *hi, I'm thinking about you* kinda text, but still. It doesn't make sense that he wouldn't respond. I mean, we had something ... I'm sure of it."

Sheri's face took on a dreamy look as she listed the things that came to mind, "He made me the best gin and tonics and French press coffee I've ever had, he's this bad-ass surgeon with a tender heart. And he has really fun taste in music. Those are meaningful things, right?" she asked her friend, looking up at her for validation. "And I taught him to paddleboard, which was flirty and fun, and he taught me how to be kinder to myself, which is huge. We had sunrises and secrets and my girls like him. Also huge. I mean, it felt like we were starting something, you know? But maybe he was just in vacation-mode, and in a heat-of-the-moment mindset or something ... I just don't know."

Sheri slowed her pace, lost in her tangle of thoughts. "*And* he was so great when Tia got sick – driving us to the hospital, sticking around through that, checking in the next day, he was amazing. But then *nothing*. Crickets. And my heart is folding. I know we've had to be discreet – but it kind of added to the fire, like we were sneaking, you know? I couldn't wait to see him again. And I haven't felt that way in a long time. And, no, Tommy doesn't count – he just can't count – I'm like damaged goods around him, not knowing which end is up or how I'm really feeling at all. Sex is one thing but it sure as hell isn't everything. It's just confusing with Tommy, so damn confusing to love someone and hate him at the same time – that can't be right. Especially since this conversation wasn't meant to be about him at all."

The long grasses swished against their legs as they walked and the sky remained a low ceiling of gray. Sheri had said so much she was half-afraid of how it all sounded, of what her friend was thinking.

"You know I love Tommy," Trudy said with a sigh, "but you two, unfortunately, especially given the number of years you have invested in him, weren't meant for forever. It's no one's fault when that happens sometimes. And I think maybe you're finally feeling closure with that, with him. Which is hard, I'm sure, but good and necessary. Do you think you could be rushing the moving-on thing? And maybe putting pressure on whatever's going on with you and Cooper? *Don't look at me like that!* With those eyebrows up to your hairline! I love you, Sheri, and Cooper seems awesome. Maybe give it space to breathe. I have to say, when you fall, you fall completely ..."

"Is there any other way?" Sheri said dreamily. A quick wind swept the fog bank away for just a minute, giving them a peek of the harbor in the distance, before the misty gray rolled back in again. That's how Sheri's mind felt, with just random bouts of clarity and vision.

"So where are you now, with Cooper I mean?" Trudy said.

"Well, he didn't return my last text. I've been tempted to text *everything ok?* But that might come across as naggy or needy. I want to let him know I'm concerned without having him think I'm asking *why hell the hell aren't you texting me back*? Which is, of course, exactly what I'm asking! The silence is killing me. Aaand apparently, his ex-wife is here now, so there's that!"

"Wait, what? You lost me."

"I lost me too. And I'm sick of losing me. And she's gorgeous. They just go together, anyone would think so. I mean, his going back to her obeys all the laws of nature."

"Sheri, *what* in the hell are you talking about? How do you know what she looks like for starters, and do you even know why she's here on-island? Why are you assuming they're back together, which is *nuts* by the way – why did you automatically go there?"

Before Sheri could confess to googling the ex-wife the other day and falling down that rabbit hole, Trudy was frantically fishing her dinging phone out of her back pocket. Her friend's restlessness was seeping into Sheri – maybe it was the weather but Trudy was definitely off, her typically carefree beauty was a mask of worry.

"It's Mike's wife, Sue, asking if I've heard from Griff. She's been trying to get a hold of Mike with no success." Trudy's fingers flew across the keyboard of her phone, her face a fall of emotions. Without looking up, she said, "See? I told you something was wrong – I could feel it. It's this unsettled weather, this fog that won't lift"

"Okay, okay, what's Sue saying – does she have any intel at all? What do you want to do?"

"She's saying that of course bluefish and stripers weren't enough for them and they wanted to go deeper for the big guys – bluefin tuna and white marlin – that they were headed at least fifteen miles out."

"Um, who's idea was that? It's been pea soup since this morning."

"Showing off for their buddy Noah I'm assuming, dragging him way out in Mike's fancy new boat, Jesus. I can just hear them – *aw, come on, men, we can catch the stripers any day right off Great Point – what we want are the monsters, like a one-hundred-pound mako shark*. I have this pit in my stomach, Sheri, and I don't know if I'm more angry or scared!"

"So, we don't know what the weather's like fifteen miles offshore, right? Could it be better than it is here? And which direction are we talking – southeast? I know nothing about deep-sea fishing, Tru."

∞

After zooming up and down the open grassy trail, alternately playing with the other dogs and racing back to check on her humans, Zuri seemed to decide to stick by their sides. Animals with their sixth sense, Sheri thought, were amazing. "Sue says they were talking about Gordon's Gully, twelve miles southwest of here. I've heard of that," Trudy was saying – as much to herself as to Sheri, "I think you can get there either through Muskeget Channel or through the cut between

Nantucket and Tuckernuck Island. But Muskeget can have some pretty huge standing waves when you have wind opposing the tide, so you have to pay attention to that. And there are sandbars that can move around a huge amount in that area year to year so you cannot rely on your charts. Also it can get to be very foggy in the worst places, even if the rest of the island is clear. Which it's not!"

"How do you know all that? And what do you want to do?"

"I'm married to a boat guy, that's how. And a thrill seeker. So, really, you'd think I'd be used to his shenanigans. I don't know what's wrong with me – hormones maybe – does it ever end with the hormones?"

"Not according to Rose. Her upper lip was beading-up into her seventies – damn hot flashes – not looking forward to *that*!"

"My mom didn't really have hot flashes," Trudy said, "and they say it's hereditary so maybe I'll be lucky in that."

"Of course – you'll just get all dewy and glowy and be as beautiful as ever while I'll be walking around with sweat dripping between my boobs and mopping my face." Sheri was glad to have gotten a laugh out of Trudy, even if it was just a momentary diversion from her friend's worry.

"And what lovely boobs they are, Sher, I'll always envy you that."

"Not when they're down to my belly button you won't. It really is lovely out here, Tru, in this peaceful wide open space with all this long, lush grass and so many wildflowers – only a mile from town teeming with people taking in the charm of Nantucket – a completely different vibe. You have the best of both worlds here in your Cliff neighborhood."

"Agreed. We'd toyed with Tom Nevers back in the late 90s but I'm glad Griffin pushed for this. It really is ideal for us and not awful for Ollie to get to Cisco or Nobadeer to surf." Trudy looked back down at her phone as it pinged, her brow furrowing at the sound. "Speak of the devil. Sir Oliver has risen. Wondering where I am. Texting from his bed no doubt or he'd have seen my note, that kid, I tell you. Looks like he's been in touch with Wyn – apparently the surf wasn't as great as reported and they're thinking of meeting up at the brewery. Of course he wants his dog back."

"Of course he does, ha, I bet Zuri is quite the chick-magnet – everybody loves a Husky. Hey, why don't we tag along, it's the perfect brewery day."

"Which means everyone and his brother will be there, you know that, right? It'll be a scene."

"Maybe just what we need. Unless you don't want to go? Are you terribly concerned about your wayward fisherman? Is he usually in closer touch on these deep-sea jaunts? I can't picture him having his phone at the ready as he's hauling in a big fish. I picture him more as the phone-in-the-bottom-of-his-bag kinda guy, I'll see ya when I see ya."

That smoothed out Trudy's furrowed brow and a laugh like little bells tumbled out. "You're exactly right. I guess getting that text from Sue just kind of messed with me, like it added to whatever weird thing I'm feeling, you know? Let's go to Cisco, can't feel anything but fine at the brewery. Right, Z? Let's go find your dad. That always sounds funny, calling Ollie a dad."

"Is he a good dog-daddy? That's a big responsibility, I'm actually surprised he was up for it."

"I was too. Especially after he and Aria split up and she took the dog they rescued together. He really loved King – it was a double loss, not a great time for him at all. I mean I was never totally on board with them adopting a dog together in the first place – that's a huge deal! But it was the pandemic ... and they sort of ended up living together by default. I think relationships and things took on a different meaning during that time. Anyway – Aria wasn't leaving King behind."

"Ouch – that was nice of him to let her take him."

"It was, but I think King was more Aria's dog anyway. She was the one who took him to play at the beach, took him running with her – she had more freedom to do that with her job. Anyway – Oliver could barely take care of himself when things ended between them, it wasn't good and we were worried about him. But once he pulled himself together, he realized he wanted a dog – wanted to rescue an animal, knowing how they rescue you right back. He got lucky with Zuri, she's a very sweet dog – you never know with a rescue."

"Well, good for him. And it will definitely teach him responsibility. A twenty-something man having to take care of someone other than himself isn't the worst thing in the world. And then there's the chick-magnet thing too …"

The ladies reversed their direction on the links trail back to Trudy's to pick up Oliver and head to the brewery. It would be impossible not to shake off their collective moodiness surrounded by happy people and reggae.

Chapter Thirty-Two

A LINE WAS ALREADY snaking past the merch tent at Cisco Brewers to get in which was no surprise. It gave Sheri time to catch up with Oliver and to wonder for the hundredth time why Wyn hadn't fallen madly in love with him. With perennially tousled hair the color of sand and his mother's green-blue eyes, he was gorgeous by anyone's standards. He was tall like his parents and the kind of accidental hot-fit you get just from doing what you love.

Sheri tried to picture Oliver's job but anything that fell under the heading of business and sales was really too broad for her to nail down. Double that confusion for anything with computers and software. Did any of it actually mean anything anyway? Careers and focus seemed to change with the breeze and no one seemed to stick with a thing or a place for long. Oliver was bright and still young – he would do ten other things, and always make the bucks enough to keep him in surfboards and skis. Wyn was not a whole lot different and would always find a way to make the money to buy the toys and take the trips.

Finally past the gatekeepers with their neon I'm-old-enough-to-drink bracelets in place, they were free to roam the cobblestoned terraces of the outdoor beer garden, listen to the band and dance if the spirit moved them. Or wait in line at one of the food trucks for oysters or dumplings or lobster rolls or pizza and fries – the place practically begged you to stay for hours. Sheri's heart skipped with a familiar joy at the sight of Wyn's sunny profile holding her favorite drink, the Madaket Mule, laughing at whatever Leo was saying. Leo – in that moment looked so much like his dad it gave Sheri a jolt. She was on her way over to Wyn before she lost her in the gathering crowd when she was stopped dead in her tracks. Cooper was coming up beside Leo at the same time, with Leo's mother right beside him.

"What are we drinking?" Trudy said, having materialized beside her after stopping at the Millie's truck first for their famous street corn. Sheri immediately changed her direction and steered her friend toward the outermost bar by the stage. "What are you doing –" Trudy started to say.

"Keep walking, I need a Dark 'n Stormy, stat."

"Wait – that was Wyn – where are we going and why are you pushing me?" Trudy said, craning her neck to get another look while Sheri kept her hand on her friend's back to keep her moving toward the opposite bar. "Ooh that's Leo with her, *wow*, he is hot isn't he - I mean, you know if I were like twenty-five. OH, wait, that's *Cooper* and—"

"Shh, Trudy, shut it, my God."

"Oh shit. That's the ex? Shit, doll, do they make couples, entire *families*, any more beautiful?"

"Not helping! What am I going to do? This is beyond awkward ..."

"Chill, alright? Let's get drinks first, then think. Where'd Ollie go – did he run into someone he knows?"

"Probably – did you think he was gonna hang with us?" But before Trudy could respond, they both noticed that Oliver had found Wyn and was now standing with the expanding group that included Leo's family of three. "Jesus – how can we avoid them now?"

"Why would you want to? Come on, pull up your big-girl panties and let's go. You have to move past this one way or another – find out what's really going on."

Sheri grabbed Trudy's arm as she started in Wyn's direction, "Stop, wait – let's get another drink first"

"Really? You think double-fisted is a mature look?"

"I'm not ready!" Sheri's pleas went ignored and before she knew it they were standing in front of Wyn, Leo, Oliver, Cooper, and the ex-wife.

"Mom!" Wyn said, embracing her, "and Auntie Tru! Yay, you're *here* – how fun is this?"

Sheri tried not to look in Cooper's direction but the harder she tried not to, the faster her eyes went straight to his. It was like in a movie when everyone around them was frozen and only she and Cooper were in real time.

Their eyes locked on each other and Sheri could neither look away nor care who else might notice. She stared into his eyes and saw that they were a flat hazel instead of the fiery amber she remembered, the light had gone out of them in the same way the sun had forsaken the day. She had so many questions. But all she saw was the way he was picking up her discomfort and mirroring it back to her. His eyes took on a sheen – maybe tears gathering behind them – making them look like the surface of some river. Was he trying to tell her something? She had no idea what it meant. Only that it meant something.

Complicated and painful feelings were pinwheeling through her. She didn't think she could stand there and be introduced to this woman, this beautiful, vulnerable looking woman who was at one time this man's wife. Sheri decided instead on the willful suspension of disbelief, like in a book when you wanted so badly to believe in a thing despite logic and rationale. That regardless of the way things looked, Cooper just couldn't be back together with his wife. No, for now she would choose the intentional avoidance of critical thinking for the sake of her own heart. .

"Cooper, great to see you again," Trudy was saying, pulling Sheri from her movie reel. And then to the woman beside him, "Hi I'm Trudy."

"Lauren Madden, it's a pleasure to meet you." *Lauren.* The name suited her, Sheri thought, sophisticated, self-possessed, but with a shadow of unveiled emotion that lurked behind her eyes. Strong but with some endearing quality in need of protection.

Taking in her white linen shirt with cuffs rolled precisely and slim white jeans, Sheri felt silly in her little dress that was really more of a beach coverup. Though stunning, Lauren's hair was a color that could only have come from a salon with its rich layering of golds and platinum that fell in rolled waves to just above her shoulders. Gold jangled at her wrists and encircled her throat, even woven into the sandals on her feet.

"Is this your first visit to Nantucket?" Trudy asked, preserving the flow of conversation.

"Yes, actually," Lauren said with a wooden smile, "I didn't grow up getting to do the island-beachy-thing. My parents brought me to Europe most summers of my childhood. For the art, architecture, culture and history, and all of that sort of thing." Sheri watched her as she spoke, chin angled high and with a cartoonishly large purse dangling from her elbow that cost more than Sheri's first car. She'd be used to elegant people in elegant clothes having stimulating conversations. She'd probably been raised in a world of restrained wealth where champagne fizzed quietly and where dignity was as essential as the right alma mater.

"Oh, you must think that sounds impossibly stuffy," Lauren continued, with a high laugh and tight face, "but there really is no comparison, of course. Don't get me wrong, your little island here is lovely. Or I should say it *would* be, out from under this fog ..."

Sheri was caught between wanting to talk to the kids and learning more about this creature beside Cooper, who she couldn't decide if she was taking back what was hers or just trying to insert herself into his good time. Either way sucked. Sheri discreetly wound herself beyond Trudy and the other grownups to stand by Wyn and Ollie, curious about Leo's place among the three of them.

Surfing bonded people. Whether it sucked or was ripping, it gave the three of them plenty to talk about and drink about. Sheri didn't feel like she belonged in that conversation either. And then Tia was texting her, pissed that everyone was there but her, like it had been arranged specifically to exclude her. When, Sheri wondered, did they grow up for real? She texted Tia back to get an Uber and join them already – it wasn't like they'd be leaving any time soon.

Then glancing at Trudy, Sheri tried to gauge her mindset. She knew Griff's silence was clawing at her peace of mind, despite trying to tell herself it was nothing out of the ordinary, but Trudy was putting on a good show. She really was a spectacular conversationalist and knew just what to ask a person to make them feel important. It was a gift, one that transferred easily to her writing. Strangers and readers alike felt uniquely chosen, as if Trudy were speaking only to them. Sheri couldn't tell if she wanted to be rescued.

It became a non-issue as Lauren and Cooper walked off in the direction of the Lobster Trap food truck and Trudy turned back to Sheri. She was consulting her phone and the lines rose up again on her forehead. It didn't look like it was going to be a good time to pump Trudy for intel on Cooper and the wife.

"This is not good," Trudy said, "Sue is telling me that the Coast Guard has had no sign of them. It's like they fell off the grid – what's going on?"

The Coast Guard? When or how had they become involved? The last thing Sheri wanted to do was worry Trudy even more with her own growing concern. And not knowing the first thing about boats and their navigational equipment or what could cause a failing there, Sheri was hard-pressed with what to say. "Could there be some kind of malfunction with their communication or navigation equipment? I mean, I have no idea how these things work or what could go wrong, but stuff malfunctions, right? And with the fog so thick and visibility so poor, couldn't they be right there but invisible? So to speak?"

"But why aren't they responding to texts or calling?" Trudy said, hysteria creeping into her voice, "Too much of this doesn't make sense if everything is just hunky-dory."

"Okay, okay, what time did they head out this morning and how long were they expected to be gone?" Sheri asked, if for no other reason than to stall the panic and to gain information. "I mean, talk to me like I'm five – I just have no idea how these things are supposed to go, like do they ever stay out longer than expected, could the guys be back already and slinging beers at Brotherhood blowing off their wives?" Judging from the look on Trudy's face, NO.

"They left at the crack of dawn, Sheri, the big fish are way more active in the low light and there's less competition while everyone else is still in bed. That gets them back by one o'clock, latest."

Sheri looked at her watch, it was barely two o'clock in the afternoon – was this really a big deal, what was she missing? And why the hell was the Coast Guard already involved?

"Sue's husband Mike is OCD about his fishing trips," Trudy said, as if reading Sheri's mind, "and more communicative than Griffin. So if she senses a red flag, it means something. Oh, and Mike's brother-in-law is in the Coast Guard. Sue's not shy about calling in favors."

"Okay – but what about radar? This Mike guy sounds pretty detail-oriented so I'm assuming that firstly, this is a decent-size boat, and second, that it has radar or GPS or whatever it's supposed to have, right?"

"I'm assuming that also. All I know is that it's a Down East Cruiser, maybe thirty-five feet, nothing outrageous. Was the radar functioning? I sure as hell hope so – especially since they went out in *this*. Were its cables corroded and it stopped working? Unlikely since it's *new*. Did they hit something and sink? Was there some huge swell twelve miles offshore? Are they in the life raft halfway to Florida? Are they all *dead*? I thought being here would take my mind off this, but the more time that goes by ... Sheri, I think I need to go home or, I don't know, get in touch with the harbor master or go to Sue's – I need to do *something*!"

"Sure, sure, of course – I'll catch a ride back with Wyn. Unless you want me to come with?" Sheri was concerned about her friend's uncharacteristic distress, she was the levelheaded one who usually didn't get bogged down or emotional. "Trudy, are you okay to drive? And, wait – what does Oliver know?"

"He knows nothing. Why haven't I kept him up to speed? What am I doing, Sheri? We're usually pretty transparent with each other. Look at him – having a good time over there with your daughter and Leo – I don't want to bring him down, you know, stress him out if everything's fine, you know?"

"Jesus – why do we go to such lengths to protect our children, our *adult children*? When does that stop? When we could and should be able to lean on them sometimes, right? I totally hear you, I do the same thing with my kids. God forbid we should trouble them, say anything that might be hard or painful, why do we do that?"

"Mom genes, I guess," Trudy said shrugging her shoulders and slurping the last of her drink.

"But are we really doing them any favors? Coddling them? And I keep making that mistake over and over – like when I didn't tell them about me and Tommy struggling. Wyn still has a hard time taking things I say at face value. And here I go again with my mother – have I told the girls the full deal with that? Or have I whitewashed things again? Sorry – this isn't about me, I'm getting off topic. What is your heart telling you to do, Tru? I mean Ollie is stronger than you think and I don't think it would be a bad idea to confide what you know. You two are in this together, can be there for each other. And you know what? Our kids *need* to do that, be that for us. They need know that they can help us, that they have something to offer. What are we protecting them from anyway? Reality? They're adults!"

"You're right, you're right. And it's not like there aren't other brewery afternoons in his future, for God's sake. Okay, I'm gonna grab him and go – I'll text you when I know something."

Fogged In

Sheri gave her friend a quick hug then watched as she parted the crowd to claim her son and his dog. Neither would be happy to leave the energy of the place and its chill reggae mood. Sheri felt the bottom of her stomach drop out as worst-case scenarios edged in.

Chapter Thirty-Three

SHERI SUDDENLY FELT ALONE in the happy sway of people. She could hang out with the kids – the brewery was nothing if not a family assortment variety pack – and Tia and Jackson were on their way. It wasn't necessarily that she felt like she cramped their style as much as feeling like an extra. And dragging an anchor with her worry about Trudy and the status of Giffin. There really wasn't space in all that for thoughts of Cooper and what the hell was going on with him and his ex-wife. Although she'd be lying to herself if she said it wasn't a stone in her gut. But she knew if she really examined the pain, she'd have to face the naked truth.

That she felt more than a little in love with him. And that while they'd shared such visceral moments of connection, he must not feel the same way. That though she'd been certain he did, and that despite her seeing a future as clear as crystal without even looking for it, the vision was melting away, vanishing into a misty fog that had her questioning whether any of it had been real at all.

Unrequited love was the worst feeling – like having your skin set on fire. One you couldn't run from. One you had to sit with until the burning stopped. Moving back around your days in rote fashion with a new numbness until it faded. And she didn't agree at all with that shit making you stronger for the next time – when what it really did was thicken the scar tissue to keep future hard stuff out. Feeling was less of an option with everything calloused over. She'd been there before.

"Mom!" Tia called out, "there you are. Where's Wyn? Oh – never mind, I see her. I thought Ollie was here, I'm dying to see him."

Sheri climbed out of the narrative she'd indulged herself in and lifted the corners of her mouth into some semblance of a smile. "Hi, guys, you made it."

"Yeah, no easy feat! Ubers do *not* want to come all the way out to Eel Point Road, I can tell you that," Tia said, pinning her mother with a sanctimonious look.

"I bet. Sorry about that. Life with one vehicle – as you'd say, *first-world probs*. You're here now, that's what matters. Let me buy you two a drink. I'm getting in line – ask Wyn and Leo if they need another round, okay?" Tia rolled her eyes as she went.

"What's the matter, Mom, you seem kind of, I don't know, off?"

Sheri forced a light into her eyes she didn't feel and told Tia she was fine. She thought of leaving it at that but then shamelessly borrowed Trudy's drama as explanation and told them about Griffin being off the grid, about the boat he was on disappearing into thick air.

"Wait – Jackson, did you hear that? Mom, our Uber driver was saying something about a missing fishing boat – do you think he was talking about Griffin's boat? I thought he had a sailboat."

Sheri's face fell again – could this really be happening? She was almost sure there'd be some logical explanation. "Seriously? What did he say exactly? Now I'm starting to freak out. I could almost picture Griff and his buddies kicking back at Brotherhood or Rose & Crown with the boat safely rocking on its mooring. I wonder if it's the same fishing boat? Are you sure he was talking about off Nantucket and not the Cape or somewhere else? Did he say *Nantucket Sound*? Because Griff and his buddies were supposedly about fifteen miles south of the island."

"Tia was on her phone and not really listening," Jackson said, "I don't remember him saying anything about the Sound – just off

Nantucket. Does this happen a lot? I mean with the fog such a presence here?"

"You know, I'm not really sure, Jackson, I know most boats have radar but I've also learned from Trudy that even radar can be skewed in fog. Add to that, severe thunderstorms can materialize out of nowhere out on the water. So I imagine high wind and waves are a whole separate issue."

"Mom – Jackson's dad has a fancy fishing boat in the Hamptons, I'm sure he knows all this."

"I don't know if I'd call it *fancy* but it's a decent size. So, yeah, I know a little bit about it. I know some guys like to fish in weather like this because the stripers are more active closer to the surface in the low light of fog. And that ground fog is different from advection fog, or *sea fog*, which is formed when warm, wet air flows over colder surface water – and can hang around even in strong winds."

"Jackson, stand in line for the drinks with Mom, you can tell her all about it *and* be useful," Tia said with a loving shove in the direction of the bar.

"She's a peach, isn't she?" Sheri said.

"A woman who knows what she wants and that she wants it now," Jackson laughed as he and Sheri took their place in the short line. "So, as I was saying, radar on boats does show other vessels nearby, but the point is that radar is only as good as its operator; that the accuracy of the image on the screen can be affected by distortion, clutter, and multiple echoes; and that the positions of targets must be manually recorded over time to determine their true location and progress relative to your boat."

"Wow, I'm impressed. So, you've been out with your dad I'm assuming."

"Many times. Not as much now, but growing up, yes. And in the summertime you see everything, let me tell you. All kinds of pleasure crafts being driven by inexperienced mariners, so when a fog rolls in unexpectedly, lots of vacation boaters get stuck. Sure, they can blindly follow their GPS back to the harbor but if they don't have radar or if they don't know how to properly operate it, they can't tell if there are other boats in the area until they're right in front of them or on top of them. The fog hides things for sure."

"I'm listening, but pause for a sec and look at the board so you know what you want," Sheri said, as they inched closer. "I can personally recommend the Blueberry Lemonade – their Triple Eight vodka is phenomenal – and the Nantucket Red – Wyn loves the Madaket Mule and sometimes the Pineapple Express, and well, I'm sticking with my Dark 'N Stormy."

Sheri was anxious to get back to their conversation, Jackson was so knowledgeable and she was intrigued and feeling some vicarious thrill thinking about Griff, Mike, and Noah – willing them to be okay but also wondering if they were having some wild adventure out there. A frenzy of emotions rolled through her and she hated to admit that she craved the softening that the booze provided – the blurring of the lines between panic and excitement. Griffin just had to be okay, it couldn't go any other way.

Navigating the crowd with five drinks between them, Jackson continued. "Of course you've heard of the Andrea Doria, right? One of the most famous shipwrecks right here in these waters."

"Heard of it, yes, ashamed to say I don't know the details. Enlighten me. Wait – let's move our little party over there away from the band, I want to hear this story."

"Yay, drinks!" Tia said, "why are we moving? What story?"

"I was about to tell your mom about the Andrea Doria – we got on the subject of shipwrecks," Jackson said.

"Shipwrecks?" Wyn said, "Is this about Griff? Tia was just telling us –Jesus, Mom, is Griff's boat missing?"

Sheri filled them in on what little was known about the status of Griff's friend's boat, then checked her phone in case there were any updates from Trudy. There was nothing. She wasn't sure if this was a scenario where no news was good news. It didn't feel that way. But part of her still believed that Griff and the guys just had to be alright – they were accomplished sailors and fishermen experienced in the Nantucket waters and no strangers to dicey weather.

"I wish we had more information. Jackson was just telling me about boats becoming disoriented in the fog and vacationing boaters who don't always know what they're doing and we landed on the Andrea Doria which sunk about forty-five miles off the coast of Nantucket back in the fifties."

"Whoa, really? I feel like I've heard of that but I know nothing about it," Wyn said.

"It was a pretty big deal," Jackson said, "for two massive ocean liners to collide in the fog like that. We're talking like seven-hundred feet long."

"How does that even happen?" Wyn asked, taking a big sip of her drink.

"Apparently both ships were approaching each other from opposite directions off Nantucket," Jackson said, mimicking the collision course with his hands coming together, "it was late at night and it was dark – but neither ship had slowed in the fog. By the time they saw each other's lights, it was too late. The other ship's bow crashed into Andrea Doria's starboard gauging a huge section of its hull – that thing was going down."

Sheri had been quiet mostly while Jackson told the tale of the sinking of the Andrea Doria off Nantucket. It was morbidly fascinating – in the same way having a cozy movie night watching *Titanic* was. Which was only okay with miles and years of separation between tragedy and real life. This story had nothing to do with Griff, Noah, and Mike – they were on a fishing boat in the middle of the day. There was just no way their boat would have sunk. She noticed the sky was darkening with heavier storm clouds and that the eerie puce light was freaking her out. She checked her phone again – still nothing more from Trudy. A stomachache was starting down low.

A deafening crack of thunder made them all jump. The skies opened up and poured out a wind-driven sideways rain. Carefree, booze-buffered brewery people threw back their drinks and ditched their plastic cups in the barrels, squealing and laughing as they ran to their cars.

Chapter Thirty-Four

THE RAIN LET UP some on the drive back to the house and Sheri was glad to be home. She was suddenly hungry despite the pit that hunched in her stomach. The kids wanted to go downtown and keep the vibe alive – Tia volunteered to be the designated driver. Sheri wanted only to heat up some Gifford's chowder and curl up on the couch and watch the storm beyond the slider over the water. She needed to call Trudy – she would, she had to – but in that moment she chose to believe that Griffin was safe and sound, with simply a lapse in communication.

She was awakened by the room flooding with pink light. It was just after five o'clock the next morning and she was under a blanket on the living room couch. She was still in that euphoric place of a dream, caught in some filmy rapture of having been beside someone, barely touching, but with a vibration so strong it thrummed through her. His face wasn't clear, but the forcefield of longing was. Her desire to return to the dream was stronger than trying to work back why she was waking up on the couch. But the feeling started to vanish like mist as the room glowed brighter with the incandescent shimmer of morning like the inside of a slipper shell.

She sat up and the questions filtered in. What day was it? How had she slept through the kids coming home? *Had the kids come home?*

Was Griffin home safe? Or still missing? Her heart picked up pace in a rattled rhythm and she was terrified to look down at her phone. But staying in that place of ignorance was neither a temptation nor a possibility anymore.

Her phone on the coffee table in front of her lay mute, having died at some point in the night. She threw the blanket off – first to look out the window to see if the Bronco was in the driveway, *check*, then hurried to her bedroom to plug her phone into the charger. She figured she'd hit the bathroom while the phone booted back up. Her parents' bathroom, with the new toilet. Yesterday seemed like a long time ago – when Wes unwittingly sucker-punched her with his news of Cooper's ex-wife being back in the fold.

Yesterday, when Griffin was happily fishing with buddies instead of missing at sea.

She brushed her teeth and washed her face before going back to look at her phone. There were three text messages and two missed calls. She opened everything up immediately to avoid playing games with herself. There was a text from Wyn from last night telling her not to wait up, then a text from Trudy telling her to call ASAP, then the missed voicemail from Trudy, and finally a text from Cooper.

She could feel her heart beating in her throat as a labyrinth of emotions rushed in. She pulled up Trudy's voicemail and sat on the edge of the bed, grateful she was alone and wouldn't have to guard her expression. The voicemail was a broken and garbled recording – Trudy must have been in a low-service area when she called. Sheri strained to hear the words and make sense of them, but after replaying the message four times she still didn't have clear answers. She caught phrases like *storm swell* and *trouble* and *rescue attempt* that made her skin prickle with goosebumps and her blood seem to sour.

She called Trudy back right away but it went immediately to voicemail. Driving straight to her friend's house was all she could think to do. She threw on some clothes, grabbed her keys, and wasn't even to the bottom of her front porch steps when Cooper rounded the corner and it hit her that she hadn't opened his text. She looked at him like a deer in the headlights as he talked. When she finally tuned into what he was saying, about his buddy, Noah, being on the boat with Griffin and Mike, he was steering her to her Bronco saying he was going with her. She'd completely forgotten about Cooper and Noah's friendship.

Sheri didn't say a word as Cooper climbed into the passenger seat and she backed down the driveway but inside her brain was on overdrive. She let him talk as they made it out to Madaket Road on the way to Cliff. She wasn't even sure why she was going to Trudy's when most likely the house would be empty.

Where did you even go while your husband was apparently lost at sea – where was the homebase for something like that? But on she drove, trying to focus on Cooper's words – about how odd it all was with three veteran mariners. That it wasn't like they were inexperienced yahoos out for just a good time, they were serious fishermen, what could have happened …

"Weather doesn't actually discriminate though, Dr. Madden – I mean Mother Nature isn't out there saying, *well these three guys have caught these beautiful marlin, they obviously know what they're doing. It just wouldn't be right to swallow them in a fog or to let my twelve-foot waves take them out.*"

"So, I'm Doctor Madden now?"

"Well, it's not like we really know each other, right? I mean who even are you?" All she could think was how well she thought she knew him, recognizing and appreciating his ability to listen when she spoke. How he'd seemed to hear her and respond in kind – was it all an act? She felt so played, so stupid! But it actually felt good to be angry instead of sad, it always did. Fuck that and fuck him – who did he think he was?

"What are you talking about, Sheri?" Cooper said.

"Seriously? Well, if you can't figure that out for yourself, then you're not as smart as I thought you were. You're not anything that I thought you were." Cooper's eyes fell to his hands in his lap.

They rode in silence and the orange glow of the rising sun was a contradiction to the dark mood. There were no other vehicles on the road, it was barely seven o'clock in the morning, and Sheri felt like they were in the Twilight Zone. Nothing felt real, especially the fact that Cooper was sitting beside her, close enough for her to smell his soap. The greatest indignity was what his proximity still did to her.

She couldn't decide what she wanted more – to pound the steering wheel and scream, or to have him reach over and give her thigh a gentle squeeze that would leave a trail of heat even when his hand was back in his own lap.

"May I?" Cooper asked, reaching to turn on the radio, "there might be news." He found 97.7, ACK-FM then clicked back and forth between that and Nantucket Public Radio at 89.5 until finally they heard a news report. Sheri felt a cold sweat start and pulled off the road and turned the radio up so they could listen with their full attention.

Three fishermen were rescued approximately twenty miles off the southeast shore of the island early this morning when their forty-five-foot vessel sank. Coast Guard Station Brant Point along with a Coast Guard helicopter from Air Station Cape Cod responded to the area around four forty-five this morning and found that the forty-five-foot fishing vessel – Night Trawler out of Nantucket – was long gone and its crew was in the water without life jackets hanging onto a Nantucket Shoals data buoy. According to Coast Guard Brant Point BM2, Charles Eaton, there was no sign of the vessel when they arrived on-scene.

Eaton said that the responding Coast Guard crews determined the safest option was to drop the basket from the MH-60 helicopter and deploy a rescue swimmer to get the three fishermen onto the aircraft, rather than take them aboard Station Brant Point's forty-seven-foot motor lifeboat. The three men were taken to Hyannis for medical care.

It has not yet been determined why the recreational fishing vessel sank in the waters off Nantucket, but that the thick fog was most likely a factor as well as the infamous Nantucket Shoals which is a vast area of shallow and constantly shifting bottom that extends twenty-three miles east and forty miles southeast of the island. Eaton said the Coast Guard was alerted to the situation when one member of the Night Trawler crew set off an EPIRB (emergency position indicating radio beacon), which provided the rescue crew with their location.

"Their properly registered EPIRB was invaluable for the rescue of these three fishermen," said Coast Guard Lt. Cmdr. Christine DeWick, search and rescue coordinator for the First Coast Guard District. "This positive outcome demonstrates the importance of maintaining vital lifesaving equipment onboard your vessel."

Eaton added that the crew from Station Brant Point recovered a few of the Night Trawler's fenders, which they believe the fishermen had also been clinging to in the water while the rescue crews headed for the scene. The helicopter team later dropped an inflatable to the fishermen for them to hang on to until they could be hoisted up into the aircraft.

"I have so many questions," Sheri said, as anxiety lifted off of her like dandelion fluff.

"This is great news," Cooper said, exhaling, his eyes brightening as he turned to her.

"So they're fine you think? No mention of any life-threatening injuries or anything? This is just so *crazy*," Sheri said, not giving him time to respond. "No lifejackets? What's up with that? And the boat *sunk*? How does that *happen* with three veteran mariners, as you said? I'm just so confused – so they'd been out there like twenty-four hours then, right? When do you think the boat sank? How long were they out there clinging to a weather buoy? Do you think they had to fend off sharks? Damn, the stories they must have ..."

Cooper waited a beat in case there was more. "Are you done?" he said with a smile in his voice.

While Sheri considered the question, her phone trilled with a call from Trudy. Glad she'd pulled off the road, Sheri asked right away if she could put her on speaker, that Cooper was in the car with her. He leaned in to listen – wherever Trudy was calling from, it was still a lousy connection. She was crying, that much Sheri could tell, which made Sheri cry too, tears of gratitude and enormous relief. As Trudy relayed the same basic story they'd heard on the radio, she got more and more emotional. She'd of course been awake since her husband had set off yesterday before dawn, having imagined the worst-case scenario for the better part of all those hours. Thank God she'd had Oliver.

"I just knew something was wrong," Trudy was saying, "he could have died! They all could have *drowned*! They should never have gone out in that terrible visibility – I'm so angry with him, and with Mike for that shit decision."

There it was again, anger trumping sadness. It helped! Sheri listened to her friend, let her vent, and tried to soothe, getting her to concentrate on the fact that all three of them were alright. Her eyes met Cooper's. They were filled with more emotion than she thought he was capable of. His hazel-gold eyes held a bigger story. He was not just some emotionally impotent, medical professional out for a good time that she'd tried to convince herself of. She couldn't tear her eyes from his.

Sheri couldn't breathe. Trudy was saying something about being on her way to Hyannis to see Griffin, Of course. Sheri didn't hear much else before the call dropped and Sheri lowered the phone to her lap. She was caught in the force field that whirred between her and Cooper. In that moment she'd forgive him everything -- the ghosting, the pretending they'd never had anything -- if he'd change his mind right now and choose *her*.

He raised his hand to touch her neck under her hair, his thumb a feather touch on her cheek. He looked into one eye and then the other before landing his gaze on her mouth. At once he was the same person she thought he was – attentive, listening, staying for the whole story.

"Why? Why can't we have this?" Sheri whispered, it taking everything she had just to form the words. She knew she should pull away.

"What are you talking about, Sheri? Have you changed your mind? Because—"

"Changed *my* mind? What about *yours*? You're the one who hasn't been answering my texts, just nothing – as if we'd never had anything between us!"

Cooper pulled away, pain and confusion darkening his features. "Sheri, you're back with Tommy now, how could I possibly come between that?"

"I'm WHAT? Don't you mean you're back with Lauren now? Why are you putting this on me? I don't know where you're getting your information but …"

"From your daughter? And then I remembered seeing you both out on your deck that night, when the girls arrived, you looked –"

"My *daughter*? Which daughter and what in God's name did she tell you?"

"Tia told me that you and Tommy were working things out, that your relationship was stronger than ever …"

Sheri sat back like the wind had been knocked out of her. What in the actual hell was going on … her mind was a typhoon of confusion. The parent trap.

"And you seriously thought I'd take Tommy back? Just like that? After you and I –"

"I struggled with it, Sheri, believe me. But when someone's kid, *your* kid, tells me something, I take it as gospel. You four were a family! And if your kids, no matter how old they are, could have that back, I'd never be the reason you don't get to."

Dumbfounded by this new information, Sheri couldn't bring a single thing into focus. A barrage of thoughts and questions fought for space inside her. She leaned forward in her seat to face Cooper. "But what about you and Lauren? I thought— I mean you two are –"

"We two are what? You can't possibly think that we –"

"Wait – you mean to tell me you're *not* back together?"

Cooper looked at her like she was a patient who'd wandered away from the psych ward. Then shook his head without ever breaking eye contact with her. "Where in the world did you get that idea? Do not tell me Leo said any such thing – because as much as he thinks he'd like us to be a family again, he knows better. He genuinely understands that as much as we each love our son, we work much better as separate parents."

Sheri scanned through the images in her mind of Cooper and Lauren the past few days and honestly couldn't come up with anything that screamed romance or intimacy. Then she remembered her dear plumber's little bomb. "Wes! It was Wes the plumber who told me!"

"What exactly did he tell you?"

Sheri thought back to the conversation they'd had in her bathroom, but all she could remember was him telling her that Cooper's wife was there at the house She must have filled in the blanks, created the whole horrible narrative on her own. "You know – I can't even remember. He just dropped it into the conversation, you know, about your water heater crapping out and how the Mrs. was in town, or something like that."

"Unbelievable, the gossip. I may have to switch plumbers," Cooper said, laughter and relief spilling into his voice.

"Well, it's not like it's *your* house – shouldn't be an issue moving forward, right? I mean, how long do you have left here?" Sheri was blindly firing questions but it was like her brain was a few steps ahead of her, trying to get to the bottom of where they'd go from here.

How bewilderingly hopeful she felt right then. How hurt she was willing to be. Her foolish heart.

"Are we really talking about toilets and plumbers? What are we doing, Sheri?"

Sheri didn't know what to feel. Or how. But she could identify feeling careful. With what they'd all just gone through with Griffin it had become staggeringly clear how precious life is, how very much is taken for granted. That the people in your life who change the way you breathe and the way you see things are people you need to hold on to.

Considering that there was a new potential reality out there, Sheri wanted to let it incubate. She was terrified that if she opened her heart too wide it might disappear. Need stretched out in every direction, waking up her skin, her nerves, her blood. Even her organs were too busy *wanting* to do anything else, every last brainwave preoccupied with the feel of his hand on her face.

Tears built up across her vision. She'd wanted to fall in love again, in her own time. It wasn't supposed to happen with a crash and a clamor that left her trembling. It wasn't supposed to happen without her permission.

The sun rose higher and hotter leaning in the windshield of the Bronco and Sheri opened both windows. Air swirled in, resuscitating them. It was as though the rest of the world was on pause, too early still for the kids to be wondering where she was and hitting her up with questions. Nowhere either of them had to be in that moment, besides this place of discovery and what might be between them.

Sheri could see in his eyes all the questions that were swimming in her own. Nothing about it seemed hopeless which was a plush blanket of relief. It was like they were having a conversation without having to pick their way through any of the words.

They leaned into each other as close as the console would allow and they met each other in the kiss. His lips moving achingly slowly over hers, teasing at the smile that grew there. It was as intimate as any naked moment.

Warmth and happiness rushed over her, nostalgia giving way to a brand-new joy, that instead of catching her off-guard, felt exactly as it should. Sheri could see it as clearly as the sun glinting in its rise up over the moors – a future of Nantucket summers with this man, all the days and years with him – with their adult children weaving themselves into this new piece of the tapestry. How their family would grow and how they would lose people too, but they would endure. And accept the presence and absence of their kids – the way it would ebb and flow with the tide.

Chapter Thirty-Five

SHERI DIDN'T KNOW HOW to feel casual about any single moment in her daughters' company. She basked in the light they brought to each day. But she was trying not to indulge in this preemptive nostalgia for the past that wasn't even past yet. And as the days trickled down of their Nantucket vacation, she tried not to burden them with the marking of time, tried not to hold each moment up to the gold of the sun like sea glass, smoothing each piece in her hands.

Rose had always told her that what she needed when she was sad was something to look forward to, that she should plan a happy thing that would come *after* the sad thing. Whether that was when the girls left for school in the fall or the paralyzing goodbyes after Christmastime when they went back to their lives, leaving Sheri alone by the magic light of the tree, decked out in a lifetime of ornaments so carefully placed with excitement and anticipation. The dismantling of which was left all to her. It came and was gone so fast. Like their childhood.

A clambake! That's what she would plan. *What do you think, Mom?* Sheri felt alive with purpose – it had been years since they'd dug out a sandy pit on their beach to cook corn wrapped in seaweed and clams and lobster. She was electric with the idea. For their last night, they'd invite Trudy, Griffin, Ollie, Cooper, and Leo. They'd have a sunset swim, play music, make toasts and new memories. She envisioned the details of their beach party – the song of the sea with its pink-tinted foam, laughter bouncing off the dunes, and the sideways spill of the setting sun. She could already feel joy spearing through the melancholy.

The kids took the idea and ran with it. Googling the ins and outs of a do-it-yourself clambake on the beach. "Oh, we totally got this," Jackson said as he recited the steps. "First we pick our spot down there on your beach and we dig a good hole – roughly four feet long by three feet deep by three feet wide, giving us a total volume of thirty-six cubic feet."

"Dude, that sounds aggressively large," Wyn chimed in, "We're not hosting a wedding."

"We'll adjust," Jackson said, "okay, then it says here to line the hole with flat beach rocks then light a big fire on top of the rocks and let it burn out. Shovel off ashes. Layer seaweed, then lobster, corn, clams, and whatever else you want like sausage or potatoes on top of hot rocks. Top with more seaweed and cover with sand. Cook until everything is done. Dig up and dig in."

"That almost sounds too easy," Wyn said, "like how do we know when it's done? How does everything cook in the same time?"

"Maybe you should take a chill pill," Tia said, "and it says here also that we can cook potatoes inside first so we don't overcook the lobster. Do we even need potatoes since we have corn?"

"I was thinking the same thing. And do we really need sausage?" Wyn said. "This is gonna be *sick*, I'm so glad we're doing this! Let's absolutely eat down on the beach too, right? Not lug everything up fifty-seven stairs."

"Duh," Tia said.

"Just make me a list," Sheri said, excitement spinning with their new plan.

"Hey, Mom – do we still have those tiki torches from a couple summers ago? That would be so cool, right?" Wyn asked, looking to the gang for approval.

"Someone having a luau?" Leo said, bounding up the deck stairs to where they all sat, growing their new plan.

They filled Leo in while Sheri savored their animated exchange of ideas before ducking inside to call Trudy. Having a thing to look forward to was so much better than letting the last of the sand divebomb through the hourglass. *Mom, you'd be so proud of me ...* And then instead of whispering things to her mother in her head, she picked up the phone and called her.

∞

The last day arrived like it always did. Everyone had their assignments: chairs, a table, music, plates and napkins, lobster crackers and bowls for shells, butter, coolers of beverages, blankets, balls, tiki torches, sweatshirts, and a frisbee.

As much as they tried to minimize trips down the narrow steps to the beach, it seemed they were countless. But no one cared, revved by their scheme they floated up and down with smiles and jokes. Their collective joy was palpable and Sheri's whole body was buzzing. It seemed lately that she kept being caught off guard by her own joy.

There was never a more resplendent dining room than their beach as the sun began its descent. The water, diamond-edged, the air cooling, and the spray lifting off the low waves rolling in. As their dinner steamed in its salty pit under the taffy glow of a July sky, flames flickered and laughter rippled. The kids whipped a frisbee with drinks in hand and their smiles glowed in the twilight. Journey's "Stone in Love" echoed off the dunes, lyrics swirling - *those summer nights are callin'* ...

Nostalgia, warmth, and happiness washed over Sheri as she looked on at the movie they made ... Tia's wide smile and sunny hair tied loosely back as she tumbled to the sand in a winning dive-catch of the frisbee, her golden skin against white cutoffs and blue hoodie.

"*Hold my beer!*" she'd yelled as she went down. Then Jackson helping her to her feet with a soft kiss and a tap of his beer to hers. And Wyn. Stripping down to her bikini in a sprint to the sea leaving Oliver and Leo in her wake before they joined her in the red-tipped waves. As Trudy and Griff shared a private look.

Sheri thought how being a mother had infused every realm of her life – the decisions she made about the roads she drove, the clothes she wore, her hopes for the future. That when she daydreamed about the future, she noticed she was daydreaming about her kids' futures instead of her own.

She could see her daughters' daughters … their chubby summer-brown hands reaching for shells and smooth stones, then their own surfboards, their own lives. Caught, as they all were, in the sweep of time.

Nothing – not the beautiful, not the terrible – lasted. Everything changed. All you could do was point yourself in the right direction and hope the wind would let you get there.

And then Cooper … watching her watch everyone else. She recognized him in the way you recognize people you are supposed to meet, the ones you've been waiting your whole life to know. And, yeah, her happiness was as important as everyone else's.

"This can't be the end," Cooper said, looking out at the scene they made.

"What?" Sheri said, startled by old insecurities.

"There's still summer to be had," he said, "this can't be the end of our Nantucket time. Let's plan a Labor Day blowout, right here, all of us, just like this." Slowly he smiled. She felt its power slam into her.

Sheri's balloon heart filled, and she caught herself before saying, *I love you for that.* But she did. Love him. For that, and all the ways he saw her. "What a perfect idea! Oh, my mom would love you." From his seat beside her, he reached his open palm down to her and she slid her hand in his. She was already imagining them meeting. Next week or next month, they would go to visit her parents together.

Sheri looked out over the sea and whispered, *I see you, Mom ... and I see me too.*

Sheri caught Tia's small smile before she had a chance to turn it on Jackson. It flooded her with some perfect mix of comfort and strength to have her daughters' support and encouragement as she explored her new relationship with herself and with Cooper.

"Let's dig this out, people!" Griff sang out as they all gathered to help plate the feast. Sheri noticed a new tenderness in the way they moved among each other. And she thought how every good time needed the fires of tragedy underneath it to keep it at a rolling boil.

They unearthed their treasure, each lobster more perfectly cooked than the next, and reveled in the beautiful orgy of perfect seafood and corn. The gilded light settled on the group as the tiki flames danced in the wind. Drinks were raised in one toast after another of gratitude and promises to meet right back there for Labor Day weekend.

"Here's to wooden ships and fiberglass ships, and all the ships at sea. But the best ships are friendships and may they always be," Griffin said, with a voice that broke just a little.

"And," Cooper added, "may your joys be as deep as the ocean, your troubles as light as its foam, and may you find peace wherever you may roam."

Everyone was looking to her, Sheri knew, for some final words of celebration, deep meaning, and cheer. It felt impossible to put it all into words, into a toast.

"Cheers to you all and this magical place. To its mesmerizing land, miles of coastline, and the sea that hugs it. To all who came before us and to those who preserve the fabric of this island's history and all the stories it holds. To the thick foggy days that remind us to focus on what's right in front of us ... and for the assurance that the sunshine always returns. To Nantucket, for being a place that we dream of as home and count down the days to return to together, we are so lucky.

I wish I could bottle this moment and wear it as perfume so it would always be with me." Tears were hot and close and Sheri noticed her heart stumbling over its next beats.

A chorus of cheers rang out as they raised their drinks. And they dug into their seaside suppers in the low purple light, quiet with their own hopes and dreams of the future but buoyed by the perfect present.

Epilogue

SHERI PULLED HER COAT tight and burrowed into her scarf as the ferry cut through the icy Atlantic headed toward Nantucket Island. She would spend the rest of the two-hour chug inside the hulking steamship on this December afternoon but she couldn't resist standing at the bow as they pushed forward from the Hyannis dock to begin the thirty-mile crossing. It was Christmas Stroll weekend and judging from the number of passengers in Santa hats, they were ready for a little Christmas right this very minute.

The cold wind blew her long hair back and made her eyes water – what a difference from that steamy day in July when she last stood there gripping the black railing with real tears blurring her view. Sheri could barely conjure the heat and despair that clung to her that day. It seemed so much longer ago than five months.

A rush of warmth blasted her as she pulled open the heavy door to the cabin, it felt like a hug. The Eagle staff was handing out fat candy canes and a line at the lunch counter was already forming. Undoing the top two buttons of her thick coat, she noticed Cooper at the front of it dropping a tip in the jar with a beer in each hand. God, he was handsome in his navy wool peacoat and two-day scruff that was even hotter than his one-day. She'd seen him almost every single day for five months and the sight of him still made her heart shimmy with anticipation.

She met him halfway to the seats they'd scored by a window, removing her coat before taking one of the Cisco brews. "This is perfect, thank you," she said, stealing a soft kiss before they sat.

"Your lips are chilly," Cooper said, taking a slow sip of his beer, "what shall we do about that?" The low sun on the water coming through the window lit up the gold ring of his hazel eyes and Sheri scooted closer to nuzzle that warm spot where the curve of his jaw met his neck.

"How about if I just stay right here for a minute," she said, "you smell so good."

"Works for me," his voice was low and sexy in her ear. "What time did you say the girls are getting in? And Jackson too, right? Was he able to get the time?"

"Yes! There's an *announcement*, remember? They all come tomorrow afternoon," she said, straightening in her seat just enough to look into his eyes, "I'm so glad they're managing to get here Friday instead of Saturday – the weekend will go by so fast." She took a big sip of her beer while her brain ticked off the list of things she wanted to do before Wyn, Tia, and Jackson arrived. "I know we'll only be here a few days but I want to get a smallish tree and decorate it ..."

"And how tall is *smallish* exactly ...?" he said with his half smile that grew into a laugh.

"You're making fun of me, I know," she said, nudging his thigh, "but I have a vision! And you know I'm used to Christmas trees of a minimum height of eleven feet, so, anything less than that would be *smallish*. Don't laugh! I want the house to look festive ... we'll go straight to Moors End Farm and get a wreath for the door, some evergreen roping for the mantle, and the tree – that's not crazy, right?" Resting her beer in the cupholder, she counted on her fingers, "I brought enough strands of little white lights to cover that, and we can add scallop shells and pinecones, string cranberries, and of course fat white candles for the mantle." Sheri clapped her hands with the excitement of a little kid, "Can you just picture it?"

Cooper wrapped his big warm hand around hers and leaned in, "I can," he said, kissing the tip of her nose. "Now if only I could order a magical dusting of snow for you ..."

"Ooh, it might snow, right? That would be so pretty. As long as it's *after* the kids are here – we don't want any travel snafus."

The partying group in the booth next to them broke into song, everyone belting out the chorus of "Jingle Bell Rock," the six of them all in matching green-and-red Nantucket Stroll scarves with a whale down one side and the iconic shape of the island on the other.

"I love seeing all the versions of the Stroll scarves from past years," Sheri said, eyes lighting up, "Ooh, let's go to TownPool and get us all matching hats and scarves!" Sheri squeezed Cooper's hand and thanked her stars again for putting him in her path, for the way he let her excitement infuse his own, and for the way he listened and let her be her.

The wintry crossing was kind to them with minimal bucking and bouncing over the low chop. Their conversation was all over the map across the two-hour trip, from coordinating a visit to see her parents and Mandy on Christmas Day to putting Sheri's house on the market next month and shopping for a new place together.

That while they were missing Leo this season, he'd granted his mother her wish by spending the holidays in Laos where, as a Foreign Service Officer with the American Embassy, she'd been stationed for eighteen months. Tommy, as ever, had been good at sharing time with their daughters – and the new woman he was seeing, and her two grown sons, seemed to bring out the best in him. The blending of their families had been drama-free, seamless.

They took turns leafing through Nantucket's seasonal newspaper, *Yesterday's Island*, pouring over the weekend's detailed schedule of events deciding which of them were not to be missed – Trudy's book signing at Mitchell's Bool Corner among them.

"There she is!" Sheri said in a voice a full octave higher, pointing to her friend's photo in the paper. "Ah, just look at her, Coop, I'm so proud to call her my friend. *On Borrowed Time* is her latest – I can't wait to get my personalized copy! She'll be at Mitchell's Saturday from three o'clock to four. That gives us plenty of time to catch Santa cruising up Main Street and the parade of crazy costumes, then make our Slip 14 lunch reservation – it's perfect! And we'll get more time with her and Griff at the brewery on Sunday which will be more laid back, how does that sound?" Sheri said, folding the paper in her lap with a satisfied smile.

"Social director extraordinaire," Cooper said with pride, "you've thought of everything, something for everyone. Of course you realize, *ma chérie*, all I ever really need is you." He put his arm around her shoulder and pulled her close bumping into her kiss just as the boat connected with the dock.

"Look!" Sheri said, pointing out the window as she gathered their things before returning to Cooper's Range in the hold of the ship, "it's snowing!" Chunky white flakes were swirling down from the sky and Sheri rushed outside to stand in it. Cooper steered her portside with one hand on her lower back and the other waving down to the small group looking up at them.

"What ... who ... is that Trudy? And the *kids*? How –"

Sheri froze in her tracks looking out at her whole world waving up at her, the best surprise. Their bright smiles lit up the silver sky, and the ice on Tia's finger was winking like a star.

The End

Acknowledgments

My third novel in three years – I'm on fire! I couldn't have done this (wouldn't have done it) when my kids were little. I kept notebooks instead. Filling the pages of journals in between the Candyland and checkers marathons, beach adventures and backyard campouts, teaching them how to pitch a tent, swim, ski, climb mountains, and what it means to love each other and be good people. The moments, days, and the years in their company were too precious to hand off. I have a hard enough time now when they are 32, 27, and 24.

So, let me thank my children: Cody, Madison, and Ryder, before I thank anyone else. You inspire me, then as now, to live large in the smallest of moments, to laugh always, and to never stop reaching and growing. I love you enormously – we have so much fun together! I feel so lucky for this.

Thank you to Ann Leslie and Sara Oestreich for your collective editing genius and for helping me strengthen this story, these characters, making them more compelling. Thanks to proofreader extraordinaire, Ciera Cox, for the last-minute polish, and to Sarah Lahay for another gorgeous cover design and for your interior formatting expertise.

Thank you to the people in my life who raise me up and keep me company – on long walks through the woods or up tall mountains, for girls' lunches and day drinking, for the piggy-back rides down memory lane – the exquisite times and the brutal – and for manic texting during The Bachelor. Michael DeNitto, Allison Soucy, Lisa Heinke, Linda Cain, Brenda Fife, Susan Jackson, Laura Whiton, Alyssa Rennie, and Lisa Ollenborger (you know under which category you fall), I treasure each of you.

And to Billy, my husband and the father of our three kids – thanks for the safety net you graciously stretch under us all, for your quiet confidence in me, and the spotlight you so willingly cast. Thanks for picking up the slack at home and for judiciously ignoring me when I'm slamming pots and pans yelling, *I'm so done with cooking – no dinner tonight!* Your patience is gold.

I'm so grateful to Tim Ehrenberg (@timtalksbooks) President of Nantucket Book Foundation and Marketing and Events Director for Nantucket Book Partners, for his generosity in including me on the calendar for summer book signings at Mitchell's Book Corner on Nantucket. It is a living dream for me. Thank you all, gracious booksellers, for the passion built into your curation – I feel unendingly lucky to have my books on your shelves and in your windows. Thank you!

About the Author

Doreen Burliss, author of *We'll Always Have Nantucket* and *That Nantucket Summer*, lives in a small town north of Boston with her husband, two fat cats and a dog. They have three grown children, for whom their Nantucket summer vacation remains etched in gold on the calendar, no matter where they are or what they're doing. *Fogged In* is her third novel.

PHOTO BY: ALYSSA BAYLEY

Printed in the USA
CPSIA information can be obtained
at www.ICGtesting.com
JSHW020005160724
66469JS00001B/2